Barren

J.J. Savaunt

BLOODHOUND
BOOKS

www.bloodhoundbooks.com

Print ISBN: 978-1-5040-8181-8

For we wrestle not against flesh and blood, but against principalities, against powers, against the rulers of the darkness of this world, against spiritual wickedness in high places.

Ephesians 6:12

Chapter 1

Cara: False Promises

When they said they were *making Ballantyne Better*, they only meant for the one percent.

The sharp morning breeze cut into her skin. Each step sent a wave of spasms gushing through her abdomen. Gasping for air, she planted her back against a traffic pole; its steel flesh sent ice up her spine, but she didn't mind the sudden chill, it was the least of her problems.

The pain hadn't always been like this, but lately, every morning started the same. It started out subtle, like a stomach cramp from exercising right after eating, but with that first onset of slight discomfort, Cara knew what was coming next. She held a breath bracing for it. Within a few minutes, that light pain evolved into convulsions, knocking air from her. The sheer agony ripped tears from her eyes. *Hell couldn't hurt worse than this*, Cara thought. Staggering through the poorly built sidewalks, Cara was within earshot of Mercy Hospital. If only she could make it.

Vehicles were at a standstill, one behind the other. The skies were a stonewall gray, cruel, and lifeless, given that the sun had not yet awakened. Cracked concrete pressed against the soles of

1

her cheetah-print flats. Blaring horns screamed in her ears, and she could not go one block without some random guy catcalling at her. Cara used to like that kind of male attention, especially when she was being filmed and paid quite well—while naked, but Cara did not do that type of work anymore. This was an average day in Ballantyne, so bleak through Cara's eyes, but that was not even the worst part.

She feared she was infertile.

Ever since her teenage years, Cara had endured this unimaginable pain. She didn't know what part of it was worse, the suffering or no one believing it. Teachers thought she was exaggerating since the pain forced her to sit out of gym and swimming classes in high school. Her friends and classmates assumed she was being dramatic and asked for tips on what to say to get the same treatment. Doctors claimed she would get used to it as she got older, yet here she was over a decade later and still the pain brought her to her knees. This wasn't a feeling she or anyone could ever label as normal. It was a mind-numbing type of agony that curled her into the fetal position and forced ear-shattering screams into her pillow until the waves had passed. If she was lucky, she would feel human for just ten days in every month.

Now her agony had reached an all-time intensity. In the past, when a doctor or nurse asked her to rate her pain from one through ten, she'd always replied with "a nine" because she'd been saving the "ten" for another day. Fumbling through the revolving doors of the hospital, enduring strangers' concerned gazes, and clenching her stomach, today that day had come.

Is this how she felt? Cara thought.

She as in her mother, Lenora.

Due to a genetic flaw and questionable job history, Cara feared she would never be able to have children. Her mother had suffered five miscarriages before giving birth. At thirty-two years of age, Lenora had decided it was time to start a family, only she hadn't realized just how difficult that would be. Lenora had suffered from stage IV endometriosis. During her pregnancy, doctors had warned that given her medical history, childbirth would be risky and that for her safety she should consider terminating the pregnancy. But Lenora was a stubborn woman, and that's what had made her an amazing captain in the Navy. Once she had her mind fixed on something, there was no changing it. That same strong will was Lenora's death sentence. She'd bled out on the delivery table the day Cara was born.

Cara often wondered if she would suffer the same fate.

Walking into Mercy Hospital, Cara took a spot in line to reach the receptionist's desk. Short of breath. Unable to keep still in line. Sweat rolled down her back. What little hope Cara had left was disappearing with each thump of her heartbeat.

Though center city Ballantyne was a booming metropolis with massive sporting arenas, organic food markets on every corner, and designer boutiques with foreign names and commas in the price tags—on the outskirts were abandoned storefronts, sketchy cash checking places, and run-down clinics. Places where the average citizen, like Cara, lived paycheck to paycheck and could not afford one of those luxury high-rise condominiums that kept appearing out of nowhere every day. But a clinic would not suffice. She had been to one, the staff had been rude, unprofessional, and judgmental of Cara's previous employment in the adult industry. Now with this whole fertility thing Cara had to deal with, the financial burden felt to her as stressful as the potential diagnosis.

"Next," the receptionist shouted as the man ahead of Cara stormed out of the exit.

Cara stepped forward in front of the receptionist, Pam—a middle-aged woman who spoke with the enthusiasm of someone nearing the end of a twelve-hour shift. No one could blame

Pam; it was chaotic inside, with too few seats and not enough employees. Still, the receptionist was the unfriendliest person Cara had ever met. Pam refused to smile, barely made eye contact, and her perfume was so sweet it began triggering a sinus headache.

"I need a doctor like right now," Cara said, sliding documents underneath the glass separating them.

Irritated, Pam snatched the papers.

Rude. Cara bit her inner cheek. This was the best hospital in the city, there was nowhere else to go if she didn't like the service.

Strike one, Cara thought.

Cara was taller than most women and never dressed out of business casual, because of a personal motto. *Dress how you want to be addressed.* A quote she faithfully lived by, thanks to her father, who, despite his functional-alcoholic tendencies, was a sharp dresser. His uniform was always ironed and layered in lemon-scented starch. The citrusy aroma always left her optimistic about the future. Even when dealing with people like Pam on days like today.

"How are you today?" Cara asked.

Pam threw her gaze over her glasses then looked down at the documents again. *Not one for small talk. Got it.*

Another wave of spasms surged through her stomach. Cara doubled over, leaning on the front of Pam's desk. Rocking herself back and forth, Cara kept her gaze down at the polished concrete flooring. Every time the pain hit her, so did regret. Both were a reminder of the dozens of partners Cara had had during her film profession. Time was slipping. *How much worse would the pain get before it... it killed her?* She needed good news and soon.

Wanting the interaction to end, Cara asked her final burning question. The humiliating question that anyone making under six figures in a place like Ballantyne had to ask. Cara had heard stories of how some people took out loans to cover a visit, but that was not her style. Yes, she worked... or used to work in the adult industry which paid for her bachelor's degree but that was months ago. Cara was responsible with her money. She was here with two months of income saved.

"How much will this visit cost me? I have insurance, I don't know what it's called–"

"You have insurance and don't know what it's called? How does that work?" Pam let out a frustrated chuckle, shuffling through stacks of papers.

One of Cara's biggest pet peeves, next to someone telling her to "calm down" when she was already calm, was being interrupted. Cutting her off was telling Cara that her entire existence didn't matter. It was a verbal uppercut. It was beyond disrespectful.

Strike two.

By now, Cara had silently and internally grown tired of Pam and her sarcasm. Cara was not one to make a scene, but inside she was screaming. No one, anywhere, seemed to be able to tell her anything. The insurance rep was unhelpful and now the damn receptionist could not even answer a simple question that only required a numerical response.

"Just ask your nurse," Pam said, shooing Cara away with a hand before sliding the blue surgical mask down to her chin. "Next!"

That answer should have given Cara some relief, but somehow, be it her desire for everything to be perfect or Pam's consistently dry tone and even drier half-smile, it did the opposite. In her head, Cara was furious.

Everyone had a breaking point and Cara had reached hers. Underneath the smile, Cara imagined walking toward the waiting area, grabbing the nearest fire extinguisher, and hurling it at Pam. She imagined the glass wall protecting the obnoxious receptionist shattering into thousands of shards. She imagined the people in line scattering upon the impact, whereupon Cara would snatch Pam's collar and slam her face into the desk over and over again until she drew a thin line of blood along her hairline.

In real life, however, Cara simply grabbed her documents and smiled back at Pam like the good girl she presented herself to be. Then she walked over to a hard cushion seat and slumped into a chair. Staring at the square light embedded into the ceiling, Cara's mind raced. She hated hospitals. The disinfectant smell that persisted through every square inch, the hours of waiting, the extravagant costs, all reminded her of one thing: Her mother's death. Her mother died in this very same building twenty-two years ago.

A few years back, Cara's father had shared the story of her birth. The cramped delivery room and condescending staff had left Lenora feeling jilted, but her father, too excited to meet his daughter, had dismissed Lenora's concerns. The big moment came and as the two doctors stood in front of Lenora, gently retrieving the baby, Cara's father noticed Lenora mouthing words. He had tried getting the staff's attention, but the nurse warned him that if he kept being disruptive he would be escorted out of the room. Instead of making a big fuss he sat beside his wife holding her hand, watching her grow weaker and her words become fainter, but he assumed this happened in birth. He had always heard a woman was closest to death when bringing forth life. He leaned closer to hear Lenora's plea, the only thing he could make out were the words *my back*. As they pulled Cara from her mother, blood had begun streaming from all sides of the delivery bed. Monitors and mechanical noises shouted simultaneously and only then had the doctors realized something was wrong. They rotated Lenora onto one side. Her entire back, the hospital gown, and table had been drenched with her blood. To this day Cara's father blamed himself for his wife's death. If only he had spoken up sooner for his wife, if only he had been more adamant regarding Lenora's declining strength, if only he had been more outraged overall, then maybe Lenora would have lived.

That same regret of Cara's father turned Cara distrustful of medicine. She did not see hospitals as a place of hope. To Cara, hospitals were places where people came to die.

A nurse opened a transparent door and yelled for the next patient.

"Mrs. Esperanza?" the nurse called out.

Annoyed from her frustrating interaction with Pam, Cara lifted from the seat and caught a glimpse of the nurse's name tag before following her.

Cindy.

Cindy was a few inches taller and a few shades lighter than Cara. Perhaps in another life, they could have been sisters.

Following Cindy into a white-floored room with a small window in the corner, Cara sat upon a thin sheet atop a beige exam table. The nurse closed the door behind her.

"Alright, Mrs. Esperanza—"

"It's Ms. Esperanza. I kept the last name."

While Cindy retrieved a small dose of foam from a wall hand sanitizer dispenser, Cara noticed the nurse's gaze drift toward her left hand. An empty left ring finger. Awkward.

It had been three months since her divorce. Married for only six months, Cara and Matthew had lived together in Jacksonville, North Carolina, where he'd been stationed at Camp Lejeune. A proud Marine, Matthew loved the south, he was born and raised in Jacksonville where tobacco fields stretched for miles and nature reclaimed whole neighborhoods. Cara wanted more for their lives, to live in a city where their children would have a diverse mix of peers and adopt a neutral accent instead of a southern drawl. The beauty of their different opinions eventually drove them apart, well that and when Matthew had found out about her prior adult film career. Cara was now jumping from man to man, hoping to ignite the embers of what she and Matthew once held.

A sudden dizzy feeling consumed her. The room began spinning. *This was new*, Cara thought. Was this her condition or the anxiety? Perhaps it was the pressure. After all, this visit would determine the rest of Cara's life. Both her fertility and the future of her health were on the line.

"My apologies, Ms. Esperanza. Gosh, you're so young, but never mind. Sorry, let me pull up your info." Cindy sat down and began scrolling through documents on a touchscreen clear clipboard. "Let's see, it looks like... hmm... that's weird."

Cara's heart sunk.

"You last saw Dr. Stevenson. It seems here your results came back abnormal."

Abnormal.

"She diagnosed you with endometriosis."

Cara covered her mouth, not shocked, not surprised, it was an automated response to her taking in the news. A part of her knew she had the same illness that claimed her mother, but she didn't want to believe it. She didn't want to live in a reality that the only thing that she had in common with her mom was how she was going to die. As daunting as her future seemed, Cara had a different concern.

"My insurance is going to cover this, right?"

Cindy smiled, flashing a brilliant set of teeth. Immediately, Cara grew self-conscious of her own.

"Endometriosis is tricky. I understand here it says you're with Argus." Cindy paused. "This morning they mentioned something about them," she pointed out, tapping a pen on the clipboard. "But hey, let's not get ahead of ourselves," Cindy said as she sat on the backless chair in front of Cara. "Let me verify with the insurance department. I'm sure everything will work out, okay?" Cindy placed a hand gently on Cara's wrist. More than anything, Cara needed those words to be true.

Once more, she waited. The white walls, monitors, medical equipment, posters, and cold linoleum floors stared at her as a reminder of how alone she truly was. With her athletic build, average means, and her average lifestyle, she felt as if there was nothing extraordinary about her at all other than her exceptional memory and crippling low self-esteem. From the outside peeking in, Cara had it all. Yet the truth, Cara was depression in physical form. The only thing that she believed would bring her happiness was the one thing out of her control: a baby. Cara's friends rarely returned phone calls and they had every right not to, given they were preoccupied with husbands and school-aged kids. All Cara had was the guy she was dating. Yet even in that direction, serious problems laid. During the day, her boyfriend was a ghost. She'd wanted her golden-haired, blue-eyed, six-foot Adonis to accompany her today, but he was busy with something at the office. He was *always* busy.

Cara pulled up a picture of her mother on her phone. A smile that looked like it was hiding something silly stared back at Cara. Her mother had the kind of body that could handle any physical challenge the military threw her way and still managed to look feminine. She stopped on a short video. It was her parents at the beach during peak summer. They were people watching and laughing at each other's made-up stories about strangers. Cara's mother was funny, the entire video was filled with her dad's wheezing laughter. There was a sparkle in her dad's eye that dwelled only in these memories. When Cara's mother died, a part of her father did as well. Cara scrolled to another picture, her mom in Dress Blues. The woman looked like she could command an entire battalion. At a certain point, Cara could no longer tell if these memories helped or hurt. It was a reminder of the mom she could have had, and simultaneously, the woman she would never meet. Although they were not yet even born, Cara could not let her imagined offspring grow up like her. She'd always envisioned giving birth naturally to three children: Zach, Zen, and Alina. She'd already mapped out their chosen schools and even the type of father they would have. She could not help it; Cara was a planner. No matter what, she would find a way to make this work.

Cindy returned with news, but she was not the same chipper person as when she'd left the room earlier.

"So?" Cara asked, both hopeful and scared of the answer.

"I am so sorry, Ms. Esperanza, we—"

"I figured, well, let me see." Cara extended an arm toward the clipboard. Reluctantly, Cindy handed it over.

As the total medical costs came into her view, showing the fees for visits, for further treatment, for everything—her emotions took hold, and a pool of water suddenly blurred her vision. Cara liked to think of herself as a strong woman, she had broken a bone or two in her childhood and suffered her fair share of heartbreaks, but this... this was too much. Her money saved would not put a dent in this total. Cara fought, but the dam broke. She tilted her head back, hoping the tears would slide back into her eyes, but they refused and fell onto the clipboard screen covering a comma and six varying digits.

"There is no way I can afford this. Is there anything else we can do? Cheaper versions of the same treatment?"

Cindy paused. Her eyebrows lifted suddenly. *Maybe she'd forgotten to mention something*, thought Cara. *Yes, that was the only explanation for the somewhat happy expression. Perhaps, there was something she could do.*

"I—I am afraid not," Cindy said and collapsed into her shoulders like a half-baked cake.

Unreal. Soon the sadness left Cara, but another fierce emotion took its place.

"You cannot be serious?" Cara said. Though she kept a low volume, there was a spice in her delivery. She usually held it together well, but in this case, Cara had had enough.

A cramp slammed into Cara's abdomen. The third one in less than two hours. Cara placed her hands on her knees, taking in longer and deeper breaths and hoped the stabbing pain would soon subside. Ibuprofen was no longer enough to keep it away, and with this expensive treatment that she needed, Cara was at a loss. It was like the entire system was set up to let her die.

"Ms. Esperanza, there might be another way," Cindy said, sifting through screens on the clear clipboard, she then handed it to Cara. On the front read:

BRT HEALTH INDUSTRIES: GET YOUR LIFE BACK

"The hospital partners with a company called BRT Health Industries. They are doing trials for fertility treatments. I think you're a great match for what they are looking for... If you're interested, I could refer you to them? They could give you a consult today if you have time. It'll only take a few minutes," Cindy said.

Cara, still sitting with her tears, only nodded in response.

"Okay, good, just wait in the lobby and I'll have him come grab you." Cindy stood, and Cara followed her.

Cara waited in a separate lobby area. It was much darker than the main waiting room. A single hallway, an unmanned reception desk, and only two mottled-oak chairs took up the small area. Despite the anxiety swirling in Cara's chest, she stayed and found a seat closest to the exit. Cindy had given her no real insight into this company called BRT Health Industries. All Cara knew was this might be her last option. A *free* option. She had nothing to lose.

An hour later, a door opened.

Though she saw no one, she heard the click of a knob and a small conversation wrapping up. Around the corner, a young woman walked past. Her heels clapped in a subtle rhythm on the linoleum surface and a hint of her perfume grazed Cara's nose. She was a gorgeous dark-skinned woman, the type of brown beauty cast as the token Black girl modeling down a high fashion runway; long slim legs, high cheekbones, not a smidge of acne, and a smile that looked bought with sugar daddy money. She was what Cara called a "glitzy girl". The type of woman who always knew what color combinations matched her skin tone best, knew how to accessorize according to each season, always wore the most exclusive hard-to-pronounce perfumes, and was never seen in sneakers and yoga pants outside the house. Now it all made sense. The glitzy girl was what was taking so long.

"Ms. Esperanza?" A middle-aged gentleman approached her.

"Yes." Standing from her seat, Cara shook his hand. "And you are?"

"Call me Mr. Khizar." He smiled and extended a hand. A jet-black suit that looked custom made by some famous designer adorned Mr. Khizar's well-over-six-foot, beer-bellied frame. He even smelled expensive, but his most prominent feature was his olive complexion with dents, bumps, and long-healed tissue, across the bridge of his nose, forehead, and the deep scars along his right cheek. The man must have won those scars in some war fought long ago or some terrible chemical accident.

Cara clasped her grip in his hand. He had a stronger-than-average handshake. Through that one moment of contact, Cara knew this man could overpower her. She was alone, in a seemingly abandoned part of the hospital with some sketchy looking man full of promises. *Is this a mistake?* In that same thought, desperation kicked in and so did the imaginary picture of her unborn children. Twin boys and a little girl. She would have the boys first so they could protect their little sister. The twins would be tall, athletic, brave, and sweet young men. They'd bring home nice girls for Cara to meet prior to marriage. While her daughter would grow into the role of Cara's best friend as an adult; they would go on wine tasting tours and brunch dates and when strangers asked if they were sisters, they would laugh at their expressions when people found out they were actually mother and daughter. Cara needed this to work. *To hell with any doubt.*

Cara trailed behind Khizar, and they found seats inside a nearby office space. She stepped in first and he followed, closing the door behind them.

Sitting across from Mr. Khizar, the interview commenced.

Mr. Khizar kept the energy light and conversational. "We are a pioneering fertility company. We offer free treatment for women in your current situation. But, Cara, above all, we're here to help." He leaned forward, placing his elbows on the wooden table between them. The lighting above him cast a shadow on the harsh lines of his face. Deeply lined sallow pouches sat under his eyes. His once-friendly demeanor had left. Mr. Khizar suddenly looked like a federal agent interrogating Cara and she had incriminated herself.

Almost instinctively Cara shifted slightly away from him. This Mr. Khizar had a terrifying talent, he managed to make her feel uncomfortable even with a smile on his face. Although her nerves were on edge, Cara could not leave. Not with her future at stake. She had to see this through.

"Well, like, how exactly does it all work? It sounds too good to be true, honestly."

As he spoke, his accent became more distinct. To Cara's ears, Mr. Khizar sounded as if he was from some island in the Caribbean. "It is very simple. I ask you a few questions. Our team reaches out to you. Then we assign you to an obstetrician in our network. Lastly, we monitor your case with care."

It sounded simple enough. It was free and required no effort from Cara. She needed no further persuasion.

"Great, now we begin with a questionnaire I have to go through with you. Apologies in advance if some of the questions feel intrusive." He chuckled, then began reading from the paper in front of him.

Are your parents still living?

Do you have any siblings?

Are you married?

Any children?

Are you currently expecting?

With all of these questions, Cara gave him the same response: "No."

"Excellent, only a few more things to cover then you're all finished." Mr. Khizar pulled a stack of papers an inch thick and dropped them between Cara and himself.

Shocked, Cara's eyes widened.

"It's a lot I know," he chuckled, "but you've got me, and I'll explain as we go."

Mr. Khizar sped through the hundreds of pages, barely giving Cara any time to read a single document completely. He spat out words like "guarantee" and "fertility" and "no cost to you" then continued to the next page and the next page. It was as though Mr. Khizar was in a race with himself. The empathetic "we're-here-to-help-you" Mr. Khizar had turned into a car salesman who almost seemed as if he didn't want

Cara reading the fine print. Everything was happening too fast.

"Maybe I shouldn't start this today. I need to think about it."

Mr. Khizar paused for a moment, and smiled, but in that short time span, Cara saw something. She didn't know exactly what it was. Perhaps it was the subtle muscle twitch in his forehead or the way he thinned his lips. Either way, there was a glint of rage that flashed upon his face. The mask he wore to the world as this philanthropist in women's health had slipped for just a second, but Cara saw it.

"What is it that you need to think about?" Mr. Khizar said, sliding the papers to the side. "I know this is a big decision, but we have a lot of other viable candidates and limited space available. If you don't want this treatment, I understand."

Cara was frozen with indecision. She did not trust anything about this man, but in truth, she had no other options. If she left this endometriosis untreated, she would never have children. She would never meet Zach, Zen, or Alina. She would never potty train her kids, never feed them their first bite of pizza, never hear their first curse word, and never watch their first steps. They would be a hope living in her heart that never happened and turned into regret. Cara could not let decades fly by wishing she had done everything possible to have kids. If this had the slightest chance of working, Cara needed to try it. If not for her, for her future children.

Cara sat upright in her seat, confident. "How many more pages are left?"

Mr. Khizar smiled without revealing his teeth and began flipping through pages once more.

As he reached the end of the packet, there was this pressure mounting in Cara's chest. This was it, time to make the final decision. She began rocking back and forth in the wooden seat. It was like she was watching someone else in this moment.

There was no way this was her life. She grabbed the pen and slowly signed.

God, I hope this is the right decision, Cara thought.

Cara left the facility. On the drive back home she looked in the rearview mirror at the glistening building that was Mercy Hospital. It shone in the sunlight like a beacon. Cara's eyes fluttered, fighting back tears once more. Life was so unfair, but this opportunity of a lifetime might mean Cara had a shot at meeting her unborn children. A shot in the dark that could have saved her mother had she had the chance.

While crossing a bridge to get off the interstate, she took note of the car behind her. A black SUV with blacked-out windows. It was one of those vehicles that looked like someone important was inside, like a senator or a celebrity, but there was something else more noticeable about the vehicle. Every turn she made, they followed suit. It was not until she'd made three turns in a row, that she really noticed their presence. This was strange. *It was mid-morning with light traffic, surely this person had better things to do?* This was happening. Someone *was* following her.

While on a lone strip of road, the mysterious vehicle behind suddenly picked up speed. They were so close they were the only thing in her rearview mirror. If she stayed like this, they might hit her or worse.

Panicked, Cara pushed her foot on the gas. The speedometer jumped from sixty to one hundred miles an hour. Her engine hummed as her car kicked up speed. Cara was not one for taking risks; she hated gambling, drinking, or anything that put her in harm's way. In fact, this was the first time she'd ever seen her speed this close to one hundred and twenty. This was life or death.

On a sharp curve of the road, the steering wheel jerked to the left, and Cara lost control of the car. Spinning out, she ricocheted against a guard rail and crashed into a ditch. The airbags deployed, filling her green sedan with a stench of smoke and sulfur. The coppery taste of blood formed on her tongue. The sheer force of the accident had smacked her against the steering wheel. Fading, her eyes began closing against her will.

A man appeared by her window. Dark haired and of Mediterranean accent; her blurry vision refused to make out any details of his face.

"Good, she's unconscious. We don't have to sedate her."

Before Cara could make sense of anything, darkness took hold.

Chapter 2

Justice: Another Girl Gone

Most considered Ballantyne a safe city, except along the outskirts of the lavish metropolitan. Outside the perfectly gentrified center city, there was an entirely different reality. On nearly every single corner sat liquor stores and fast-food restaurants. Schools were riddled with bullet holes and graffiti. Drug stores served as community supermarkets since the health food stores were too afraid to open shop in these parts of town. The interior of poorly built neighborhoods were roach-infested apartments, one of which Justice had called home during his childhood. This was Officer Justice Reeves' reality. Life was cruel. As a high school junior Justice was forced to become the man of the house when his father died, some ten years later he had become a mountain of a man, all resilience and sheer will. He needed to be that, not only because of his job as a police officer but in order to survive this part of Ballantyne.

Justice, with his partner, Goodchild, were five minutes away from their destination, Mercy Hospital.

"Suspect's name is Ivery Johnson, eighteen, African American female," Goodchild said from the passenger side.

To describe Goodchild, Justice had one word: naïve. Green-eyed and green in his experience, Goodchild was Justice's new partner. Justice swore the Chief had assigned Goodchild to him as a prank, perhaps even in retaliation, though no one had told Justice this, they didn't have to. Goodchild seemed like the type who never had to work for anything. Granted, Justice had only known him for a week, but his constant complaining about the free office coffee, sitting with his feet up on his desk and his mom's special brown-bag lunches all highlighted to Justice how spoiled the guy was. Justice gave him a month before the Chief fired him. Still, Justice trained him like any other newbie.

Justice and Goodchild entered Mercy Hospital which sat right off the corner of Thirty-Fifth and Claventine. By Claventine, there was a yoga studio, a frozen yogurt shop, and a farmer's market along with a blond girl jogging along the newly paved sidewalk. Right on the other side of the railroad tracks were a run-down gas station, an all-Black school where the students couldn't give a damn about test scores, a recreation center with a net-less basketball court and a homeless man panhandling oncoming traffic at a stoplight. Here, two worlds collided.

Only a little over a week ago, after the events at Easthampton strip mall, Justice had dropped off a suspect at Mercy Hospital. Had he taken her to the precinct instead, she would not have lived—at least, that was what the nurses had told him when he'd brought her in.

While Goodchild waited by the door, Justice stepped around the teal curtains covering half the room. Justice pushed the light fabric back with one hand. To his surprise, the suspect was gone. The only other person who knew her whereabouts, besides himself, was his partner, Goodchild. This was bad.

Searching for answers, Justice ran across a nurse walking past the room with a clear clipboard.

"Excuse me—"

"Cindy," the nurse said.

"Cindy," Justice repeated, digesting it.

Justice sensed a hint of Spanish when Cindy spoke. She came to his shoulder in height. He noted her glossy lips and naturally long eyelashes. If Justice had any courage outside of his job, he would have asked her out. *But no, not now.* He had a job to do and that was his focus.

"Have you seen this young woman?" He pointed at the bed. "She had, ugh... bright red hair. Her name is Ivery Johnson."

The nurse glanced through the window, looking into the room. Her eyes narrowed, attempting to bring forth a face matching the name.

"She shouldn't have been able to go anywhere. She was cuffed to the bed, standard procedure," Justice reminded. He glanced over his shoulder and examined the bed once more. The handcuffs... they too were missing.

The nurse sifted through the names on the transparent clipboard clutched in her right arm. Justice entered the room once more and studied the bar of the bed where the handcuffs had once been. No stains, no streaks, no sign of struggle, or any mark of that matter remained. *Either this suspect took the cuffs, or this was a new bed.*

"Officer—" the nurse said.

"Reeves. Call me Justice."

"Yes... Justice," Cindy paused a moment, eyed Justice up and down. She then threw her attention back to the clipboard, a slight blush on the ball of her cheeks.

"Have you found something?"

"The patient you brought in last week, let's see here. I'm just going over the sign-in log from that period. Hold on a second... Ivery Johnson. Yes I see. She came in at 5:40pm. Last Monday. It seems the doctor discovered a severe heart condition. These things happen sometimes, no need to worry,

Justice. She is with Dr. Dowey. She went for additional testing just to make sure she's squared away for release tomorrow. I believe she should be back in the afternoon."

"Why did Dr. Dowey not follow protocol and follow up with the police department right away?"

Cindy sucked in a breath and drew the clipboard closer to her chest. Being a six-foot, athletic-built kind of guy, Justice tended to have that effect on people, his words often came out harsher than his intention.

"That part, I don't know, Officer Reeves, but I can give you a call when Ivery returns."

All of this felt out of order, but with nothing except a gut feeling, there was not much else Justice could do in the situation.

As he handed Cindy his business card, her delicate fingers grazed his. He hoped she would make good use of the phone number but based on the lack of eye contact Justice doubted it. He left the hospital with a specific place in mind.

Justice parked outside a manor house built with bricks as red as dirt and ivory trimmings, and they climbed up a never-ending driveway. Justice stared at the well-kept lawn shimmering under the sun's touch. A memory resurfaced of his father and himself at their old home. A three-bedroom apartment off Jefferson Parkway. Outside, they used to play catch in an open grassy area behind the leasing office. The grass was the same awkward shade of green as the lawn beside him now. Countless days he and his dad had tossed a football back and forth. Justice had once harbored plans of going pro. Schools and scouts were already looking at him even as a sophomore in high school. However, one fateful evening changed everything.

Justice recalled the memory, his last memory of his father. On the way home from one of Justice's football games, they had stopped at a local gas station. If it could have been called a gas station, there were only two parking spots and dim canopy lights wrapped around the pavilion above two gas pumps. Every other gas station in town was better than this one, but this was the only location that had his dad's favorite treat. Two minutes, his father motioned with two fingers and a clever smile on his face. By that combined gesture, Justice knew exactly what his father wanted. Some damn smoothie-flavored Skittles. Forty years old and the man still had a sweet tooth. Those two minutes changed his life. A gunman, dressed in all black attire and a ski mask covering everything but his eyes, stormed the gas station.

Justice watched the gunman and as the door to the convenience store opened, a man was leaving. Justice prayed it was anyone but his dad. As faithful as his father was preaching the gospel every Sunday, surely this one time God would intervene.

A man emerged.

When Justice saw the brown leather dress shoe, his heart fell into his chest. It could have been anyone else. It should have been anyone else, but it wasn't. It was his dad. Faced with death, his father lunged for the pistol.

Boom.

Next moment, blood splattered against the store windows like confetti.

Over a decade had passed since his father's death, yet the pain felt fresh as yesterday. There was a belief in Justice's family, that they were cursed and anyone who got too close was doomed to suffer a horrid fate. That, among many reasons, was why Justice kept to himself.

Barking rang in Justice's ears. A giant ball of angel brown hair and a long pink tongue ran full force toward Justice and Goodchild. It was Lucky, a big, brown-eyed golden retriever. He slammed into Justice, knocking him on his back. Lucky must not have realized he was no longer a puppy and by the force with

22

which Justice hit the dirt, he imagined there must now be a grass stain on his uniform somewhere.

"Wow, you've gotten so big," Justice said, avoiding Lucky's tongue from smearing all over his face. His long tail swayed back and forth so fast, it was hard to tell which way it was moving.

"Lucky, leave him alone," a frail voice shouted from the porch. Lucky obeyed, bolting towards his owner.

Justice stood and brushed himself clean. A smile appeared as he spotted his mother.

"Hey, Ma." Justice waved from afar, and she motioned for him to come closer.

Her hair was an ancient gray, a deep shade of silver like a crown from her ancestors. She walked with a slight limp, but her mahogany complexion was wrinkle-free.

"It's good to see you." She patted him on the back. "Now who is this?"

Goodchild took a step forward. He removed his hat upon entrance revealing a short, dirty blond Afro and fiddled with his hat in both hands.

"My partner—"

"I know who he is. I mean what is he doing here?" Ma said, crossing her arms.

"It'll only be a second," Justice pleaded.

"Fine." Ma sighed. "Anything happens to him out there you have to answer for it," Ma said, pointing her finger at Goodchild like she was his mother too. "Come on in. Y'all letting my air out. I'm not trying to cool down outside."

Stepping into this home, Justice felt as if he was walking through time. To his left, Justice found a picture triggering the most embarrassing time of his life. Middle school. His features dominated his small face. Ears too big for his head, nose too wide for his cheeks, and lips so pronounced kids teased him relentlessly. He sighed, embarrassed she still had photos.

Ma fixed a small cup of ginger lemon tea, then sat in the squeaky reclining chair in the living room. The cracked brown leather on the arms and back looked like stretch marks. The handle on the side barely functioned anymore. The chair had a permanent cigarette stench engraved in it and someone should have tossed it in the garbage by now. But no one in the family had the heart to throw it away. That used to be his father's chair.

With the TV softly playing in the background, Lucky plopped down on the carpet in front of Ma.

"You know what the news isn't talking about? Those missing girls. Have you heard about Tawnya, Shania, and Maria? Three weeks ago, they all went missing and no one has seen them. Have you?"

"No, I haven't. What's that about?"

"You tell me Mr. Officer," Ma said.

The disdain his mother held for local law enforcement often showed up as sarcasm. Justice didn't blame her. Ten years later and the police still hadn't found the man responsible for killing her husband.

"I figured those idiots at your job wouldn't know. The police only care when Black folk are the criminals. God help us." Ma took a sip of her tea, changing the subject, "I heard about what happened at Easthampton mall."

Everyone in the locality seemed to have heard about what had happened, but there was a different side to the story. Justice's side. But being a police officer, the public judged him with an unrelenting eye—none more so than his own community.

"Ma, look, I can explain. It's nothing—"

"Let them not rule over me, then I will be blameless, and I shall be acquitted of great transgression," Ma said.

Justice was always impressed with how effortlessly his mother could recite scripture. Back when his father had passed, his mother had dived deeper into the Bible, but Justice had found himself too angry to listen. Too bitter to care.

"You don't have to. I believe you. It's just... I've known Ivery her whole life, she didn't deserve that." Ma darted her eyes at Goodchild.

A long silence passed between the three of them. Justice knew Ivery too. Feisty little Black girl with that fiery red hair, Ivery was hard to forget once you'd met her. He was ten years her senior. He used to give her loose change to get snacks from the ice-cream truck and keep an eye on cars that drove a little too slowly through the neighborhood. She was practically a little cousin of his, which was partly the reason why he'd taken her to the hospital first. Still, once she had recovered, Justice had to take her into custody. It was his job. There was no way around it.

Ma let out a bone-breaking cough. It was so loud it scratched Justice's eardrums. That sound was becoming too common. Ma refused to get herself checked out, she claimed, "if it pleased the Lord it pleased her" and Justice had to live with her decision. That cough was a constant reminder to Justice of her mortality.

Justice glanced around the room. Sitting upright on the coffee table was a picture of his little sister, Grace. When his father had passed, Justice had become the man of the house at seventeen, so hanging out was out of the question and so was attending a four-year university. At least his little sister would have a chance.

"Justice?" said a familiar voice, as Grace came from down the steps and stood at the entry of the living room. Justice stood and hugged his sister. She was a twig in his arms, all bones. Grace had previously undergone the transition from relaxed hair to embracing her natural curls. She'd had it cut and dyed it a soft lavender. Grace could rock any hairstyle, and, in all honesty, Justice thought she looked better with it short. Her hair reminded him of hundreds of tiny tulips growing from her scalp. In celebration of the drastic change, on her seventeenth birthday, she'd got a butterfly tattoo behind her left ear. It was a strange place for a tattoo, but Justice respected her decisions.

"It's good to see you, Grace. How's school?"

As quickly as the words came out of Justice's mouth, Grace's happy expression dissipated.

"Well, about that, so... I have some news," Grace muttered. "I got accepted into Carden University."

Anybody in their right mind would be excited to be accepted there. Carden was the premier Ivy League institution. An acceptance letter there meant any and every door to the future was within grasp. Yet, Grace seemed less than enthused.

Grace rubbed her elbow awkwardly. "I am happy, I am, truly... it's just... it costs seventy-eight thousand dollars per year."

The entire room slipped into a sorrowful silence. Tuition. Justice knew it.

"Well, there is financial aid, right?" Goodchild chimed in.

Again, Ma sent Goodchild the death stare. Justice knew that look. Even as a grown man his mom could correct his behavior with a simple glance. For Goodchild's sake, it would be wise to be quiet.

"Yeah, I got scholarships and grants to cover forty thousand dollars of it, and that is hard enough, but I'm short thirty-eight thousand."

Justice and Grace were siblings who shared a borderline clairvoyant bond. Whatever Grace felt, she didn't even need to express it, but he could sense it. He could feel her stress or whatever bad news clung to her spirit emitted it from her like heat. Justice knew that Grace was going to be somebody, maybe the next tech billionaire that would create jobs for millions one day she'd always been good with that computer stuff. Grace had a 4.5 G.P.A. She was not the type to go out all night partying and drinking and doing drugs. She had a good head on her shoulders. Yet, she was learning the hardest lesson: life did not reward you because you stayed out of trouble.

"We'll figure something out," Justice said, laying a hand on her wrist. That was the best advice he could offer and that often frustrated Grace. It was a burden to be the first one in the family to have the grades and opportunity to go to school.

"Can I talk to you about something, Jay?" Grace said, motioning for him to step into the kitchen with her. Justice followed behind his little sister. "I think I just discovered a way to help pay for it, but I'm not sure. There is this company called BRT Health Industries and they are offering enough monetary compensation for an experimental trial thing where they, like, do something with your eggs or something. I dunno the details. I just know if I get that money, I could pay my tuition and then some. Do you think I should do it? The problem is, I can't verify the reviews online about the trial. They all trace back to bots and invalid IP addresses."

Anything within his reach he would do for Grace, he would give a kidney for her if she asked. However, this school stuff was out of Justice's element. School applications, student loans, the FAFSA, all of that was a foreign language.

But Grace could never know that.

He was her older brother, protector, financial advisor, mentor, and anything else she needed when she needed it. There was no room for inadequacy.

The kitchen fell quiet. Justice crossed his arms, tucked his head into his chest and prayed for the right words to say. It was his job to make sure Grace didn't end up on a pole, so what he said next had to push her the right direction.

"Grace, you have to do your research before you just jump into things. Especially when it sounds this good."

"But you don't—"

"And if it was that easy. Why isn't everyone doing it? Why don't more people know about it?"

"I guess that makes sense, but how else am I—"

"That's all I have to say on that." Justice stormed off into the living room. That was the beginning and end of that conversation. He would figure out a way to help pay for her school and Grace knew better than to ignore his advice, no matter how incomplete or unfair it seemed. Justice always knew best.

A voice cut through the old-school television set. A bright blue screen flashed, then a young woman with blond hair appeared. The news caption at the bottom of the TV read: POLICE NEARLY KILL A BLACK UNARMED TEENAGER. It snatched the attention of the room.

"Earlier last week, events at the Easthampton mall left the community devastated as two police officers from the thirty-fifth precinct almost killed a young woman after an altercation at the local strip mall." As the reporter delivered the news, a recording from a camera phone played. Immediately, Justice recognized the two officers. It was Goodchild and himself.

Watching the news, Justice's stomach spat into a free fall.

"As you can see, the owner of the hair store strikes her first and when she manages to avoid his blow, she assaults him. We then see an officer pull her from attacking the store owner, throw her onto the concrete on her stomach, and drive his knee onto her shoulder blades, leaving this teenager, Ivery Johnson, with no room to breathe."

Though terribly edited, the recording painted a clear story. Goodchild's knee was on Ivery's back for much longer than necessary. Justice yanked Goodchild from Ivery, but the camera missed that moment. Instead it captured Justice shoving Ivery's face that was flushed with red and a myriad of bruises, into the scorching hot concrete. Justice threw handcuffs on her, and though the video lacked audio, the deep veins lifting on Justice's forehead, arms, and neck painted a clear image: police brutality. There was no disputing it. Ivery's high school physique did not stand a chance against him.

The news media needed an enemy and for some odd reason, they'd chosen him.

"I gotta go, Ma," Justice said, leaving a peck on her cheek.

Justice left first with Goodchild right behind him.

"Where are we going?" Goodchild asked.

"To the precinct, we need to tell our side of the story to Chief Glassman's face. I'm sure he's already working on the press release of how to cover his ass, which means, he might hang us out to dry."

The two hopped in the squad car and pulled off onto the road with Justice driving faster than normal.

"Hey, Reeves, I'm sorry what happened last week. I am, I didn't—"

"Don't," Justice stopped him, raising his right hand. "It happened. No one died. No need to re-live it."

Goodchild had been just one week out of the academy when on his first day on the job he'd damn near killed somebody. Justice had always thought there ought to be a test that prevented people like Goodchild—clumsy, clueless, and with no sense of awareness—from joining the force, and that day had been proof.

Justice wished he could have his old partner back; Goodchild was nothing like Mason. Though Mason was a typical pastel-polo-shirts-and-chino-pants-wearing college frat boy, he was aware of his privilege and used it for good. The man was a damn good cop and even better partner.

One night the two of them had arrived at a scene of a drug bust. They'd received a tip that these people had stored 50 kilos of cocaine inside their place, and as this was Justice's case, he and Mason were determined to find it. Two suspects had been present: the woman, a shy blond female, her skin was covered in dark spots and mottled flesh. She clearly had been on some type of illicit drug. Then the man: a balding, lean figure with tattoos covering his neck down to his wrists. Their townhome was a wreck. Inside, filthy clothes were tossed everywhere, papers, dirt, leaves, and all types of children's toys filled the hardwood flooring, so no matter where Justice stepped his foot landed on top of something. The ivory walls had gained a pale-yellow hue from years of cigarette smoke. Gray smudges were plastered along the flooring and kitchen walls. Dishes were stacked to the window seal, and an overwhelming scent of garbage hung in the air like a camera watching the police and their every move. Dog poop was scattered up the steps to their second floor, and what Justice found there left him speechless. He'd searched through mattresses, sofas, cushions, pillows, suitcases, drawers, under tables, beds, and linen, but nothing turned up, not until he looked in the baby's room. These people had stored the drugs inside old diaper boxes, wet wipes, and children's old toy containers. Justice would have taken a bullet for that man, but on that day, searching through those boxes for drugs, Mason took one first.

Now, Mason would be in a wheelchair for the rest of his life. From that day forward, Justice had learned the importance of staying alert, no matter how run-of-the-mill a situation may seem.

"You're right... Watch out!" Goodchild pointed past the dashboard.

Justice slammed on the brakes and came to a screeching halt in a near-empty parkway. A woman staggered into the middle of the street crying hysterically without regard for her life. Oncoming traffic on both sides came to a rubber-burning standstill.

Justice forced the door open and rushed to the woman in need.

"Ma'am, I need you to go back to the sidewalk."

She refused to listen to him. In place of reason, her bright pink acrylics latched onto his shoulder.

"My baby! Someone took my sweet girl!" She broke down and fell to her knees.

Justice then escorted the woman back onto the safety of the sidewalk. Goodchild stepped into the driver's seat and steered right, turning the patrol vehicle onto the curb.

First, his mom had mentioned missing girls, and now this woman.

"How old is she?" Justice sat eye to eye with the woman.

Disoriented and with her hair disheveled, the middle-aged woman could barely form a sentence.

"She's... she's... She just turned eighteen. Her name is Briana."

Justice nodded, thanking God that the woman was finally responsive. "And when was the last time you saw her?"

"Three days ago... she said she went to an interview with some company about donating her eggs..."

"And what was the name of the company?"

"I don't know," she said, rocking herself back and forth. "And I haven't heard from her since." The woman broke down into tears once more and tossed herself into his arms. Her sobbing warmed his chest like a furnace. There was a deep guttural pain in her tears, and as Justice held her, he found himself being swallowed into the black hole of her agony. This woman was not much older than his own mother and until her daughter was found, her suffering would know no end. Justice ran a hand along her back, comforting her. Whatever had happened to this girl, right then and there, he had made up his mind to find her.

First, it was Tawnya Reese, then Shaina Boyce, and then Maria Edmond. And now this girl, Briana... all in a matter of weeks. Something was going on and he intended on finding out exactly what that was.

Chapter 3

Jacqui: Enemies In High Places

Jacqui, only one phrase could describe this woman: burned out. Jacqui had given her youth to the study of medicine, but now, she was an echo of the doctor she once was. These days she wore a lab coat, worked in a hospital, and merely went through the motions. She had such an air of mystery surrounding her that no matter how close someone believed they were to Jacqui Stevenson, they never really knew her. Life had taught her to keep everyone at a distance.

Usually, Jacqui handled stress well, but today she was nearing her point of no return.

Nurses in burgundy scrubs scrambled inside the small room readying the defibrillator machine. Jacqui took lead.

"Charge to two hundred."

Even with nearly two decades of experience, moments like these were proof, no two days were the same in Mercy Hospital.

Jacqui wiped the sweat off her forehead with the back of her forearm. A river of straight black hair woven into a single braid fell down her spine, its thickness carried heat on her back. It had been nearly thirty-six hours now; she was running on fumes at this point.

The whirring of the machine sucked the air from the room, and the nurses jumped back from the bed. Rubbing the defibrillator pads together before slamming them onto her patient's bare chest, Jacqui watched as the patient's pregnant belly jerked from the charge.

"No pulse," a nurse announced.

Quickly, Jacqui kept up compressions. Each pump pulled her closer to exhaustion, but none of that mattered, not in the slightest. Not only was Irene a Premier Care patient—people who paid top dollar for the best services—but Jacqui had delivered Irene's third child only five years previously, there was no way she could let her die. The love between Irene and her husband, Donovan, was the kind that stuck with Jacqui. The day Irene had given birth to their first child, her husband, Don, had brought a two-foot bottle of wine to the delivery room and Irene had laughed so hard that her face had turned as red as her hair. Unfortunately, Jacqui had to be the bearer of bad news and advised that drinking would prohibit breastfeeding. Instead, Don had given the bottle to the staff.

"Please help my wife," Donovan now pleaded, his voice cracking under the strain of heartache. Tears streamed down his cherry-red face. Jacqui could feel his pain; it fueled her all the more.

"Clear."

Everyone in the confined space backed away from the bed. Jacqui shocked Irene again. Her body reacted to the jolt. In utter silence, Jacqui watched the black screen above her bed, anxious for any sign of life.

"She's stable," Jacqui said. Watching Irene's chest rise and fall brought relief. Yet, Jacqui had a feeling Irene was not home free.

"What's happening to her?" Donovan asked. "She was feeling fine until a few weeks ago." His disheveled tie nearly fell from his neck. Sweat permeated his expensive gray-black suit. His dirty blond hair was matted from sleeping against a wall in the waiting room, but his only concern was his wife, Irene.

"We were at an Italian restaurant, she tried a new wine there, and um... She only had one sip, some doctors said she can do that even though she's so far along. I should've brought her here sooner when she first mentioned the chest pains. And then just like that, she stopped breathing." Donovan lost his cool, cries consumed his words.

"Sir, we need you to wait outside," Ivan, a nurse, said as he guided the husband out of the room. "When we have an update, we'll let you know. Your wife is in great hands, I promise."

Confused, Donovan agreed and stepped outside, and Ivan slid between the two transparent doors before they closed shut.

Inside the room there was disarray. Nurses scattered along the walls searching for syringes, watching blood pressure monitors, and injecting IVs with pain meds. A barely conscious patient, and Jacqui without a clue as to what kept stopping Irene's heart. Every test came back normal. If she didn't find the root, Irene would bear the punishment.

On the monitor, Jacqui waited for Irene's chest X-ray to appear. The sight stunned her.

"Wide mediastinum," Dr. Isaiah muttered.

"Her aorta," Jacqui said, locking eyes with Dr. Isaiah, fully realizing what this meant. Jacqui yanked the handles to the hospital's bed upward and Isaiah repeated the same on his side.

"She needs surgery now. Have anesthesia meet us upstairs!" Jacqui yelled, hurrying the staff.

The three nurses in the room nodded and went to work. The thick glass doors opened as Isaiah and Jacqui rushed Irene through the room and into the elevator. Mr. Donovan entered before the silver doors closed shut.

"Don't worry, sweetie. It is going to be alright," Don

whispered to his wife, holding her hand in his. Though he fought fiercely against the tears, they won.

"Don," she whimpered. Her shallow voice barely held together.

Hearing her speak brought a smile to Don's face.

Jacqui stepped forward about to touch Don on his shoulder from behind him, but Isaiah grabbed Jacqui's forearm, stopping her. And by the look on his face, he knew, and now Jacqui knew a frightening truth. A truth she could not tell Don.

"I... love... you," Irene struggled. For a brief second, they both wore smiles on their faces.

"I love you too, Irene. You're going to be fine." He ran his fingers through her hair.

"Do you remember that time last year when Jon Jon was in the fifth grade and asked what an orgasm is?" Don asked and Irene smiled in response. "And you told me to leave it alone, but he kept asking so I had to tell him something. So, I said it's when you're having a really good time and you feel really good, and you cannot explain it."

Irene nodded and half-smiled.

"And then later that month, we went to New Funland. When Jon Jon and I got off that roller coaster, he ran over to you and do you remember what—"

"He said, *Mommy, Mommy, guess what? I just had an orgasm!*"

Irene and Donovan spat into a chuckle.

Jacqui covered her mouth in a failed attempt to disguise laughter, but the story was too hilarious.

"Kids, man, they really listen to you," Donovan said, looking at Jacqui, then turning back to Irene. "I need you here, Irene. I realized I am not the best at answering those types of questions," he said, and she cracked a smile. Irene fisted his collar and Don leaned closer as she parted her lips to speak.

"I... I." Irene's eyes rolled into her skull. The elevator was only on the second floor. Jacqui knew that they were running out of time faster than predicted.

"Irene?"

She said nothing, but something was off. Jacqui placed two fingers between Irene's neck and chin.

"Come on." Jacqui started compressions, but this time there was no backup, not until they reached their destination on the fifth floor. Jacqui pumped hard against her chest, watching Irene's body jump in reaction, but no life came to her. Then Irene's head fell limp and her eyes closed. This time for good.

"No, no, no," Donovan said as though it was the only word born to him.

The harder Jacqui pumped, the angrier she became. Not at Irene of course, but herself. Then memories of placing those bright-eyed children in Irene's arms fueled Jacqui's hands. If she had saved her from near-death at childbirth, then she could, without a doubt, do it again.

The elevator doors finally opened. Jacqui kept going, no matter the burn in her biceps, until Isaiah's hand landed on her wrist.

"Jacqui," he uttered.

In that one word, Jacqui knew what he was about to say, but she could not listen. She could not bring herself to believe that this time Irene's heart had stopped—permanently.

"This is a tragic incident, please don't blame yourself," Isaiah said and walked off as more nurses rushed to Irene's now lifeless body.

To brush off a patient's death with such cold-hearted ease was something Jacqui had never been able to master.

Stepping behind the front counter, Jacqui watched as Cindy wrestled through a stack of clear clipboards, nearly dropping them in the process as she was so clumsy. That was one of Jacqui's favorite things about Cindy, the girl could always find a way to make her smile.

"It's not as bad as it looks," Cindy joked. But her humor fell on silent ears. Cindy pressed on, "Is everything okay?" Cindy asked, leaning into Jacqui's peripheral vision.

Now was not the time.

Jacqui stayed silent as she tapped on the touchscreen monitor in front of her. Like an annoying little sister, Jacqui's quiet demeanor had sparked Cindy's interest. Countless wine nights, crying sessions in the employee bathroom, and lunches filled with gossip of their ridiculous co-workers had formed the entirety of Jacqui and Cindy's friendship. They were best friends born twelve years apart. The two had become telepathic they spent so much time together. Even if Jacqui tried hiding something, eventually, Cindy found out.

Cindy stepped closer to Jacqui.

"I am fine." The dull and dry tone of voice had failed to convince Cindy it was the truth. It barely convinced Jacqui herself.

"You know, the last time you had that look on your face was right before you told me about your mom." Cindy's words stopped Jacqui in place. Only a few years had passed since Jacqui's mother had died from cervical cancer. The day before her death, they'd gotten into an argument about something so small and meaningless, but at the time it had been enough for Jacqui to refuse all conversation. Now, Jacqui would carry that regret to her grave.

"It's nothing, Cyn," Jacqui said, darting eyes at her. "Fine, since you insist. You know my patient, Irene?"

"Yes, I heard. You know how news travels around here. I'm sorry to hear about it."

A sudden warmth stung the back of Jacqui's eyes as she withheld tears. "There was something off about the way it all happened. It was something I had never seen before. Like some sort of underlying pre-existing condition must have..."

It hit her.

This was not the first time this pattern that mothers, wealthy mothers at that, suddenly lost the ability to carry a baby to term. Jacqui had scanned through hundreds of pages of peer-reviewed documents on birth-related complications. Perhaps this was a public health issue? Maybe something nearby had contaminated their water source? Like the Flint situation, prolonged lead exposure could cause birth defects. However, people like Irene had the best access to everything and that was not an exaggeration. They had organic food markets on every corner, alkaline water fountains, sea moss supplements in their bread, running trails, and cycling studios everywhere. Only non-fat, gluten-free, dairy-free, vegan, eco-friendly, anti-aging and antioxidant products entered their homes. What could possibly cause the healthiest people to suddenly lose the ability to have children? It just didn't make sense.

"It did what?" Cindy said, her words jolting Jacqui back into the present.

"I don't know yet... shoot, I have a meeting with the director in a little bit. I'll see you later," Jacqui said as she extricated herself from behind the desk.

AS THE METAL CHURN of the elevator doors eased open, she marched onto level eight—the Premier Care floor of Mercy Hospital. This was the floor exclusively designed for patients who owned eight-figure hedge funds and million-dollar life insurance policies. The ivory marble floors were so well polished that she could see her reflection anywhere. Though the exquisite floors and white hall lights shot a blinding pain through her eyes, combined with the angelic music over the intercom, Mercy Hospital tended to feel more like a five-star resort at times. At least the Premier Care floor did. It was a luxury establishment of its own and by comparing floors everyone knew that was where all the funding went.

As Jacqui continued through the halls filled with peers dressed in suits and lab coats, the porcelain white walls showed ads from skincare to weight management supplements. Overlapping conversations overwhelmed her ears. It was 5:00am, but Jacqui could not tell how early it was, other than from the bags under her eyes. They said New York never slept and neither did Mercy Hospital.

Every floor had a bathroom, but none like that of the Premier Care level. With its marbled-terrazzo flooring, the delicate scent of vanilla and grapefruit disinfectant that perfumed the refined halls, combined with the bamboo stalls, the place always gave Jacqui the feeling of an unspoken elegance. Above all, she had total and utter privacy. Most people went years working at Mercy Hospital and never knew of this sacred space. It was her secret haven.

Nearing the ladies' room, a digital screen right outside the entrance stood out to Jacqui, mostly because of the twenty or thirty faces on it. All of them were young enough to be just starting high school. At the top it read:

Have You Seen Me?

Strange.

Jacqui could not remember this virtual missing person sign being here in the first place, let alone that there were so many young women missing in Ballantyne. She took a moment to look at their faces. *Wow.* They were all brown-skinned girls. One girl had these hazel green eyes so stunning she looked like she should be a singer or an actress, but instead, she was gone. Jacqui dropped her head and placed a hand on her chest. She could not imagine anything like this happening to her daughter, her sweet Ashley. Her heart ached at the sleepless nights their parents must have endured. The worst of it all... when brown girls went missing in Ballantyne, they were never found.

Jacqui walked towards her meeting with the Director. Before she reached the boardroom she passed by the maternity sector: her area of expertise. She stopped when she noticed something. Usually, she heard newborn cries. Their little high-pitched screams could sometimes be so loud that they gave her a headache, but right now all she heard was silence.

Slowly, Jacqui walked over to a floor-length glass window. Here, she typically found dozens of tiny bodies sleeping or kicking in their tiny transparent bassinets, but, instead, she found one single baby dressed in light blue. Last week, she'd had a hundred patients, and all of them had given birth to either a stillborn, lost the child well before their due date, or were like Irene, died giving birth. And now looking at this single baby boy all by himself, the child was worth more than gold.

Jacqui reached the meeting room where she expected only to see the Director, Eric, but there was a surprise awaiting her. Inside the meeting room, they were not alone. Several men dressed in expensive black suits surrounded the table.

"Dr. Stevenson, please," an older gentleman said, gesturing at a chair.

On his wrist was a watch costing six-hundred thousand dollars. Whatever they wanted with her, these men did not waste time. They meant business.

Jacqui cast her gaze across the meeting room. In front of her stretched a blackened-wood table that took up entirely too much space. Jacqui found Eric stuffed in a corner like some intern. Between Eric's designer suits that showed off his wisdom-tooth-shaped figure and his dusky-scented cologne that smelt more like his musk than anything else, Jacqui could not stand him, but she noted something strange about Eric at this moment. Usually, Eric made his presence known by sitting at the head of the table like the head football star of a high school team but in the presence of these other men, Eric was a puppy with his tail between his legs.

Besides Eric, she counted six of them; all strong jawlined men with no-room-for-mistakes expressions on their faces. Her throat closed with fear. From where Jacqui stood, she was on trial, and if these men were her jury, she was, without doubt, guilty.

Anxious, she slid into a seat. Her heart was beating so hard she could feel it through her lab coat. What could they possibly have to talk about?

"My name is Arnold. I own Lanzran Inc. You're familiar with us, yes?"

He was a tall, silver-bearded man with dark eyes that looked like they had something devious to hide. Even with his pleasant smile, there was something off-putting about him. She searched his entire ensemble for the origin of her angst. Did it lie within the smirk he made whenever he mentioned his business? Or was it the gaze of his colleagues drilling into her from all sides without saying a word? Whatever it was, everything about this room, filled with these silent and intimidating people, scared her to the bone.

"Yes, I am familiar. You all provide medical equipment among other things."

"Yes, that we do. By chance, do you know why we've called you here?" Arnold asked. A deafening silence swelled within the room. The kind of silence that came before a judge handed out a life sentence. *What did little Dr. Jacqui Stevenson do to draw the attention of the top CEOs in the region?*

All eyes fell upon Jacqui. She cleared her throat, trying to stop her voice from trembling. "No, I don't."

"I don't imagine you do," he chuckled. "Well, I will get right to it. We've noticed you've been trying to access classified files. I am curious. Why is that?" Though he kept his tone light and friendly, Jacqui could feel the threat on his breath.

Jacqui sat upright. "I was researching some abnormalities."

"And what has your research led you to?" another man around the table interjected. His accent sounded Japanese to her. Did the man fly over fourteen hours just to talk to Jacqui? Whatever had caused this conversation went much deeper than some flimsy research. Jacqui was certain of it.

"Nothing, I hadn't enough time to understand exactly what's going on."

"Not yet," Arnold added. "How would you like to come aboard my company, BRT Health Industries? I started this program with hopes to further understand these *abnormalities* as you put it. Now keep in mind, we are a pioneering fertility treatment company. We are inclined to take certain risks on this specific project."

The men seated near Arnold shot their gaze at him like Arnold was revealing some precious recipe.

Though the voices in her head were screaming at her to excuse herself from the room, she stayed. Glancing at Eric, she recalled the last time she had an opportunity for advancement snatched from her. The Chief of Surgery position had been vacant since Dr. Dowey had retired. She was beyond certain she was next in line. She had the most amount of time served. It was her right. One morning, when she'd walked into work only a few minutes late, she'd realized something important was about to happen. The entire floor of nurses, technicians, and her colleagues had gathered in a circle of roaring applause. Eric stood at the center and with an arm around Dr. Isaiah—Jacqui called him the good ol' boy, a real teacher's pet. It had been pathetic to watch. Dr. Isaiah had rolled his shoulders back and stood up tall, smiling so hard his eyes appeared closed shut. Then Eric said those fateful words that sent fury into the pit of Jacqui's stomach. "Everyone welcome our new Chief of Surgery."

Jacqui could not let the past repeat itself. She placed her elbows on the table and leaned forward with intrigue. "What project?"

In response, Arnold stood. His chair scuffed the marble flooring.

"I have clients that are leaders in their fields. From government, finance, and information technology, but all that wealth means nothing if you have no one to pass it down to."

That newborn boy dressed in light blue came to her in a single flash. Then Jacqui remembered all of those empty bassinets around him.

"You would be on the frontlines; our program aims to provide a solution to the delicate situation we're in. Without healthy children, we have no future. I believe a woman of your talents could assist us in this endeavor, given the right resources," Arnold said, pacing around the table, his steps slow and calculated as he eased closer to her side of the room and glided past the wide-framed windows behind him.

Jacqui threw her gaze to her right, towards Eric. He sat quietly in the chair. His suit swallowed his body like a punishment, the top three buttons of his blazer barely held his jacket closed. He fiddled with his fingers, idly. This meeting was above his pay grade. The coward could not even look her in the face. He may have passed her up for that promotion, but this was her chance. Her focus went back to Arnold.

"And I will have access to everything I will need?"

"You'll have more than enough," Arnold said, smiling slyly.

He stood over her, extending his right arm. "What do you say, Dr. Stevenson?"

Without hesitation or even discussing her intuition, Jacqui leaped from her seat. Confidently, matching Arnold's eye level, she shook his hand.

"Welcome to the team, follow me," Arnold said.

"Oh, you meant right now?"

"Do you have somewhere else you need to be?" he replied with an eyebrow raised. His colleagues stood and followed them.

Jacqui glanced back at the men, who together formed a wall behind her. The hairs rose on the back of her neck. *Where is the contract? Shouldn't I get at least a day or two to make the decision final? Why the rush?* Jacqui thought, but the time for asking questions had passed. Arnold and his colleagues were the equivalent of congressmen in their fields. Jacqui didn't want to come across unprofessional, perhaps later they would hammer out the details. She then faced forward, holding eye contact with Arnold. Telling them *no* was, without a doubt, off the table.

"Good." He smiled.

Arnold led her to the elevators. Walking behind him, Jacqui caught a glimpse of her reflection in the white halls. Arnold at the lead, the men trailing behind, and her, crowded in the middle. The only thing missing were shackles along her wrists and ankles. Everything was happening so fast. Too fast.

Upon entrance of the steel box, Arnold took the spot near the dim-lit numbers. His hands slipped past every single digit and stopped beside the emergency icon. He slid a square panel to the side, revealing a hidden black button. It took them to:

LEVEL UG

Jacqui had worked at this hospital for almost two decades; yet she'd never known this was here.

The elevator doors split open, and immediately she wished

she could go back. White translucent lights illuminated the mysterious level. Two thick transparent doors stood in front of them. As Arnold walked, an optical device emerged from a wall panel and scanned his retina. The doors parted allowing passage. All of this gave Jacqui the feeling that if she continued, only something horrible was waiting for her. She had been in all types of laboratories, but this... she could not pinpoint what it was, but this feeling had begun lifting the hairs on her arms.

"What is this?" Jacqui asked.

"It's called the Colony. Fifty floors dedicated to research and development all right under Mercy Hospital. You'll be working on this level. Disregard the other floors. They have separate purposes."

Fifty floors?

"Why go underground? It seems like a hassle compared to having your own building beside the hospital."

"Working here, privately, gives the company certain *freedoms* the surface just can't compete."

Perhaps he had a point. Mercy Hospital's third floor, the research and development department, could use some work. Systems often went offline for hours and made it difficult to service patients. Jacqui had a few horror stories of her own when dealing with all the new tech. However, one question remained.

"Why haven't I heard of this before? Why the secrecy?"

Arnold ignored her and kept walking. The place was never-ending, and he sure knew how to power walk for his age. There were no windows, only one or two black doors with Roman numerals on them. With every corner they turned, the long, gray-tiled hallways began to look alike. Soon, Jacqui could no longer distinguish the front from the back. She had no choice but to follow Arnold.

Arnold stopped in front of a charcoal gray wall. There was

no entryway, no windows, no signs, no wording of where she was—nothing but the thick wall of cold concrete in front of them. He had led her to a dead end. What in the hell was going on?

He stepped into the corner and a small square panel appeared from the wall. Arnold entered a password into a wordless keypad. Moments later, a horizontal line split down the middle. The entire wall folded into the sides like elevator doors. There were so many levels of security to this place, like it had a secret to protect.

Jacqui entered the room behind Arnold. The sight before her stole both her breath and words. She should have listened to that inner voice. This was a mistake.

The room was the size of an industrial warehouse. Strips of blaring ceiling lights illuminated every inch of this enormous space. The floors were a pale hue of blue, cold and lifeless. Soft mechanic noises of monitors filled the silence. A sickening chill lingered in the air. However, the most shocking thing of all were the dozens upon dozens of unconscious women chained to hospital beds. There were too many to count.

Jacqui moved closer to a bed.

Wait a second. Jacqui recognized her. Curious, she moved even closer. Her light skin was without a blemish, her face was slender and full of something that could only be described as youth. Though her eyes were slightly open, she was not awake.

Jacqui took a step back.

Fear began to take root, shaking every part of her body and Jacqui found herself incapable of moving. Jacqui *did* know her, that girl was the same, brown-skinned girl with the piercing hazel-green eyes. *No. No this could not...* She was the girl from the **Have You Seen Me?** digital screen that Jacqui had just read on level eight of this very same building. *Oh. My. God. She was a missing person!* Bile rose from the pit of Jacqui's stomach. *If that were the case, then who were all these other women?*

There was another door, one of many, in the far corner. Arnold saw Jacqui looking at it. Casually, he whistled while walking over to it and he unveiled the inside.

Jacqui knew she should not go inside, the smarter part of her had long realized that this project was nothing like what Arnold had told her only moments ago, but she had to know.

Stepping through the entryway and flipping on the blaring ceiling lights, Jacqui covered her mouth. There was only one word to describe what she saw. Horror. Pure horror.

Like pillars, there were countless thick glass tubes filled with a liquid substance. Inside each, were pale-skinned babies. She was in complete disbelief at what her eyes were feeding her. Okay, this was a dream, and she must have fallen asleep at her computer, and she was imagining this. However, right now, she was about to wake up in three... two... one—

"We haven't been able to figure it out," Arnold said, walking between the lime green pillars. "Something is forcing women, in particular, Premier Care patients, to physiologically spontaneously abort their unborn children, and the ones that make it full term are stillborn." He stopped in front of one pillar, examining it, staring into the closed eyes of a baby boy. Was it sorrow or anger coming from his eyes? Perhaps it was both. "This is why I recruited you. To handle our current predicament. You will have access to anything you need right in the Colony. On the main floor, this floor, of course."

Jacqui turned around and found Arnold staring at her, smiling. He wanted this. Then she put the pieces together. The Black women were chained to beds. The stillborn children contained. It all suddenly made sense. She was the missing link in this experiment. This was why Arnold had chosen her.

"My research from my thesis, that's why you need me,"

Jacqui said, dropping her head into her chest. "It is purely theoretical: a full womb transplant including the fallopian tubes and restructuring the recipient's DNA. This procedure has never been done before. It is far too dangerous, and there is still so much that could go wrong."

"What do we have to lose? A few bodies? Imagine how we could change the world if this works? The life you would have if it succeeded?" As Arnold spoke, his expression lit up, like he was a genius on the cusp of brilliance.

Jacqui looked back at the brown girl with the green eyes. Her work had led her here.

"Besides, we've already begun. We're not stopping until we see results. The Aphaia Corporation will not take no for an answer. And now that we have you, that won't be a problem, will it?" His words cut Jacqui to the bone.

Aphaia Corporation. Jacqui committed the name to memory.

There it was. His true self. The evil she sensed in the conference room had fully bloomed in front of her. She should have trusted herself and left when there was time. Now that she knew about this place, there was no way to unsee it.

She could not hear another word from Arnold's mouth. This man had floating bodies of stillborn babies and Black women chained to hospital beds stored underneath a hospital. Jacqui could care less about any explanation he used to help himself sleep at night. Despite her inner rebellion, she was so shocked. She was stunned at the scale of success in his operation, and having gone undisturbed for so long. The number of resources necessary to make this work from the beds, monitors, lights, and high-level security measures to the hospital staff involved, and investors who poured money to ensure its success. With all this working in Arnold's favor, Jacqui had no words.

"When we created the Premier Vaccine, we knew there

were risks," he whispered to himself, placing his hands in his pockets.

"Premier Vaccine? What are you talking about?" Jacqui crossed her arms. "You know what? I don't want to know. I'm done. I rescind my offer. I can't do this." Jacqui stormed off towards the exit.

"Oh, I think you can," he smirked. "If you refuse, I will ruin you. First, I'll take your house, savings, and retirement. You'll be homeless by the end of the week. I'll make sure of it."

Jacqui kept walking, paying him no attention. Her possessions meant a lot to her, but they were not worth her dignity and peace of mind.

"Then we'll come after everyone you care about. What is the name of your daughter's father? Is it Damon Velasquez? You two did make a beautiful couple. So sad to hear you two couldn't work it out. It would be a shame if he was deported. And how old is your daughter again? Fifteen? Or is it seventeen? Either way, I think she would do great here."

Jacqui stopped mid-stride.

Arnold knew no limits; the man would stoop so low as to involve her family for this. Damon earned amnesty at eight months old when his mother brought him to Ballantyne. He had no other country as his home. But more than that, how could he drag her baby girl into this? Arnold was the devil.

Chilling screams cut through the air. Five rows down and nine beds from the entrance, a young woman with natural bright red hair cried in pain. To Jacqui, it was an unusual sight to see a woman of deep mahogany complexion with red hair atop her head that blended seamlessly at the scalp. *Another young girl who'd been brought here because of her own research?* She had to help the girl. Her forehead glistened with heat despite the freezing temperatures in the room. Sweat soaked her hospital gown and tears streamed down her face. Without any hesitation, Jacqui rushed to her aid.

"Her heart rate is spiking, what did you do to her?" Jacqui yelled.

"Nothing, they are instructed to give her injections every week. Or every hour. I'm not sure." Arnold's cool composure remained even as he watched the girl suffer from his doing.

"Injections?! With what?"

"Do I look like a doctor to you? Figure it out."

Jacqui turned back to the girl in pain. Arnold was useless here.

"What's your name, sweetie?" Jacqui asked, trying to distract her from the pain.

"Ivery."

"That's beautiful." Jacqui smiled, but her soft tone failed to calm the fear in Ivery's eyes.

"Am I gonna... die?"

Jacqui ran a hand over Ivery's forehead. "I will do everything in my power to make sure that does not happen, Ivery, okay?"

Ivery nodded. That one subtle movement shocked her into a seizure. Adrenaline rushed through Jacqui as she searched her body for clues. What was going on with Ivery?

"Help me hold her down!" Jacqui yelled.

Though her command was directed at Arnold, two nurses in black scrubs, gloves, and surgical masks appeared and assisted Jacqui. They reacted in such a calm manner as though they had done this before. They probably had, thought Jacqui.

Ivery foamed at the mouth. Her eyes rolled to the back of her head. Sweat poured from her brown skin. A nurse handed Jacqui a syringe. At first, Jacqui merely stared at it, a clear substance dripped from the needle edge. She could not use that; she had no clue what was in there.

"It will calm her," the nurse said sternly through a surgical mask.

Jacqui then looked back at Ivery struggling. She knew that she was partly responsible for her being there, she needed any help Jacqui could give her. Finding a vein on the girl's arm, Jacqui buried the needle into it.

Ivery's erratic movements calmed, and her breathing stabilized.

A sigh left Jacqui, as she assumed the worst had passed. She cleaned off the fluids from Ivery's lips. However, she still had some choice words for Arnold.

"If she dies, it's on you," Jacqui said calmly, but rage infused her words.

"With you here, I'm certain that won't happen." He turned to walk away but stopped himself. "By chance, Dr. Jacqui, do you know how many abortions this girl has had?"

"Knowing that would be a clear violation of her privacy."

"Three."

A gasp escaped from Jacqui's lips. The girl had to be no older than seventeen, maybe eighteen. Jacqui knew plenty of women who had made that same decision, her mother was not exempt from that group. Still, Jacqui always felt it was not her place to judge.

"Every woman has a reason why they do things."

"The girl graduated high school last week. Just think about it, Dr. Stevenson, what kind of woman would she become? What kind of mother?" Arnold looked back at Ivery, scoffed, and walked away.

Jacqui turned back to Ivery and stroked her bright hair softly, hoping it eased her suffering. She looked so young; her adult features had hardly formed on her face. Watching Ivery's chest heave up and down reminded Jacqui of her daughter's first moments. When her daughter, Ashley, had been born, the doctors had said she would not make it, and looking at Ivery, right now, brought her back to that moment, as she'd watched her own daughter fight for her life in this same hospital. Ten days later, Jacqui had brought her bundle of joy home.

When Jacqui had become a doctor, she'd vowed to help people make their lives better and worthwhile. However, *this* project crossed a line, despite the outcome it would produce, giving healthy living children to those struggling to get pregnant. That had been the central argument for her graduate thesis, that the ends justified the means, but this was different. These girls were patients too. They needed help to survive this torment. They deserved a life.

Rapid beeping noises snatched her attention. The numbers on a screen near Ivery's bed began drastically falling from double digits in green. Before long, the numbers turned into a red zero. In less than a minute, a straight line took form on the screen. A high-pitched noise pierced her ears. Ivery's hand dropped from the edge of the hospital bed, and now, she laid motionless. All her breathing ceased.

The two nurses moved quickly and pushed Ivery's bed into a separate room. Like there was a procedure for this. Like they knew Ivery was not going to make it. More than that, they *anticipated* that she would not survive. Jacqui knew she should not stay, but now that she saw Ivery's lifeless face, like that of Irene's... there was no way she could leave.

Chapter 4

Cara: A Fresh Start

C hilly air crept along her flesh. Slowly, she tried moving her legs, but they protested her command, something else had control. Cara was stuck. Then her eyes fluttered open. And dear God, she would give anything to be anywhere else than here. Was this a dream? It had to be. Because what she saw next struck fear through her spine.

Piping hot ceiling lights burst through the sheer skin of her eyelids. A heartless gray ceiling stared down a mile above her. The room was spinning, an endless loop of gray patches and a flashing light.

Where the hell was she?

She moved to prop herself on her elbows, but a resistance stopped her from fully sitting upright. Clinking noises accompanied her struggle. That soft metallic sound brought to her attention that something was terribly, terribly wrong.

Cara was chained to a bed. Her hands were bound to each side of her, attached to a steel bar. Her feet were strung apart with each foot secured to the side of the bed, leaving her legs open to the unforgiving air conditioning. She was tied down by metallic restraints that dug into her skin with merciless consistency. Cara had been stripped of all clothing except a thin white material that resembled a hospital gown, the sheet of white fabric felt like paper against her, and it barely covered past her knees, but left a giant slip exposing her backside.

A constant beeping sound drummed in her ears in a steady flow as it served as a quiet clue of her whereabouts. She turned her attention to the bedside and there was a monitor filled with green digits and lines along with flashing numbers and symbols of hearts, gears, and bandage icons plastered on the screen. It was in that moment her last memory surfaced.

She'd jammed a foot on the brakes as her car swerved off the road and crashed into a swampy ditch. That putrid stench of rubber road burn still clung to her nostrils. The airbag had deployed, shoving Cara back into her seat—hard. Water had poured into the car from a nearby runoff. Grasping at her seat belt now stuck in its place from the sheer force of the impact, Cara had been trapped, losing air and time. Helpless, afraid, and with adrenaline fueling her anxiety. Cara had genuinely believed that these were her last moments.

Then, her driver-side window had been smashed open. Shards of glass scraped against her forearms as she shielded her face from the shrapnel. A firm hand had pulled her from the wreckage. Her head pounded. At the touch of her scalp, blood oozed from her temple. The coppery taste of blood filled her tongue. She'd been grateful to set foot on the ground again.

"She's in no condition..."

The accident made no sense, and she could not even recall whose voice she had heard. Then the darkness had reclaimed her and in the next minute of her life, she was here, trapped, wherever *here* meant. Between passing out and ending up in a sketchy warehouse remained a complete blur to her.

Looking to her left and her right, she noticed something that had evaded her at first. On each side of her, there was a girl, a young Black female, suffering the same fate. The girl on her right had skin so light that there were visible freckles all along her forearms and cheek. Around her wrists were chains wrapped twice, and her feet endured the same, as the girl's body was so small, she might have had the chance to slip out if her captors had not been as smart. The young woman on the other side probably wore a dress size twelve if Cara had to guess and merely had handcuffs binding her feet and hands. They were secured so tightly that her wrists had begun swelling from the contact.

A breeze forced a shiver through Cara, the kind that made her shoulders, legs, and elbows shake without her permission. The sudden wind felt like a reminder that her life was now out of her own control, that someone else could take her body and use it for whatever they wanted, while she laid there, completely, and utterly powerless. She had none of her possessions, no phone, no clothes, and no idea of where she was, nothing but stone-gray walls surrounding her, and the faces of other women trapped in the same predicament.

A set of footsteps closed in. The rhythm sounded like that of a dress shoe, a man's dress shoe. Before long, the owner of those feet came into her view. The overhead lighting behind the man cast a sinister shadow. Dark circles rested beneath his eyes, blocking Cara from seeing his entire face. She could only make out a dark figure wearing a white lab coat and a stethoscope around his neck. He was facing her with a slight grin. But even worse, who knew what this man had in store for her.

"Ms. Esperanza, so lovely to meet you."

Chapter 5

Jacqui: Hidden In Plain Sight

Jacqui's work had now claimed the lives of innocent women, there was no other way to possibly look at it. Seeing Ivery's body dragged out by those two nurses, should have pushed Jacqui to the local police station. It should have made her tell the news, reporters, bloggers, anybody that could get the truth to the public. But be it her desire to help women still trapped or her feeling guilty of creating the whole mess, she stayed and learned. She spent hours trying to figure out what the hell was in that injection she'd administered to Ivery, and if it indeed did cause her untimely demise.

Entering work that morning, not her usual halfway-happy self, the bitter reality of what Jacqui had signed up for with BRT Health Industries weighed on her heavily. She had made worse decisions before, such as divorcing her husband without at least trying couple's therapy. He cheated and to Jacqui that meant the marriage was already over. In that case, she'd refused to seek help as she had already made up her mind. But this topped it all. Jacqui was being forced to keep an unbearable secret from everyone, her daughter, her boss, her best friend, Cindy. Never had Jacqui felt so alone. And every time she closed her eyes to sleep at night, all she could see were their faces; young, barely having reached adulthood and most of them had just graduated from high school or dropped out altogether. All of them were stuck just below the surface of freedom. The only consolation Jacqui had was the fact that these women were unconscious; at least they would never know what was happening to them.

The instant Jacqui closed her locker, her pager went off. She sighed hard through her nostrils. Jacqui knew exactly who was trying to reach her and he was the last person she wanted to see.

Jacqui rushed down to the ground-floor elevator. Twisting the key in the secret compartment, she waited patiently as the steel box lowered into her second home: Level UG. As she stepped off, Arnold stood there awaiting her.

"Good morning, Dr. Stevenson."

Saying nothing, Jacqui glared at him. This man had the nerve to smile in her face as though her presence was voluntary. Between his ebullient cocksure attitude, his entitlement, and the need-to-show-off kind of attire, Jacqui found the man repulsing to be around. Every compliment was filled with a backhanded aftertaste. Every assessment Jacqui submitted to him was met with doubt and a need for reassurance from another source. The micro-managing never ended. The more she learned about Arnold through working for him, the more she wanted to kill him.

"Are you a fan of ants, Dr. Stevenson?"

"What are you talking about?"

"Their efficiency and seamless execution is impeccable, like no other creature on earth. Anyway you're not a morning person I see. This way."

Arnold led her through thick glass doors. This time, however, instead of traversing back to the chained women in the Transition Room, he took Jacqui somewhere much worse. He led her down a long hallway to an elevator big enough for four people. He scanned his ID badge and the doors slid open. Inside was lustrous stone flooring. The stainless-steel interior shone to perfection. Arnold stood next to the button panel. Fifty black squares, one for each floor of the Colony. Each floor was an enigma housing unfathomable secrets.

"Level Three."

Level UG had the Transition Room storing abducted women. Jacqui's stomach twisted, wondering what lay on the third level of this underground operation.

They exited the elevator and right away Jacqui heard voices. Indistinct conversations of numerous people, the sound reminded her of an audience. Then Jacqui realized, in the short walk between elevators, she had not seen a single person. No one except Arnold. For an organization with so many floors, so much secrecy, where was the manpower that kept it running?

Arnold then stepped inside of what resembled a lecture hall large enough to house at least three hundred people. In this case, it was students. The room was at capacity. Hundreds of faces stared back at Jacqui upon entrance.

Jacqui froze in place, realizing that there was no way out of this. This operation, BRT Health Industries, was much larger than Jacqui could have ever originally imagined. Arnold had managed to convince a hospital, the safest place anyone could think of, to build warehouse-sized rooms to store women like canned goods. He had machinery moved down to fifty secret levels to treat these women, external technicians to concoct experimental drugs on these women, and now a room similar to that of a college campus to onboard more people into this project. The success of BRT Health Industries went beyond alarming. In this place, Arnold could do whatever he wanted and there was nothing to stop him.

Beyond the shock and disgust, Jacqui was confused. She

glanced at Arnold who stood in front of the students. With the lights shining down on him, brightening his fair skin from where he stood, the man looked like a mogul on stage. Had she not known any better, she would have fallen for his charisma as well.

Still, Jacqui could not fathom how these recent college grads could willingly sign up for this. Unless they had not. *Were they completely unaware that people were being held against their will? Surely no one willingly signed up for this? Perhaps Arnold had convinced them that it was something else entirely.* Just like he'd tricked Jacqui. And once they had seen too much, he would threaten them, if he'd not done so already.

"This morning I have a special treat. I am sure you're all aware of the work of Dr. Jacqui Stevenson?" Arnold said.

A deafening applause consumed the room.

Many of the students lit up when they laid eyes on Jacqui. She usually enjoyed their admiration, but given the circumstance, the adoration made her sick to the stomach.

"Today she will introduce her theory of the next step in the fertility treatments and how it can be used to help our patients fulfill their desire to have children. Dr. Stevenson."

Hesitantly, Jacqui stepped forward in front of the sea of faces. This was not the way she wanted to influence the next generation. She remembered being in their seats. Whenever a figure who stood on one of these stages spoke, she'd listened eagerly, taken down notes, and absorbed every word. Now, looking back, Jacqui wondered if those same people she'd listened to were in her situation, bound by circumstances out of their control. Either way, standing here and now, with the attention on her and people watching, Jacqui needed to wake them up to reality. But she would have to be smart about it.

Behind her was an image displayed from a projector secured

to the ceiling. The image was of a pale woman enveloped in vines and leaves from her shoulders upward. Between her sea foam green eyes was an opening filled with black space like a slit into a parallel universe. In place of hair were peach-colored flower petals blossoming atop her head. It consumed an entire wall of the room. Jacqui had seen this imagery before, it was the Aphaia Corporation's logo. Jacqui assumed it was some abstract take on having a "third" eye, but she refused to look at the woman for too long. It made her skin crawl.

"Before I dive right into it, I have a question for you all."

Arnold stood a few paces behind her. If she was going to do this right, she would need to tread a delicate balance between lecturer and alarmist. She only had one shot. It had to count.

"Why are you here today?"

A few hands shot in the air. She searched for a face that looked honest.

"You, in the middle. What's your name?" Jacqui pointed to a young blond woman who was obviously texting under the desk.

"Irina," she said, cleared her throat, and spoke, "Through research, experimentation, and analysis, I am here to help women who cannot conceive naturally." Irina shuffled nervously in her seat. "With your research about complete female organ transplants, we can retrieve the entirety of the womb and transfer it to a completely different host. With accurate stem cell research, we can form new eggs, essentially creating embryos from a simple blood sample of the new host. What decades ago we would consider magic, is now a reality."

Within that moment, it was clear to Jacqui that Arnold had blatantly lied to these young adults. This was not some laboratory type of position; this was the Henrietta Lacks experiment all over again. He had founded an entire organization that was committed to using Black women as lambs to be degraded, slaughtered, and dissected, all in the name of scientific innovation.

"So, basically, the removal of a viable womb and injecting a foreign organ into someone else's body, right? Well, doesn't that turn the organic material into a parasite? Assuming the host's body, correct?" Jacqui exaggerated the details for a reason.

Irina cleared her throat once more. "Yes, but no, I think you're oversimplifying it. With advancements in technology and medicine, we're able to do a full transplant of the uterus. But not only that, we can regenerate the fallopian tubes and eggs of the recipient. Now, we can help all women who've ever had a less than favorable diagnosis."

Pacing back and forth, Jacqui made eye contact with every student on the front row. Some with glasses, some with hope in their eyes, but most of them despite having spent so much time in school were still oblivious to the world around them. One thing was clear, Arnold was abusing their naiveté.

"Irina, is it?"

The student nodded in response.

"Out of curiosity, do you think those animals wanted their organs removed?"

"Well... it is difficult to say but—"

"You think they willingly donated their bodies to science?" Jacqui stopped in front of Irina, seated in the front row.

"Um, well, I don't..."

Jacqui stepped down from the platform, locking eyes with Irina, intentionally trying to intimidate her. Step by step, Jacqui inched closer to the bright student, deliberately raising her voice, and stomping her Crocs into the hard-tiled floor.

"But if you are to guess, Irina, what would it be?"

Smack.

Jacqui slammed her palms into the desk in front of Irina. All of that smugness Irina once carried in her face had left the lecture hall.

"I would say, if they had a choice probably not—"

Jacqui began walking along the front row, passing students one by one.

"Since BRT Health Industries is looking to begin human trials, I think there is a question you all are overlooking."

Stopping again to look another student dead between the eyes—the girl was a young Black woman—one of three in the entire room of three hundred students. Jacqui sucked in a breath. Oh no... would this woman, or any of the three of them, be the student or the studied? Jacqui made a vow to herself to ensure that those three women left the premises right away after the lecture, not only that but she would make a point to escort them to the elevator—personally. It would kill Jacqui to see another face tossed onto those chained beds, especially ones she could have prevented.

"Whose wombs are you transferring?"

The room fell dangerously silent.

Sometimes being so smart came with a blind spot. By the eerie quietness that sat idly in the room, Jacqui knew she had proposed a question none of them were thinking.

A hand landed firmly on Jacqui's back. The contact sent a spasm through her spine. A feeling only Arnold gave her. For a moment, Jacqui was so engulfed in warning the students in front of her that she forgot the threat behind her.

"Can I speak with you for a second?" Arnold whispered in her ear. He walked briskly between the double doors. Jacqui followed him out of the room.

Once a safe distance from his recruits, Arnold began.

"What the hell are you doing?" Arnold said, keeping the fury in his voice to a low whisper.

"I am doing what you asked." Jacqui crossed her arms. She

needed to be smart about this. Arnold held her future and her daughter's life in his grasp.

"Asking them why they are here? C'mon, did you truly think you'd get anything out of them? They don't know anything more than they have to, they are just here to run samples. Nothing more, nothing less."

To Arnold that may have been enough to keep his peace of mind, but for Jacqui, any involvement was already too much. Knowing that she would be training these students for anything related to those women in chains was enough to drive her insane, but Jacqui had to stay strong for her daughter, Ashley. Jacqui always believed it was easy to die for your children, but to suffer this torture every day and lose sleep at night was another strength entirely. As long as her work meant keeping her little girl safe, she would do it for Ashley without a second thought. Every. Single. Time.

"And another thing. I may not be a doctor, but I am sure as hell no fool."

Jacqui turned to face him as Arnold stepped beside her, whispering in her ear with a threatening grin.

"If you think you'll get out of this, you're in denial. You see, Dr. Stevenson, when you agreed to work for us, I had other assurances in place to make sure you didn't try anything out of the ordinary. When you get a chance, Dr. Stevenson, check your bank account. Several perks come in addition to your new position."

If this was true, then Jacqui's reasoning for not going to the police was no longer out of moral obligation, she was as guilty as Arnold. He had pulled her waist-deep into the quicksand of this nightmare. There was no escape. Arnold could prove that she was receiving kickbacks and no matter what Jacqui said to the authorities to prove her innocence, now, the blood of those women, like Ivery Johnson, was on her hands.

"You don't want to go there with me. Things may seem bad, but trust me, they can get much worse. Consider the ant, Dr. Stevenson." Arnold stormed off in the opposite direction of Jacqui.

Staring at his black suit as Arnold walked off, Jacqui knew there were only one of two outcomes if she continued to play by Arnold's rules. One: once he no longer needed her, Arnold would set her up to be sent to prison for the rest of her life. Two: he would put a hit on her, killing both her and her daughter. Arnold seemed like the type to do it. At this point, both outcomes were equally likely.

Hearing Arnold's words just now was supposed to break Jacqui, to make her bend to his every whim no matter the cost to her self-worth and ethics. However, for some strange reason, it did not. Instead, his threat filled her with a refreshed rage that could only be described with one word: retribution.

Leaving the Colony, Jacqui rushed back to Mercy Hospital.

FUELED WITH A SUDDEN ambition, Jacqui went to the lab and investigated Arnold's companies, specifically BRT Health Industries. The elevator doors parted on the third floor—research and development. There sat a receptionist desk and rows of white desks with a transparent screen in front of each rolling chair.

Sitting down behind a silver-white desk, a thin outline of a standard-size desktop screen took shape in front of Jacqui and green words emerged in what looked like mid-air to the untrained eye. Placing her face right in the middle of the transparent screen and without moving an inch, the system outlined her face. Soon, the words *welcome Dr. Stevenson* appeared. This was one update Jacqui didn't mind, she had a nasty habit of forgetting passwords.

Jacqui dove into files, data, and statistical information on BRT Health Industries. Anything stored on the company shared drive, it didn't matter how innocuous it seemed, Jacqui reviewed it.

In a few short hours, Jacqui learned Arnold's company BRT Health Industries was founded in 2019 in response to declining birth rates and BRT Health Industries was created for the betterment of all life starting at the moment of conception... And that was it. She didn't know exactly what she was searching for, but commercial brochures and pamphlets didn't quite fit the bill.

She should have known better.

The information she needed was not going to be stored on a hard drive. Arnold was too smart to leave evidence unsecured and Jacqui learned her lesson from her first encounter with Arnold. She was being watched.

Jacqui signed out and stopped by the reception desk.

A heavyset man with a hairline starting behind his ears sat behind the marble circular desk. Wireless earphones in his ears and clearly not paying attention to anything other than his phone, Jacqui grew annoyed with his lack of professionalism. She was often offended by poor service. He seemed like the type to coast until he reached retirement.

"Hey, I need to access some files—"

"Go to the archives, straight back, last room on the left," the receptionist said without looking up from his phone.

Jacqui found the archives room. It should not have been called that. It was more like someone had projectile vomited documents inside of a storage room. Overhead, there were only two sources of light barely clinging to life. The walls were a dingy green that had chips and cracks in the paint. A series of double rivet shelving units were placed so close beside one another that Jacqui had to sidestep between units. Mold and wet cardboard smells dangled in the air. Manila folders stuffed with documents dating back to the fifties were stacked sloppily atop the shelves. It was going to take a while before Jacqui made sense of anything in front of her.

She pulled a folder, sifting through the dirt and coffee-stained papers she took note of the letterhead. Spreadsheets, pink slips, company memos, email printouts all had the same name front and center—

Lanzran Inc.

It sounded familiar to her.

The sister company to BRT Health Industries, Lanzran Inc. specialized in medical supplies, or at least that was what Arnold had the public believe. Buried in an old cardboard box, Jacqui found minutes to a high-level meeting of executives for Lanzran Inc. which included a peculiar topic: *Premier Vaccine*. The overview didn't offer much insight, only stating that the Premier Vaccine was to be marketed as a one-stop shop. Permanent immunity. It was claimed that you'd never need another vaccination flu shot again. However, it was only available exclusively to the one percent at the affordable price of $49,995 per dosage and per individual. No insurance covered it. At the bottom of the document was a date: June 24, 2005.

"When we made the Premier Vaccine, we knew the risks." Arnold popped into her head.

But what did he mean by that?

Jacqui could not deny there was a connection right away— whoever could afford this vaccine, definitely could afford a womb transplant.

There was something about this vaccine that left Jacqui uneasy. *Why was Arnold so secretive about an incredible medical innovation unless something had had happened. But also, what was the relationship between this vaccine, BRT Health Industries, the Aphaia Corporation, and this whole underground operation in the first place?* Something other than the BRT Health Industries' project was going on inside the Colony, Jacqui just could not figure it out yet.

Chapter 6

Justice: The Car Accident

Yesterday replayed in his mind. Blaring car horns of bumper-to-bumper traffic, blinding headlights, and a middle-aged woman wailing in the middle of the road. The floral headscarf, the blue denim jacket darkened with tears, the house slipper and sandal mismatched shoes the woman was wearing as if she was in a hurry to go outside. A new case and the victim who was now missing for over three days. No leads, no witnesses. The only way to find the perpetrator was to learn as much as he could about the victim: Briana Wilson.

Justice had interviewed Briana's mother. Briana was eighteen, a cheerleader with above-average grades. A senior in high school, headed to a great college out of state. Briana was much like his little sister, Grace. And like many girls from where Justice was from—the north side of Ballantyne with cracked concrete roads, buildings that hadn't been remodeled in decades, and sketchy gas stations—Briana had needed money for tuition *also* just like his little sister, Grace. According to Briana's mother, her daughter had attended an interview. When Justice reviewed a copy of Briana's emails, a company named BRT Health Industries had popped up in his investigation. After this said interview, Briana was never seen again. It seemed to be a disturbing turn of events. A string of events that needed to be brought to Chief Glassman's attention today. And Justice knew that he had to be the one to do it.

Along with his partner, Goodchild, he'd barely entered the precinct that morning, when right away, as if on cue, Chief Glassman had called him into the office.

"Close the door behind ya," Glassman said.

Twisting the knob to shut the door, Justice took a seat in a black leather chair in front of the Chief.

Chief Glassman was a bigger than average man in both height and weight, with a receding hairline and a thick gray mustache that turned upright at the corners slightly. The man had once been a great cop, but he sure was a lousy boss. Glassman did the bare minimum for his workers, but made his employees work overtime so he could be the face of awards and acknowledgments. Even in this conversation, Justice already knew how it was going to go. First, the Chief would pretend to care about his psychological well-being, then some vague analysis of Justice's performance, finishing with the Chief's favorite saying: *Keep your nose clean.* Rinse. Wash. Repeat.

"Reeves, how are you holding up?"

"I'm good, thanks for asking," Justice responded without any meaning in his words. These two were the epitome of alpha men. There was no relationship outside of catching criminals, police ceremonies, routine procedures, and of course paperwork. Justice knew that it was best for both of them to keep this conversation short and to the point.

"I assume you know why you're here, right?" Glassman said.

"Yes, and the events of the Easthampton mall were documented in my report thoroughly, but before that, Chief, there is something much more important going on I think you should be aware of." Justice pulled out a black-and-white map from his pocket. As he unrolled the piece of paper, Glassman slipped on a pair of glasses over the bridge of his nose and leaned forward.

"Between MLK Boulevard, Twenty-Second Street, Claventine Ave, and Rockhill Road, what do you notice?"

Glassman inspected the eight by eleven sheet of paper under the desktop light. Nothing stood out to him. By the blank look in Glassman's stoic blue eyes, Justice realized that if his boss was going to understand the point, he needed a little help.

"What am I missing?" Glassman said, looking at Justice over the rim of his glasses.

Justice took a pen and drew circles around the four separate locations. All four lines collided forming several overlapping spheres meeting at one place in particular.

"All of these intersections are within a fifty-mile radius of each other, there is a trend."

"What kind of trend?"

Justice swallowed back his nerves. Knowing how lazy the Chief was and how new investigations were not typically approved unless the Chief had concrete evidence, Justice was not sure how the Chief was going to respond to this. He took a chance.

"All of the victims are Black women between the ages of eighteen and into their mid-twenties. They've gone missing at alarming rates."

Glassman fell back into his chair and knotted his hands together in his lap.

"Reeves."

At the sound of his name, Justice knew he was losing. It was as though he was climbing a mountain made of metal in a thunderstorm. The fight was already over.

"Chief, before you say anything, I know how this sounds, but look at the facts. I don't have much evidence to form a case, *just yet,* but, Chief, everything I've gathered so far has pointed to a clear pattern. Someone is hunting near the—"

"May I speak?" the Chief said.

Between Glassman's sudden nonchalant attitude and the sarcasm in his voice, Justice was nearing the end of what patience he had left. Justice leaned back into the spine of his chair. Though not wanting to accept defeat, today, he feared this battle was already lost.

"Reeves, I appreciate all you do around here, and I know you did not get enough credit on that welfare scandal case, but even you have to admit this sounds slightly ridiculous."

Offended, Justice kept a cool composure. Even so, this was the frustrating part of Justice's job; the politics, the presenting the facts in a way so that the higher-ups could see his perspective. Race played an implicit role in this pattern, not in a way that makes victimization beautiful, nor suffering somehow virtuous. This problem was much bigger than winning awards from the city council or state-wide recognition. Justice had a little sister to protect. A little sister who looked and fit the profile of all these women who were disappearing by the dozens every day.

"With all due respect, sir, which part sounds ridiculous? The part that there are dozens of Black women missing or the idea that I am right about why they're disappearing?"

Glassman scoffed. That sound was all too familiar around the department. If someone made Glassman utter that sound, they were thirty seconds away from losing pay, being suspended, or simply fired. Justice wondered which fate he would receive.

"All I am saying, sir, if this was happening to white women and if every day, and *they* were being snatched off the streets, the community would react to this much differently."

The only thing admirable about Glassman was the fact he

afforded time for Justice's rant in its entirety, but the man was not actively listening. After a while he began texting on his phone, looking at his computer screen pretending to check for emails. At the end of the conversation, ultimately Chief Glassman refused to budge on his stance. He was not going to fund an independent investigation on a reputable company such as BRT Health Industries, especially not with all the funding from other governmental agencies relying on the success of the company. This was and would never be a top priority and Justice knew that. When was it ever a crisis when it came to missing Black women? Only a month previously a state governor had come under fire for his comments about the maternal health crisis. The governor claimed that if you excluded race, in particular Black women who were dying at three to four times that of their white counterparts, then the numbers were not as bad as they appeared. *The audacity!* Everything Justice said sounded no different from a crazy conspiracy theory to Glassman.

"Reeves, all I need from you right now is to keep your nose clean, in fact, that was why I called you in here today. You're on desk duty until further notice. You let a suspect slip through your fingers. Last name Johnson."

"She didn't slip, she is still at the hospital—"

"I don't care, get it handled."

Justice stomped out of the Chief's office. *That had gone about as well as to be expected.* Glassman always claimed everything was out of his hands and now Justice had to figure it out alone. It was the welfare scandal situation all over again, only this time, his little sister could be a casualty if Justice failed.

AFTER WORK, JUSTICE HEADED downtown to grab a drink in a live-music bar. The place was a nightlife paradise. Around the inside of the establishment were couches in place of booths. They were so soft it was like sitting on air. Abstract art covered the walls adding to the relaxed ambiance, with warm shades of burgundy, cream, and violet, and the sweet scents of honey and vanilla floated around the elegant room. Best of all was the soothing music at the perfect volume where he didn't have to scream in the bartender's ear to order a drink. It was a nice place, except for the annoyingly loud trust-fund adults and Ivy-League graduates who were still drinking despite having passed their limits. Sitting at the bar, Justice tried to ignore the belligerent frat boys beside him. They were like the people he worked with who were blind to the reality of poverty, ignorant to the struggle of not knowing where your next meal was going to come from, and oblivious to life below the six-figure income level. A part of it infuriated Justice. Maybe it was just jealousy. Maybe he was justified in feeling that way. The better and more mature part of him downed the rest of the brown liquor in his short glass and let it go.

"Hey, handsome," a sweet voice said behind his ear. The voice belonged to Cindy.

Cindy sat down next to him. She wore a knee-length black dress with a high slit up to her thigh showing off her long legs and a leather moto jacket covering her shoulders. Outside of work, she enjoyed binge-watching reality housewife shows, secretly envying women who were so beautiful they did not have to work. That was the life she'd always wanted and could have had, for she was without a doubt pretty enough. But life had forged her path here, with Justice. Though their connection had started with a work-related phone call about Ivery's whereabouts, their conversation had ended with Justice asking Cindy out for coffee. Tonight, however, was date number three.

"You clean up nice," he teased her.

"Thank you. One of us has to be presentable in public." Cindy reciprocated his taunting tone.

They knew enough about each other to want to explore more, but neither was ready to call what they were doing anything more than simple fun. Even so, the chemistry between them was boiling. Cindy sat with her legs between his at the bar, while Justice had his arm wrapped around the back of her barstool.

Justice chuckled slightly at her remark, as the bartender dropped another short glass in front of him.

"You never told me what Cindy was short for," Justice said.

"You're going to laugh when I tell you." Cindy looked at her drink then back at Justice. "Okay fine I'll say it, it's short for Cinderella. Go ahead and laugh. What can I say, my mom, *really*, enjoyed Disney," Cindy said as she started laughing at herself.

Justice smiled, silently adoring every little detail about Cindy. From the sound of her laugh, her spicy personality, her toned feminine legs, her independence, the subtle accent, all the way down to her French-tipped toes, he could not find a single flaw about her.

In the Reeves' household, Justice's mother always spoke of a curse. A hex that if anyone grew close to him, they were destined to inspire tragedy. Justice's last girlfriend, Kia, he'd dated for six months before she'd passed away from a rare heart condition. Doctors had said the odds of her survival were one in a million. Then what happened with his partner, Mason, had only further served to prove the curse was real. With Cindy, he feared something terrible was going to happen to her. He could feel it creep into his soul slowly like frostbite. He feared if Cindy became something more than a friend, he would be putting her life in danger. Justice was at the age when men began looking for wives, but he was too focused on his career to think about settling down. Every day there was a new criminal, a new drug, a new threat. If he started his own family, who would look out for his mother and sister? He could not become a husband or a boyfriend, not right now at least.

Cindy's phone rang. She took a moment to look at who was calling her. She paused, looked at Justice, then back at her phone. Her entire demeanor changed when she glanced at her phone. Justice supposed that it was probably an ex or something, so he pulled away and sat back in his chair.

"Um, hey, Grace, what's up?" Cindy said, before she covered her phone and whispered to Justice, "It's your sister. Does she know we're like... a thing, ya know?"

Justice's private life was so exclusive that his mother and sister thought he liked men because he'd never brought a woman around to meet them. There was no way Grace would know about him seeing Cindy. Plus it was too soon in their relationship to tell anyone about it.

"I'm on a date. What's going on? You sound scared. Are you okay?" said Cindy into her cell.

Justice seized the phone from Cindy and spoke into it, "Grace, where are you?"

"Justice? What are you doing with Cindy? Okay, never mind that, we'll discuss that later. But I'm driving home from this interview thing that I told you about with BRT Health Industries and—"

"Grace, I told you not to go to that. I hate it when you don't listen. No reputable company I've ever heard of has an interview so late at night."

"Are you done, Dad?" Grace added extra sarcasm on the "dad" part. "Look, I know what you said, and I'm sorry I should have listened, I needed the money for school, Justice, but that's not why I'm calling you right now. I think someone is following me, I did the thing you told me about make three rights and don't stop at red lights, but they are still behind me."

Fuck.

Justice knew this day would come. But knowing this day would happen had not prepared him for it. Now his sister was wrapped up in all this.

"Don't go home, go to my place. I'll meet you there."

"Okay..." Grace's voice softened until something came across on the phone that Justice had not heard from his sister in years. It was tears. "Justice, I'm so scared and, oh crap, I think they are speeding up, I think they're gonna hit me."

Boom.

The line went dead.

"Grace? Grace! Are you still there?" Justice pulled away from Cindy's phone only to find the home screen looking back at him. He dialed Grace's number. No answer. He tried again. Nothing but her voicemail. He called her once more and this time, someone answered, only it was not Grace.

"Grab her legs."

"Grace, are you there?" Justice said, but all he could hear was a single male voice.

"The phone, stupid!"

The line went dead, again.

Justice pulled up "Find My Friends" on his phone, and right away he searched for Grace's name. Moments like this were the real reason he insisted she downloaded the app. The loading icon appeared next to her name but waiting for that little icon to update felt like an eternity. Every passing second, someone was doing something horrible to Grace. Finally, the app opened, and the loading icon disappeared revealing Grace's last whereabouts.

No Location Found.

Cindy, seeing the look on Justice's face, said, "I think you should talk to Jacqui, she's a doctor at Mercy Hospital, an incredible woman. Her daughter, Ashley, is best friends with Grace. If anyone would know anything about where Grace was last, it would be Ashley."

All Justice could do in response was simply nod. This was his failure. His greatest fear had come to life, not only that, but he'd heard it all happen over the phone. Justice was supposed to be Grace's protector, to keep his little sister from harm, but all he did was sit and listen to these grown men take his sister. No telling what they would do to her or what they had planned. The thought alone tore at Justice.

These people who'd taken Grace were stupid enough to let Justice hear their voices, yet sophisticated enough to disable her GPS. Whoever they were, Justice was going to find them.

Chapter 7

Jacqui: The Perfectionist

The porcelain white walls carried the echo of Jacqui's footsteps as she reached her next patient. Glancing down at the transparent clipboard, she saw the name: Angela Liu. Jacqui read her file. All Premier Care patients had a file, it was necessary, these people kept the lights on in Mercy Hospital. They had earned the right for anyone who came in contact with them to already know their expectations. And high expectations these people had. Angela was one of their most demanding clients of all.

Angela Liu was the shining example of minority women in science, technology, engineering, and math. Born on a U.S. military base in Okinawa, Japan, the half-Japanese, half-American girl had taken an interest in what her mother had always claimed were subjects for boys. By age thirty, not only had Angela pioneered quantum computer technology in the field of cybersecurity, but she was the youngest woman in history to do so. Now Angela was the kind of person who had earned enough to retire and donated annually on average a million dollars to the hospital alone.

Angela preferred the room temp at a cool twenty degrees

Celsius with the window open. Of course, a nice breeze kept her nerves calm. Only one hundred percent sheepskin rugs and a one-thousand thread count on all sheets and linen. Warm tea was expected by Angela upon her arrival and if the first sip was too hot or too cold, someone would lose their job that day. Career-driven, beautiful, and with plenty of life ahead of her, Angela was still missing something in her life: a legacy. Despite Angela being the most stringent of patients, Jacqui hoped she could help her in this new endeavor.

Jacqui knocked on the door.

"Come in," Angela said. She was a beauty past her prime but had not yet fallen into aging. She stood at five feet tall and wore a knee-length navy pencil skirt with a peach long-sleeve button-up. Her hair was a black bob cut with unnatural precision that stopped right at her shoulders. From her appearance alone, she expected perfection from herself and everyone around her.

Slowly, Jacqui opened the thick gray door. "Ms. Liu?"

The inside of Angela's Premier Care patient room looked like a presidential suite. It was equipped with a dining room for four, a living room, a kitchen, and a terrace overlooking the city skyline of Ballantyne. Her patient room was better furnished than Jacqui's home.

"Yes," she said, rubbing her shoulders with both hands while sitting on a loveseat. She was probably one of the richest women in the city and yet, the woman sitting before Jacqui was anxious, insecure like a teenager who'd been caught stealing.

"I assume you know why I'm here. And what happened to my last doctor."

"Yes, of course," Jacqui replied. There was no meaningless chitchat about the weather or formal exchange of "how are you". Instead, Angela went straight to the point.

Jacqui took the seat across from Angela. The plush one-seater synced to the middle of Jacqui's back, instantly relieving a knot that had formed since her involvement with Arnold. Finally an ounce of peace.

"I've reviewed your medical history. I can see that you've tried nearly every option to have a child naturally. Steroid injects and in vitro is the last option," Jacqui continued, scanning the transparent clipboard. With a simple touch of a finger, Jacqui was able to find every finite detail about Ms. Liu's health. It was not until Jacqui found a curious diagnosis that she had a few questions for her client. "Ms. Liu, has anyone told you about your condition?"

"Dr. Pravesh said something about my lady parts, but he didn't get too specific." Angela said. She tucked a loose strand behind her ear then ran both hands down her hair in one single stroke.

Angela sounded like she was at a job interview. Her tone was stiff and restrained as though this was a presentation for investors. From what Jacqui was reading, she realized that the woman sitting before her had no clue about the wall of truth she was about to run into.

"You no longer have a... uterus."

"What?!" She paused, cleared her throat, and took in a deep breath collecting herself. "W-what do you mean? That's not possible. The nurse said... umm... she said something..." Angela wrapped her arms around herself, stroking the backs of her arms.

"Well, Ms. Liu, based on what I saw in your results, it seems your body, naturally, has performed its own version of a hysterectomy. I've never seen anything like this. It was not an overnight occurrence; you probably experienced intense menstrual cycles, bleeding much heavier than normal, I'm guessing."

Angela nodded, reluctantly agreeing.

"I would say this took months, perhaps almost a year to occur. Essentially, to sum it all up, your reproductive organs have atrophied so far that there is nothing left." As nicely, slowly, and delicately Jacqui tried to deliver the news, it felt evil to say out loud.

An emptiness took shape on Angela's face. If hopeless had a look it would be Angela in this current moment; she was dead behind her eyes.

Sifting through her files, Jacqui looked for good news to tell her, but she came across something else.

"Hmm, that is interesting."

"What?" Angela sucked in a breath.

"About twenty years ago you had a procedure."

A small chuckle escaped Angela. She looked down then stood up and walked over to the oriel window. Her high heels sang a slow rhythm as she sauntered away from Jacqui. The soft sheen of her short dark hair captured a glint of light.

"Do you have any children, Dr. Stevenson?"

"Yes, one girl."

"Oh, girls are precious." Angela's voice cracked slightly. "They are carriers of culture as my mother says." Angela grabbed the red mug seated on the window ledge. "How old were you when you had her?"

"I had just graduated college, I was twenty-six. It was hard going through med school with a newborn. Thank God, I had help from her father at the time."

"That's admirable." Angela turned around to face Jacqui. "I don't think I could have done it."

"It is unfair. I agree. Our society often forces women to choose between a career or a family."

Angela turned to stare out the window once more. "A clinic right off campus performed the procedure for next to dirt cheap. The doctor who removed the fetus from me told me had I waited a week longer it would have been too late. Two decades later, I still don't know if I feel relieved or sad about it." Angela took a long sip from the coffee mug. "When my success took off, I was glad I had the abortion. I don't think I would've had the luxury of time to work and study with a child growing in my belly. As time passed, my college roommates got married and had children; I convinced myself that my work was my baby. And for a while it was."

Jacqui nodded along. She knew that feeling. Though she loved her daughter, Ashley had not been planned either.

"But in the back of my mind, when I am alone in bed, with no little voices bickering over toys and no crayon markings drawn into the walls, I find tears falling from me in the night. The guilt steals sleep from me. The times when I do manage to keep my eyes closed through the night, I swear I see her face. Sometimes she's a cute little baby girl tugging at her little toes in a bassinet. Other times she's learning to ride a bike for the first time and scraping up her knee in the process. By now, she would be a teenager, defiant against every one of my rules. But when I wake up, realizing it's all a dream, I burst into tears. I feel like the soul tie or whatever connection that had formed never went away. And no matter which way I look at it, I took a life. My baby girl's life. She will never get a second chance because of me."

The guilt in her words was difficult to hear. All those years Angela had been carrying this alone. Jacqui could not even begin to understand.

"Ms. Liu, I am going to help you in any way I can."

"Thank you." Wiping tears from the corners of her eyes, Angela cleared her throat. "I'm glad Arnold referred me to you. I knew he would put me in the right hands."

Arnold had referred Angela... what? Jacqui straightened slightly, muscles tensed. At the sound of his name, it changed everything. This meant that Angela was here not for fertility treatments like acupuncture, injections, or natural options. She was here for something else entirely.

"You are here for the in vitro program, correct?"

Angela narrowed her eyes at Jacqui as though disappointed. "I thought he went over this with you. No, a few of my friends have told me about BRT Health Industries. And Arnold spoke very highly of you, saying you are the one whose research the program was founded upon. So, there is no one better to walk me through this than you. He advised that the process simply requires a donor and some other scientific stuff, but I'm no medical professional." Angela took a seat in front of Jacqui.

Speechless, Jacqui nodded.

"Perfect. I can't decide if I want a boy or a girl. Oh, my mother would love a granddaughter," Angela said. "Arnold said we could get started with the whole process today, correct?"

Angela's words fell into background mumbles. Right away, Jacqui nodded because she knew telling this woman *no* was not an option. For whatever Jacqui said, it would get back to Arnold in one way or another. Jacqui was about to perform her first surgery, her first theft, but she had no other choice. With a sudden realization, this whole consult made sense to Jacqui. Arnold expected that Jacqui would take a womb from one of those innocent women who were chained to a bed in the basement of this hospital and give it to the highest bidder. In this case, it was Angela. And if Arnold told this woman, there were countless others headed in Jacqui's direction. The worst of it was, if she did not help this woman, then Arnold would take Ashley. By satisfying Angela's request, Jacqui was killing someone else's daughter.

Jacqui finished her appointment with Angela and went to her secret haven, the bathroom. She enclosed herself in the bamboo stall, sat atop the toilet with the clipboard on her knees.

She buried her face into her palms as her mind raced, replaying the meeting with Angela. Jacqui was caught between two worlds. One was servicing clients like Angela, the other was helping girls like Ivery. *How is this my life?* Jacqui thought. Only weeks ago she was complaining about being passed over for a promotion, and now she was about to perform an involuntary surgery.

A flashing red symbol cut through her eyelids. She looked down at the clipboard screen and at the top read:

Two minutes until you are timed out of this session

Of course, that's it!

She snapped out of the self-pity. If Jacqui was to make a move, she had to do it now.

Scrolling through Angela's medical records, Jacqui got that feeling again. That subtle rage, yearning for answers and a way out of the trap Arnold had stuffed her into. There had to be some clue, some reason that Angela could not have a child.

Client>Medical History>Immunizations
Premier Vaccine: 11/09/2018 500ml dosage vial #07925

Just like Irene before her, Angela had received that same high-priced vaccine and now, neither of them could bring a child to term naturally. Jacqui believed that in science, there were no coincidences, only connections. Right now, she had a clear, nefarious connection between BRT Health Industries and Lanzran Inc.—the Premier Vaccine.

Chapter 8

Cara: The Doctor

"Ms. Esperanza, so lovely to meet you," a man's voice said.

The mysterious man was dressed in a white lab coat that nearly touched the floor, a plain navy button-up underneath it, and green leather gloves covered with a slick sheen of clear coating. As he took his seat at Cara's bedside, he placed a silver briefcase in front of the monitor. From the single blue eye that Cara could make out, deep crow's feet ran from his corner eyelids down his cheeks. Hiding behind his thick aviator reading glasses were age spots splattered along his neck and hairline. Based on the full head of ghost-white hair atop his head, the man was long past retirement.

"Who are you?" Cara asked. "Where am I?" She demanded the truth, but despite her vicious delivery, the strange man kept at his work. Slowly, the man began removing every medical tool in his arsenal and delicately put them in place, not touching. As he stationed each item he hummed a subtle tune, completely ignoring Cara's presence.

Dr. Dowey, Cara read from his name tag.

Paralyzed with terror, Cara watched the man place a

surgical mask over his mouth then unpack each shiny instrument. One by one from the incision scissors to varying scalpels, clamps, syringes, vials filled with clear substances, whelping and obstetrical forceps. When each item touched the soft blue cloth in its designated place, anxiety grew deeper and stronger in the pit of Cara's stomach. Every move Dowey made was so deliberate. Now with every tool in its rightful spot, he snapped the briefcase closed and gently placed it on the floor like this was all some ritual of his. And with Cara being unable to move, fight, or distance herself from whatever Dowey had planned for her, she fought with the only weapon she had left. Her tears.

"Please, Mr. Dowey." Cara burst into a genuine cry for her life. "Please, please, don't do this." Never had she ever begged this hard for anything. Tears flowed from her effortlessly as she screamed and begged and pleaded with Dowey so hard that she choked on her own saliva.

"Shhh," Dowey said, comfortingly.

For a moment, Cara's erratic breathing calmed. Even though her eyelids began to swell, and her face had become flushed with a soft hue of red from her outburst, Dowey managed to end her sobbing all with a single word. Perhaps the man had had a change of heart. As much as she wanted to believe that this man would not hurt her, the soulless look behind his dead blue eyes told Cara she would not be so lucky.

"This is for your own good," he whispered, carefully running his fingers through her long dark hair.

Chained to the bed, isolated, and with help miles away, Cara realized not only was this man not going to let her go willingly, but that the one thing within her control were her eyes. If she lived through this, she would make sure this man paid for what he did to her. Every little detail about him she committed to memory. How Dowey's sleeves were cuffed and sat perfectly on his elbows. The wispy hairs on his arms were trees bending in a hurricane and especially the giant age spot that sat right at the center of his neck near his Adam's apple, it was like a tattoo on his flesh. Every tiny aspect of this man she would remember, for her life now depended on it.

Cara continued observing Dowey. He had mixed a vial full of some clear substance with the contents of a separate container. Upon shaking the small vial, the contents had turned into a blood-orange serum. He placed the serum back on the cloth, then he glanced over at Cara, grinning.

Behind Dr. Dowey was a nurse pushing a bed swiftly down the aisle between the sea of beds. Laying atop the crisp white sheets was a young woman, unconscious and unclothed. *Wait a minute.* Cara recognized the woman. She looked strangely familiar. Then Cara remembered her. This was the same woman she'd seen right before meeting with Mr. Khizar. Cara could never forget that model-like face. The "glitzy girl". But today the woman's appearance was far from glamorous. Naked with a white sheet flung carelessly across her right arm and abdomen, an opening from her navel down to her bikini area ran across the woman's body. It was evident that the woman's womb had been removed entirely. The nurse tossed a white sheet over the young woman, covering her and turning her into nothing more than a carcass. The woman was interviewed right before Cara, which meant Cara was next in line for the same ending.

"It may all look scary down here but trust me. Do you see these IVs? They are giving you a lovely concoction of nutrients, vitamins A-Z, folate, and your basic needs, and it will give your immune system a little boost to make sure you are ready for the procedure in forty-eight hours," Dowey said as he ran his palm over Cara's forehead. His wrinkled hand was so cold to the touch it made her skin crawl.

"Procedure... In forty-eight hours?" Cara's plight went unheard as Dowey went back to whistling once again.

Dowey pulled a small jar from its placement and turned the liquid vial on its head, holding it between his thumb and forefinger. Carefully as if performing surgery, he stuck a wide cylindrical syringe through the thin roof of the small bottle. Slowly, the blood-orange serum seeped from the container down through the thin needle. Dowey pulled on the lever and drew the sickly-colored fluid out of the container. An amorphous substance shifted frighteningly within the bottle. Seconds later, the bright liquid filled the syringe to capacity.

Shaking her entire body with the hope of loosening her restraints, Cara's attempt to free herself failed. Dowey watched her and could hardly stop himself from chuckling. The smile on his face infuriated Cara, like he had seen this same song and dance countless times before when he encountered new patients. Cara imagined that though he would never say it to her, the fear of his victims absolutely thrilled Dowey. He was some psycho who enjoyed having that power over someone, especially women, and studying them as they kicked and screamed to no avail. Now with Cara in his grasp, she knew the blood-like substance between his fingers was only the beginning of his experiment.

"This, however... is my secret little recipe of course."

Lowering his hand to her bicep, he grabbed her forearm with his free hand, forcing her still.

"Don't move or you'll lose feeling in your arm permanently," he said, his words muffled behind his mask.

For an older gentleman, his grip on her was too strong to stop him. No matter how hard she squirmed, she gained nothing. Cara's arm was locked into the steel death trap that was his hand.

He plunged the weapon into the muscle of her arm. As the

syringe's needle punctured her skin, a pinch cut into her left shoulder. The serum poured into her body, hot as molten lava seeping into her, burning its way through every cell in her body. As the liquid meandered through her flesh, every vein lifted from under her skin showing its bright burgundy color. From her face down to her ankles, every part of her felt like fire. She screamed, but slowly as though someone had lowered the volume in her ears. Her mouth was opened wide, and she could feel a vibration scratching her throat on its way out, but her ears told her nothing. The heat spread throughout her body like metastatic cancer. This serum was microwaving her from the inside out and as her insides boiled over, her skin had turned Arctic cold. Moments later, she lost strength in her muscles. Before long, Cara slipped out of consciousness.

Chapter 9

Jacqui: No Such Thing As Mercy

Maintaining a child's basic necessities was different from parenting a child. Every waking moment Jacqui spent in the Colony with those women kept against their will and keeping her daughter from suffering the same fate, she was missing so much of Ashley's life. From watching Ashley lead the cheerleading team at football events, making sure her prom dress was not too risqué, to helping her with her anatomy homework, and college applications, Jacqui had become a zombie to herself and a ghost to her daughter. This job of trying to protect these women and somehow stop Arnold through finding a concrete connection between BRT Health Industries and Lanzran Inc. was tearing her down physically, and even more so, consuming Jacqui's life.

Waking up at 5:00am to another chilly morning in Ballantyne, Jacqui made herself a cup of coffee. The loud footsteps rushing down the stairs startled Jacqui, but then she found relief in seeing who the sound belonged to: her daughter. Ashley was the spitting image of her father. They were both rosewood-complexioned and brown-eyed—and with an Afro as big as her bold personality, she attracted lots of friends and enemies alike. Ashley was the kind of pretty that did not need makeup or a lot of facial products. She was outgoing and smart, she was the daughter Jacqui hoped she would become, except she had the nasty habit of trusting too easily—a trait she had unfortunately picked up from her mother.

"Bye, Mom, have a good day!" Ashley said, giving her mother a gentle peck on the cheek before heading out the door.

Jacqui touched her cheek where Ashley had kissed her, and without provocation, tears ran down Jacqui's face. Seeing her daughter walk out the door for another day of school was the only thing keeping Jacqui sound of mind. Ashley's sweet voice was a whisper of hope and the kiss a touch of peace. Every day before Ashley left for school, Jacqui wondered if this would be the last time that she saw her. Or was she going to get a phone call in the middle of the night with her baby girl on the other end crying for her help? Or would the next time she heard of her daughter be the news stating they found her body in the middle of the woods. Countering the torture of the unknown every night, was each morning when Jacqui heard those loud footsteps, Ashley's routine "have a good day" saying, and soft touch on the cheek. Today, Ashley was okay and that was all Jacqui could pray for, one moment of peace at a time.

AT WORK, 7:32AM, JACQUI MARCHED through the halls of Mercy Hospital toward her next delivery. Over the past few weeks, a disturbing trend had emerged. Her last patient had labored for twenty-three hours. Middle-aged woman, a marathon runner, vegan diet, height-weight proportionate, she was a picture of health. Her pregnancy could not have been better, all lab results were within normal range. As she laid on the birthing bed, her body had twisted in pain every two minutes, as if someone was breaking every bone in her body all at once. Giving birth was a portal opening from another universe, it was only natural for such strain to accompany it. Then the woman pushed and pushed until her face flooded with crimson and nearly all breath had left her. Slowly Jacqui pulled the baby from her mother and the nurses placed her onto a bassinet. It was quiet in that room, too quiet. The child's chest was not moving, not a single breath. Then the nurses gave Jacqui a solemn look. Even though their faces were all covered by their surgical masks, Jacqui could sense their full expression. The child was pronounced dead upon delivery. This became a vicious cycle, and every time Jacqui entered a delivery room she prayed there would be a different fate. Each delivery resulted in more of the same, but strangely enough, only among Premier Care patients. Only the wealthiest of Ballantyne could not have children. Today had to be different.

Jacqui looked at the name of her next patient and her heart dropped into her stomach. She could not fail this woman. Her next delivery belonged to not a stranger, but to someone she had known for nearly twenty years. Her college roommate: Evelyn Bellfont.

Evelyn had been Jacqui's roommate in undergrad. The two had shared class notes, textbooks, ramen noodle cups, and unknowingly a boyfriend—at least until they'd found out about him and kicked him to the curb—all during their freshman year. Evelyn was a woman who'd never had a shortage of men wanting to date her, but in Jacqui's opinion, her problem had always been picking the right guy who would not treat her like shit. The right guy had appeared to be Liam Bellfont, a billionaire who'd turned Evelyn from a simple college graduate into an extremely wealthy housewife. They'd tried for years to have a child; the first two pregnancies had not made it past the first semester. But this one, her precious baby boy, had made it all the way to thirty-eight weeks. Jacqui wondered if he would be their only child since Evelyn was turning forty this year. Either way, this child was Evelyn's last hope. Jacqui could not fail her old friend.

"Okay, Evie, I need one last big push," Jacqui said, bracing herself to grab hold of the child's head upon first contact.

A sudden rush of intense heat enveloped Evelyn's body. Ragged breathing consumed her every inhalation as she pushed with what little energy she had left. As she'd been taught in her prenatal classes, she tried not to hold her breath, but to go with the back-breaking spasms surging inside her.

Jacqui knew that Evelyn's pregnancy had been rough. She'd had swollen ankles, constant morning sickness and heartburn throughout every trimester. At seven months, she'd caught the flu, and could hardly eat enough for herself let alone for her baby. She'd scraped through the lab tests with borderline results. Passing her final checkups from her doctors, Jacqui had tried to stay positive for her friend, hoping that this time she was going to be a mom.

But now Jacqui could see that Evelyn was utterly exhausted from a painful labor. She willed her friend on, knowing from her own experience that the effort would be worth the miracle about to arrive. Evelyn's baby boy.

A few more pushes and at long last he had arrived. With his thick thighs, lots of tiny rolls, a butt chin, and chubby cheeks like his father, he looked perfect to Jacqui. But as she lifted him from his mother, with the umbilical cord still attached, she noticed something terribly wrong.

"He's not breathing," a nurse said.

As she said those words, it felt like all the air had left the room. Jacqui glanced at a barely conscious Evelyn. Her friend had endured so much suffering for so long.

This can't be.

Jacqui grabbed an air compressor and placed the clear piece over his small mouth and nose, pumping air into his lungs.

While she pushed air into his airways, Jacqui took note of the rest of his appearance. The black-reddish film smeared over his face and body and the churned-up earthy smell had at first glance seemed normal, but now it concerned her. The thick coating of liquid all over his pale skin, held a black undertone. It was as though someone or something had dipped him in tar and tried to wash him clean but had failed miserably. It looked like a stain of death attached to his skin.

As Jacqui kept pressing on the air pump, she then added two fingers to aid in cardiac compressions. Still nothing. Jacqui could not let him die. Evelyn would never forgive her. Covering his soft, fair complexion, the thin layer of mysterious black-crimson liquid was slippery and left a gritty residue against her blue latex gloves. It had formed sludge inside his umbilical cord. Patches of red and black rashes twisted and danced along his flesh like a bird's feathers doused in an oil spill. It reminded Jacqui of a creature recovered from the Deepwater Horizon disaster.

A nurse approached Jacqui, with a familiar expression on her face. Jacqui knew that look all too well.

Jacqui pulled away from the child.

"What's happening to him? Someone, anyone, answer me!" Evelyn shouted, but her angry commands fell on deaf ears.

No one, especially Jacqui, could look her in the face.

Evelyn's little boy was gone.

Jacqui rushed out of the room and snatched her gloves off. Running through the halls, she could not get the image of Evelyn's son out of her mind. That thick coating of black liquid over his skin. The sludge inside his umbilical cord. The scent of decaying grass and burnt copper drifting about. The boy had looked to Jacqui more like a prop from a horror film than Evelyn's son. It was sickening to remember and each time she did, it made her skin crawl. But what had stood out more than anything was his face, and that look in his eyes that could only be compared to the regret of having formed inside his mother. Like he was sorry he'd ever existed, apologizing for letting them down.

He would never draw his first breath, never learn to walk, never scrape a knee on his bike. He'd never graduate from high school. Never go to college, and never bring a girl home for Evelyn to shower with disapproval. The weight of the things he'd never do slammed into Jacqui all at once. She was broken. Choking sobs followed the tears pouring from her eyes. Evelyn's son's death stained Jacqui's memories.

After de-scrubbing, she made her way to the break room, where she grabbed a cone and pressed down on the water cooler lever.

She sipped the water for a while to calm herself.

Jacqui put herself in Evelyn's place, imagining it was her own daughter, Ashley. When Ashley had been five years old, she'd come home acting very secretively. An hour later, during one of their little tea parties, Ashley had confessed to her mom that she had a boyfriend. Instantly they'd both started laughing. Though Jacqui wasn't thrilled at the prospect of some boy holding her little girl's hand, all she could remember most about that day was Ashley's laugh. She wouldn't trade a million-dollar lottery ticket for that laugh. It was pure, happy, full of life and goodness like the smell of Sunday breakfast filling a house with love. Then Jacqui thought of Evelyn. Jacqui sighed heavily and dropped her head to her chest. Evelyn would never have a moment like that or any other with her son. The death of a child, Jacqui wouldn't wish on anyone.

"Something is happening here," Jacqui said to Farra, a trauma nurse seated at a nearby table.

Farra was a thirty-something-year-old woman with a brown bob and bangs who loved gossiping just as much as she loved carbs. She was the kind of woman who was always on a diet, but never lost any weight.

"I'll tell you something," Farra said, before chomping down on a lettuce and tomato sandwich.

Jacqui took a long sip from her cup. The last time she'd seen Evelyn, her baby had been fine and completely healthy. *Her last visit had only been three weeks before her due date... Wait. Like Angela and Irene, the answer must lie in Evelyn's medical records.*

"May I?" Jacqui kindly asked Farra for the clear clipboard beside her water bottle. Farra handed it over, watching over Jacqui's shoulder the entire time. Signing in with her ID badge, since Evelyn was still her patient, Jacqui had access to Evelyn's records for the next five minutes which was enough time for her to find it.

The file read:

Client>Medical History> Immunizations

02/02/2019 Premier Vaccine 500ml dosage vial #41916

Another victim of this vaccine. Now that Jacqui found a pattern, she needed proof. HIPPA would prevent her from using her client's records in a research design study, but the origins of this problem had to have been documented elsewhere.

"You've been trying to access classified files, why is that?"

Arnold had said those words to Jacqui the first day they'd met. The answer had been sitting in front of her the entire time.

That database must have the answers she needed, the only problem was, she did not have access. Jacqui realized how she had been used this entire time, but what she did not have figured out was the correlation between Lanzran Inc. and BRT Health Industries outside of this vaccine. It had to be bigger than that. Knowing Arnold, he was probably fully aware of this whole vaccine situation and had done nothing to stop it, so long as he continued to make money. God, Jacqui hated that man. And once she'd found the smoking gun to this mess, she was going to point it right at Arnold's head.

Beep. Beep.

Jacqui's pager went off.

The high-pitched noise reminded her of the hellhole beneath the hospital. The fifty floors of lies buried underground —the Colony. At times, she forgot it was there, but Arnold loved using the pager. If she refused to answer within five minutes, he would make do on his threat to her daughter. Just the other day when Jacqui had taken too long to respond, he sent a picture of Ashley while she was in class at school. He did not send an ambiguous picture that could have been anyone's child, no, that was not Arnold's style. That picture was Ashley from a window seat in class, and it looked like she was daydreaming. Jacqui knew it was her girl by the music note tattoo on her wrist. It was Ashley, definitely.

Terrified, Jacqui rushed downstairs to the main floor of the Colony, but what she found surprised her in the worst way. Not only did she find a wealth of new faces added to the group of chained women, but one of them looked familiar. With the short curls of her lilac hair, Jacqui already knew who she was. She was the girl who had spent countless days in Jacqui's own home. She was a high school senior child with aspirations to go to college and establish her own tech company. An ambitious young girl with her whole life ahead of her. Someone free of any wrongdoing except for being at the wrong place at the wrong time. She was Ashley's best friend—Grace.

Jacqui remembered the first day she'd met Grace. The girl had walked through the doors of Jacqui's home as a shy sophomore, but she could tell she had a good heart. One night during a sleepover, Ashley thought her eyebrows were too bushy, so she'd decided to do something about it and trim them, and not with tweezers or waxing but with Nair—a hair removal cream. Jacqui had woken up to screams that night only to find her baby girl with one eyebrow. Ashley had been hysterical; crying and yelling as though her life was over. Jacqui had been at a loss for words. Grace, however, without a moment to spare, had sat Ashley down, grabbed some eyeliner and a fine-tooth comb, and somehow created magic. In a matter of minutes, Grace had drawn on a very natural-looking eyebrow, and ever since Ashley had drawn them in the same way. Most teenage girls would have just watched and/or laughed at their friend's expense, Jacqui knew how cruel girls could be in high school, but not Grace. To Jacqui, Grace had always been more than Ashley's friend, she was a second daughter.

At that very moment, Jacqui questioned every life decision that had led them both here. She should have gone to the cops. This had gone way too far. She had to get Grace out of there. But what could she do? There was twenty-four hour security, surveillance cameras on every corner, and clearance levels that Jacqui still did not have access to. Not only that but she was too deeply rooted in this system to separate herself. If she blew the whistle on this operation, she would incur more prison time than anyone else given that the entire project was based on her thesis. No one would have her back in court. Arnold would surely use his charm and turn the jury against her, saying that she had come to him with the idea. Heck, all his ideas led back to her research papers. If he could find enough people to support his story, he would win, and there was no doubt he had the resources at his disposal.

Nothing else mattered other than getting Grace out of there; Jacqui needed to find evidence and fast. For now, she had to plan accordingly.

WHEN JACQUI ARRIVED HOME, she pulled into her driveway and turned off the engine. Taking in a long deep breath, she sat in the car, contemplating life. Going cold beside her was a box of Ashley's favorite takeout pizza.

All the lights inside her home were off and the windows black. Ashley did not have practice today or a game to attend, yet her car was not in the driveway. Panic raced through her veins. Immediately, Jacqui called Ashley's phone.

The ringtone sounded for several seconds. Each passing moment a suffocating breath slowly wrapped around Jacqui's chest. Time seemed to have slowed down. If anything had happened to Ashley, Jacqui would never forgive herself. She had already failed her daughter's best friend, Grace. Her breathing began slipping from her control, picking up in pace and intensity, like a panic attack was creeping up from behind her in the back seat. A rush of heat overtook her body. Jacqui shed the lab coat hoping to cool herself down. It didn't work. Jacqui's chest suddenly weighed a ton. It was quite a strange feeling to be suffocating on her own breath. A flash of light hit the corner of her eye. Jacqui turned to her left as a car passed by. Looking in the driver's side window, she searched for a face. It was so dark she could not make out anything. It was probably Arnold's hired help sent to spy on her. She would not put it past the man. He was a micro-manager. Nothing would stop him from hiring someone to watch her at all times, just like he had someone tailing her daughter at school. This was bad and only getting worse. Jacqui could not even sit still for a moment without feeling panic moving inside her all while waiting for Ashley to answer her frickin' phone!

"Hello?" Ashley said in her usual condescending tone.

All breath returned to Jacqui. Inside, Jacqui was jumping and dancing in her head upon hearing her daughter's voice. But now that she had relief, it was time to be angry as her parent.

"Ashley, where are you?"

"I'm chillin', why what's up?"

This was strange. Ashley never spoke in such a cavalier fashion with her mom. She always used ma'am at the end of a sentence, no matter how angry she was with Jacqui. Why was this time different? In all honesty, at this very moment, Jacqui did not really care about her daughter's vernacular, she only needed to know she was safe and out of Arnold's reach.

"I got some pizza, pepperoni, your favorite."

Jacqui waited for her daughter's excitement to shoot through the phone. Then she waited a little longer. Still waiting...

There was a pause, before Ashley said, "You know what, I have to tell you something."

"What's that sweetheart?" Jacqui replied.

"Got you!" Ashley burst into an obnoxious laugh.

Jacqui sat on the phone, confused.

"I can't get to the phone right now, but if you leave a message, I will get back to you asap. Peace."

Beep.

At the sound of the tone, Jacqui's mind still could not process what had just happened. The automated voice faded into an abyss of silence. Above all, Jacqui could not believe her daughter would play such a cruel prank on anybody, but now of all times. She was too old to have this kind of voicemail. Worst of it all, the options laid before Jacqui were a choice between bad and terrible. If she called the cops, they would not take her seriously; a teenager out later than curfew did not raise serious concerns. But if Arnold found out that she'd called the cops regarding her daughter, no doubt she would suffer even worse consequences tomorrow. Jacqui ran both hands through her hair, pulling on the follicles. The stress of keeping this secret while trying to protect the people closest to her, was chipping away at her sanity.

Jacqui slammed the car door shut and ran inside. She dropped the heavy greasy pizza box on the countertop then dialed the number for Damon, her ex-husband. As Ashley's father, maybe he knew something that Jacqui did not. After two rings, a familiar voice answered.

"Aló?"

Hearing Damon's accent relieved Jacqui.

"Hey, have you heard from Ashley?"

"Yeah, I'm at the basketball game and—Oh come on, ref! Hey, I got to go, I'll call you back in a few."

She heard the buzzer go off just as Damon ended the call.

Jacqui called him again, but knowing Damon, his phone would be the last thing on his mind. It went to voicemail.

This cannot be happening.

An eerie silence swept through the living room. Jacqui had never seen her place this quiet before. Usually, Ashley left every light on along with every screen she owned. Now, there was nothing. There was nothing but a thick quietness that hung in her condo like humidity.

A knock at the door caught her attention.

It was now ten o'clock.

The number of people who would be knocking on Jacqui's door this late was a noticeably short list, in fact, only one person would be approaching her house at this time of night, and that one person had a key. Jacqui was not expecting company, nor any delivery, not even a package requiring her signature. This left only one option. Whoever was behind the door was sent by Arnold.

The stranger knocked again.

Jacqui had a decision to make. She could either pretend she was not home and hope that they simply went away; or answer and face the consequences of her actions. After all, she was a key part of this human trafficking ring, and no matter how much she tried to convince herself she was helping women, the only person she was helping was herself.

Jacqui thrust open the door.

It was a police officer.

Strange. Jacqui found herself wondering, *why does he look familiar?*

"Good evening, ma'am." His deep voice paralyzed her. His skin was as dark and smooth as coffee beans. He might have been in his early thirties, too young for Jacqui, but he was satisfying to her eyes. A nice smile and symmetrical face that had an uncanny resemblance to someone Jacqui knew but could not place.

"Good evening, officer. How can I help you?" Jacqui asked.

Her smile suddenly faded, realizing this could be it. The moment she was brought in for questioning. This was the day Jacqui had feared would come and the moment Arnold threatened her entire being. She should have gone to the police weeks ago, but now it was too late. What if Arnold had called the cops on her? What if they were done with her services and now this was the second part of Arnold's plan to use her as the scapegoat for the whole operation? They had her file and personnel information; they could easily alter her actual level of involvement with a few forged signatures. Or this could be a test of her loyalty. Either scenario terrified her. Sweat slid down her underarms. Her throat clenched with fear. *Be calm. Act natural. Relax.* Despite her inner thoughts, anxiety consumed her body.

He cut his radio off and locked eyes with Jacqui. "I am here on a personal call. It is about your daughter, Ashley."

As Ashley's name left his mouth, Jacqui's heart dropped to the floor.

Chapter 10

Justice: A Friend of a Friend is an Enemy

Grace had been missing for thirty hours now.

Like fine grains of sand, the last moments of Grace's life were slipping through his fingers.

Click.

With a twist of his car keys, Justice shut off the engine. He parked his Camaro outside a two-story condominium.

"Justice, I'm so scared... I think they're speeding up."

Remnants of Grace's words echoed in his mind. He ran through the police timeline for a missing person in his head. The first forty-eight hours were crucial. Leads were more accurate, potential witnesses had a fresh memory; the police could act on information. It had already been over a day since Grace disappeared. Even with his training, a sickening feel twisted his gut. What if his recent conversation with Grace was the final one he ever had with her?

Justice took his fists and struck them against the steering wheel. Frustrated and ashamed, there was nothing he could do to protect his younger sister. Their entire lives she'd looked up to him. After their dad passed, he'd taken on not just the role of an older brother but had become almost a father figure as well. And now listening to those words—her last words to him—and hearing the fear in her voice, it cracked the tough exterior Justice wore everyday. Each hour he grew weaker. Knowing there was nothing in his power to stop the evil headed towards her, the fear began seeping through those cracks. It was the unknown that plagued him worse than any illness or injury ever could.

Justice looked at his reflection through the rearview mirror, pulling himself together. Right now, Grace needed him at his best. With their mother worried sick, he was the only sane and level-headed individual left in their family. He could not lose his shit.

"If it's not one thing it's another."

His father used to say that nearly every damn day. It was his little routine with his morning cup of coffee. As a boy, Justice would sit with his father, and they would have their little talks about manhood. His father's raspy voice and tart delivery always reminded Justice of a stand-up comedian, so naturally, it was a little difficult for Justice to take him seriously. If only Justice had realized at the time how precious those moments would be. Now that Justice was an adult, he understood there was nothing fun about that saying. One out of every twenty-two Black men died not from an illness or natural causes, but from murder. That was the reality he had to face every day as a man coupled with being a police officer. He was one wrong comment away from losing his job. His mother's health was declining. His sister was missing. Life had its knee on his neck.

Still, despite it all, Justice *had* managed to find a lead. A girl. Grace's alleged best friend, Ashley.

Closing the door to his car, he rushed across the narrow road. The cool breeze of night and pure silence guided him to his destination. Long-legged light poles kept darkness off the streets. Freshly cut lawns, polished mailboxes, and stretched driveways sat in front of every condominium. Even the air smelled like premium healthcare.

Justice knocked on the door and took a few steps back. As he waited, he looked at the gold numbers above the door frame ensuring that he was at the right address.

The door swung open.

The woman before him had to be over thirty-five years old; more of a "black-don't-crack" type of older look to her. But with her smooth brown skin, dark eyes, and jet-black hair down her spine, she had the sort of face that made Justice consider dating an older woman. For a moment, he forgot why he was there in the first place. Then he took note of the lab coat. *Yes!* He remembered now and soon her name surfaced right on time.

"Dr. Jacqui Stevenson. Mother of Ashley Stevenson?"

Defensive, yet vulnerable. The woman responded the way anyone would react if the police showed up at their doorstep late at night. Justice had given countless parents bad news before; it never got any easier. Only this time the child was the one he was looking for.

"What's this all about?"

Good, Justice thought. He had the right place and the right person. The only thing he did not have were the words he was going to say to her.

"It's a personal call... It's about your daughter, Ashley. Do you mind if I come in?"

Jacqui allowed him inside and secured the door behind him.

"I will be quick, actually," Justice said, giving a half-smile. He stood near the front of the home, not wanting to step too far into her space.

She stopped in front of the beige sofa. Her lab coat fell quietly behind her as she came to a standstill.

"What's this about? You said something about my daughter?"

"Yes." Justice stepped toward her. His boots pressed against the hardwood floor. "It's nothing serious. I just have a few questions for her. Is Ashley here? She knows my sister, Grace Reeves."

Life had a funny way of working. Justice had no reason to suspect this woman, but this entire time he'd known nothing about her, and Grace had spent most of her time in these four walls. Why had they never met before? He doubted this woman could offer him anything of substance, but all he needed was a breadcrumb. Anything would help.

A long and awkward pause landed between the two of them.

Justice was fluent in two languages: English and body language. People learned to lie with their faces from an early age, but their bodies *always* told the truth. Two years back, Justice and his partner, Mason, had been assigned an arson case. Almost immediately, a security guard had come under suspicion. They'd sat the suspect in a room with a single strip of overhead light, ashy concrete floor handcuffed to a slate gray table while he awaited his fate. During the interrogation, Justice had focused on the man's eyes, searching for any signs of squinting, shielding, closing, or blocking. Justice believed it was the brain's way of protecting itself from the undesirable. He'd asked the man specific questions such as "Did you start the fire?" but the security guard's face had remained neutral, smooth, confident even, not troubled by it at all. Yet at the question "Where were you when the fire started?" the suspect had begun blinking at double the speed and squinting as Justice dove deeper into his alibi. Most would have ignored this, not Justice. A few hours later, the security guard admitted he'd left his post, which in turn had given the arsonist opportunity to set the fire. The guard was not guilty, but he'd unintentionally provided the police with enough insight needed to break the case. Justice had learned that day to always trust in body language.

From across the living room, he studied Dr. Stevenson focusing on her face. Dark circles under her eyes and a subtle imprint of horizontal lines embroidered into her forehead revealed she was indefinitely sleep-deprived but also something else. Her posture changed entirely at the sound of Grace's name. When she'd walked toward the kitchen only moments ago, her arms had moved freely about, but now, her right hand covered her left elbow, and her left hand desperately grabbed the necklace at the center of her clavicle. She literally shrunk before his eyes. Most notably, her face froze in a rictus of surprise. All of this was a clear sign of stress. It could have been nothing, but her distress placed Justice on high alert.

"Yes, my daughter knows her. She spends quite a lot of time over here."

"When was the last time you saw Grace?"

When Justice had arrived at Jacqui's place, he'd expected a light five-minute conversation, something to point him in the right direction. Anything would suffice. But what happened next shocked the hell out of him.

"I don't know maybe a few days ago?"

"And where was that?"

"Here. She spent the night, like usual."

As Jacqui talked, Justice observed her every move. Each time she said Grace's name, her neck sank into her shoulders like a turtle. Talking about Grace made this woman beyond anxious; like she was terrified. When Justice asked about the last time she'd seen Grace, the woman took a few steps back and rubbed her hands down her thighs in a pacifying manner.

That's odd, Justice thought.

Most people missed non-verbal cues, but these subtle movements, her self-distancing and soothing herself, told him more than her words. This woman knew something about Grace, but either could not or would not tell him.

Standing in Jacqui's living room, Justice looked around. Everything had its place. The décor and furnishings were minimal: one sofa, three pictures, a TV, a fireplace, and that was it. No art. No decorations. No mess on the hardwood floor. Not even a damn plant. Only the gentle smell of a vanilla-flavored candle on the coffee table in front of the sofa accompanied the two of them. *How long has she lived here*, wondered Justice. The place almost looked staged. Behind the sofa was an area housing a kitchen bar. Sitting atop the earth-toned granite work surface were two wine glasses and a large pizza box riddled with grease stains. Who was Jacqui expecting at ten o'clock on a school night?

"Can I look around?" Justice asked.

Jacqui drew a breath as if to answer, then hesitated for a few moments, her pause heightening his suspicion.

"I guess so," she eventually agreed.

Justice searched the living room. The L-shaped sofa in front of the fireplace took up most of the space. Above the fireplace was a wall-mounted sixty-inch television. Under the TV were three pictures placed exactly six inches apart. Two of them were of Jacqui and a young girl. Justice imagined this must be her daughter, Ashley. The last one closest to the window was a selfie of Jacqui with a man. Hispanic, over forty, and in running shape; the girl's father? If he was, why didn't Jacqui have a picture of all three of them together? He glanced back at Jacqui's left hand. No wedding band.

"Ashley's father?"

"We co-parent." Jacqui said it with shame mixed in her tone. Almost regretful.

In his head, he began to put a profile together on her. She was a doctor. Grueling work hours, six-figure income, technical expertise, and physicians in Justice's experience, were trained to remain detached from their emotions.

"How long have you lived in Ballantyne?" Justice said, examining the timber floorboards. The floor glistened under the dim touch of light from above, Justice could see his clear-cut reflection looking back at him.

"Fifteen years."

"How do you like it?"

"It's... Nice." She gave a restrained polite smile.

Her answers were vague, giving Justice the impression that Jacqui was a highly compartmentalized individual. What was she trying to hide from him? He doubted anyone knew the true woman underneath.

A hint of lemon-scented bleach greeted Justice at the entrance to the kitchen. This room was much smaller than the living room, with all-white flooring, cabinets with gray handles, and cream walls. Utensils sat in their proper place beside the spice rack next to the oven. There was not a single dish in the sink and not a crumb along the countertops. There was nothing wrong with keeping a clean house, thought Justice, but this was too clean, too neat, just like Jacqui's answers. *This woman is hiding something.*

Justice took the switchback staircase up to the second floor. Jacqui followed him a few paces behind.

She watched him closely as he walked around but said nothing.

He made a right and entered the first room. Beside the window, there was a full-sized bed layered with a white comforter holding a portfolio of precious electronics: a laptop, iPad, wireless headphones, and a fairy pink throw blanket. Jacqui said nothing as Justice searched but stared at him as if she were afraid he'd find something. A faint whiff of sweet mango and peach body spray drifted around the room. He could barely see the floor as shoes, dresses, cardigans, shopping bags, necklaces, earrings, and books cluttered his way.

Hanging above the closet was a blue and orange cheerleading uniform. Even without someone wearing it, the garment emitted a certain sassy attitude that only a high schooler could replicate. This room belonged to Jacqui's daughter. Perhaps that's who the pizza was for?

"Did Ashley or Grace ever mention a program called BRT Health Industries? Apparently, they are a very generous organization."

Watching Jacqui standing in the doorway, Justice swore he could see straight into her soul. With every question, it was like he already knew the answer. Was this woman blatantly lying to the police? Would she dare? What did Justice truly know about this woman? Just because her profession helped people, it did not exempt her from breaking the law. Perhaps this was her doing the best she could to keep herself out of prison. With this stiff silence between them, Justice had already made up his mind that Jacqui was a link between his sister and this BRT Health program.

Before she could answer, something caught the corner of his eye. A gray and yellow book bag that he knew belonged to Grace.

As he picked it up, Jacqui finally spoke, "Don't you need a warrant, officer?"

Out of all things she could have said to Justice in that moment, she mentioned a warrant, and that fact alone strengthened his suspicion further.

Justice replied, "Look, you see that butterfly emblem by the zipper here? I know this belongs to my sister. I'm just returning it." And with that, he was done searching, but not done with the mysterious Dr. Jacqui Stevenson. Whoever those men were that had kidnapped Grace, they were somehow connected to Dr. Jacqui Stevenson. They had to be.

As Justice headed back down the stairs, he heard a car pull up outside.

Jacqui escorted Justice to the door. A deafening tension sweltered in the space. Only the sound of their shoes against the hard surface held a conversation. Given her passive posture, Justice assumed she was an accomplice. Even so, she was completely complicit in whatever the hell had happened to Grace.

She opened the front door to show him out.

Justice paused before leaving and said, "One last thing, if you see or hear from Grace, you'll let me know?" He handed Jacqui his card. "That's my direct line and an email address to the precinct."

Though Jacqui hid her countenance well, Justice had a feeling that the woman was indeed lying to him, and Justice always trusted his gut instincts. He imagined that she must have been relieved to see him leave. She should enjoy what little freedom and time with her daughter that she had left, he thought. If he only had solid evidence, he would have arrested her right then and right there. This Dr. Jacqui Stevenson was up to something. Justice vowed to himself, that the next time he saw her or came to her home, that woman would be leaving in handcuffs.

A car had pulled into the driveway. Through the windshield, Justice counted two people. A middle-aged man and a young woman. Justice waved down the car and the gentleman turned the headlights off.

Justice approached the young woman's side; she rolled down the window.

"Is there a problem officer?" she asked.

"No, not at all." Justice looked back at Jacqui who was

standing in the doorway, watching. The face of the young woman in the car resembled that of Jacqui's and matched the photos in the living room. He guessed this must be Ashley. "Have a good night," he replied.

From the door, Jacqui hugged herself so tightly that the seams of her lab coat began showing. Her brows were drawn together, and she was chewing on her fingernails. *What is she hiding?* Justice got the sense that what Jacqui was involved in, her daughter knew nothing about. He had gleaned enough intel from this encounter. The lead had given him his prime suspect: Dr. Jacqui Stevenson.

Chapter 11

Jacqui: The Poor Give To The Rich

The previous night had offered up the perfect opportunity for Jacqui to tell the truth. Jacqui knew that as soon as she'd seen Grace's brother, Justice Reeves, standing at her door, earnestly asking for the whereabouts of his sister. The same sister who Jacqui remembered seeing less than twelve hours prior to that moment; unconscious, stripped of her dignity, and chained to a hospital bed.

In less than forty-eight hours, Grace was going to be cut open, her womb stolen and sold to the highest bidder, while her remains would never be found. If Jacqui was deeply concerned about all the missing Black girls, and if there had been any moment to come forward and help Grace, yesterday had been the time.

But she hadn't.

She'd just sat there and lied. What was this place turning her into?

Jacqui walked into Angela's Premier Care patient room. She was standing in front of the floor-length window, watching the colorful cars maneuver through traffic as she brought a warm glass of tea to her lips.

"Ms. Liu, it's a pleasure. How are you feeling?"

As Angela turned toward her, Jacqui studied Angela's stomach area. The guilt hit her all at once. Jacqui had done the unthinkable.

Side by side in the operating suite, Angela and Ivery had been unconscious, unclothed. Light blue hospital fabric had covered their upper body and legs and left their reproductive organs unbothered. After this, there was no turning back. Once Jacqui stepped into that surgery, she would leave that room a different woman; a woman consumed by evil. She was now the epitome of what she feared was going to happen to those girls. *For Ashley*, she thought as she'd kept going. Monitors rested on both sides of them tracking vital organs. Oxygen masks were strapped to both faces. Disposable head caps were attached to their heads. The both of them were mere women, but in the eyes of society, only one of their lives mattered. *For Ashley*. Once Jacqui had finished, she'd ripped off her gloves, stood and looked down at Ivery. She'd mouthed the words "I'm sorry," but Ivery was long gone; nothing more than a corpse. Two nurses had quickly placed a white sheet over Ivery's body and removed her from the room. Ivery would never be seen again.

And now, as Jacqui stared at Angela—who was in possession of a womb she was not born with—the memory of the transaction made Jacqui's stomach turn.

Angela looked down at her belly, rubbed it, and then looked over her shoulder at Jacqui. "Dr. Stevenson without your help I wouldn't be here. Thank you."

Angela was right. Jacqui was an accomplice whether she liked it or not. How did it go this far and so fast? Working on the inside, Jacqui was supposed to help these women, but now, Jacqui had come to question herself: Was she any better than Arnold? Pulling her attention back to the clear clipboard, Jacqui continued with Angela Lui's prenatal appointment.

"Alright, Ms. Liu, so as you are aware this will not be a normal pregnancy. With BRT Health Industries' fertility program, you will have your baby in about half the time of a traditional pregnancy. You will experience all three trimesters in about four and a half months. So, we must monitor you very closely," said Jacqui. "Let's get started, shall we?" Jacqui smiled as she adjusted the stethoscope around her neck.

Though BRT Health's methods were rotten, the science was impeccable. They'd created a format to shorten pregnancy and postpartum all while giving the parents the ability to choose their child's genetics like ordering from a restaurant. A woman at forty-five years old could select an eighteen-year-old's womb and have an expedited pregnancy. This was far more efficient than freezing eggs. It was brilliant. If only it did not require kidnapping and killing women to do so.

Jacqui stood at the bedside and Angela lifted her blouse, revealing the tiniest baby bump. Smearing a thick, clear substance across her skin, Jacqui then placed a wireless device on her abdomen. The remote transmitted a black-and-white image onto a monitor beside Jacqui.

"Hmph, that's strange," Jacqui whispered to herself, leaning into the monitor.

Between the last visit with Angela and right now, was night and day difference, thought Jacqui. This woman beside her had a light around her, an aura of optimism. Jacqui could not bring herself to be happy for her. How could she? Angela had paid half a million dollars for Ivery's most precious organ. Worst of it all, Angela would never know how her money had killed someone's daughter. A daughter just like the one she desperately wanted to have herself.

As Jacqui continued the scan, Angela spoke quietly of her fears, "When I was four, I lost my oldest brother. His name was Jin. I only mention it because well... He was the last important person I lost in my life. The anxiety before I found out feels like right now. The night my brother didn't come home. The moment I saw my parents' faces as they carried what remained of my oldest brother, back from the crematorium. At the time I prayed and prayed, begging God so hard that I thought he would bring him back somehow. At four years old, my mind couldn't process the finality of cremation."

Jacqui had no words, instead she merely kept at her work. All of her empathy had gone to Ivery, she had none left for a woman who had it all.

"Ms. Liu, your baby looks healthy. Give me a second and I can generate a preview for you."

Though Angela was speechless, joy took shape in her expression. She covered her mouth as happiness streamed from her eyelids.

"That's such a relief." She laid her head back into the pillow. "What do you mean by a preview?"

"A preview is... How about I just show you."

After a series of scans from the remote device, a video appeared on the monitor. On the screen was a black-and-white virtual moving image. These slowly moving pictures were Angela's future.

"This is a growth projection. You'll be able to see where he/she is right now and how he/she will look by the time he/she is ready to meet you."

As they both watched the screen, the small embryo inside of Angela began shapeshifting, and what started out as a very alien-like looking creature soon formed into a human child with its tiny legs and arms. From the moment it became only a heartbeat to the current size of a grape, the video stretched into the future, where their true features started to develop.

Angela gasped.

"Congratulations, you're having a girl."

Angela then moved closer to the screen. "The resemblance is unreal."

Though Jacqui could only see the corner of Angela's eye, tears poured from her. It could have been the hormonal changes, or seeing her child grow in front of her, but Jacqui got the sense it was something more.

"She is someone I prayed so long for. A lovely face I never thought I would see again."

"I can't imagine how you must feel, Ms. Liu."

"No, I don't think you get it." Angela laid a hand on Jacqui's wrist. Angela was known as a cold-hearted, non-emotional perfectionist from what Jacqui had heard about her. Yet, sitting in front of her was nothing more than a woman, a soon to be mother. Children had a way of doing that to people.

"Even down to the mole in the middle of her right cheek, just like him."

"Like whom?"

Angela leaned into the monitor. "Wow, Dr. Stevenson, this is a miracle. You know I'm not very religious but seeing this... Wow, I'm literally speechless. I had lost faith, but Arnold and his program have given me something much more than I paid for."

Jacqui handed Angela a tissue. She dabbed her eyelids with the soft material. Recalling Angela's story about the abortion she'd undergone in college and the grief that must have torn at her conscience, Jacqui softened. After all, Angela was merely a patient seeking medical expertise. She'd done nothing wrong.

"Not only does she look like my brother I lost, but..." Angela began to get choked up on her words. Her lips quivered out of her control as she played with the torn tissue between her fingers. This woman was responsible for the cybersecurity infrastructure of the entire city. But sitting beside Jacqui right now was just a woman who wanted to be nothing more than a mom.

"You gave me my daughter back, and for that, I can never repay you."

Chapter 12

Cara: Three Phases

S he was awake!

Then... nothing but silence.

This was the kind of mind-numbing quietness that drove someone insane. At times, the only thing Cara could hear was the beeping monitor at her bedside and the casual swivel of nurses pushing carts. Other than that, absolutely nothing.

Cara looked to her left and found the same girl with the freckles all along her nose, cheeks and arms, but to her right, the woman who had the handcuffs too tight around her wrists and ankles was gone. A nurse had come in yesterday, rolled her bed out of there and Cara had never seen her again. The worst of it all, she never caught her name. She'd been sedated the entire time. *Wait... was she supposed to be under for as long as the girls around her?* If so, whatever stuff they put in those syringes, for some strange reason Cara kept waking up. Though there was not a clock or any way to keep track of time near her, it seemed like only hours had passed each time she awoke.

Her last moments before passing out surfaced. The scorching heat of liquid rushing through her veins brought the painful memory with it. Being strapped to this bed, Cara thought of her mother. She wondered what she had thought of in her last moments.

Click. Clack.

Cara quickly shut her eyes as footsteps approached her. A nurse in teal scrubs, a surgical mask, and a clear clipboard had stopped at Cara's bed. Turning her head very slowly towards the nurse, Cara studied the woman. The nurse stared at Cara's monitor for quite some time. She began sifting through various screens as though comparing something, all the while glancing down at the clipboard and then back at the monitors in front of her. In fact, the woman seemed confused. She squinted her eyes and raised her eyebrows. She called another nurse over to look at the same screen, paperwork, and clipboard. Cara had the sense that something was wrong. And anything that had gone wrong for them, surely, meant something good for her. Right?

"Her lab results came back abnormal."

Abnormal?

It wasn't the first time Cara had heard that word and her name in the same breath. She then remembered her endometriosis diagnosis. The same illness her mother had suffered from. Proof enough that she was going to be just like her. If she could ever even sustain a pregnancy, she knew she would never meet her child. This was her fate. She accepted it because believing anything else was another form of suffering. The chill of the metal restraints against her wrists and ankles seeped into her bones. The overhead light stared at her with an unforgiving glare, like it was judging her, like it knew her transgressions. Cara refused to believe in religion but being trapped down here must have been a punishment from above.

At no cost to you. Mr. Khizar snuck into her thoughts. This could not be the treatment he'd been referring to? Then again, what did Cara truly know about BRT Health Industries? What did she know about Mr. Khizar?

"Her iron levels are far below the minimum." The nurse standing in front of her monitor said. Her voice thrust Cara back to the present.

"If not today, she'll be ready by tomorrow, don't worry, I've seen worse."

Those fateful words crushed the little hope Cara had mustered. Closing her eyes, tears began falling absent of her consent. Cara now understood the meaning of her life flashing before her eyes. She saw them, her children, two boys, and one girl. Her twin boys, Zen, and Zach, were athletes involved in every sport imaginable. Zen's favorite was Track and Field and that boy, could he run fast. Like, Zen moved so fast it was embarrassing for the other students, but you think Cara gave a crap about the other kids? Nope, not when her boy made history as the first student at their school to run the mile in under four minutes. Zach was a little jealous, but Zach shined in football. He was always in rough housing growing up so it came as no surprise to Cara, but every time when her eldest twin boy would drop someone on the field, in sleet, snow, or summer, she would stand up and scream as loud as she could, "That's my boy!" The other parents got annoyed with Cara, but she did not care because each time Zach would find her in the audience and give her a high-five from afar, that was their little thing. Then her youngest and only girl, Alina; Cara's daughter was so pretty at times Cara was in disbelief that she created her. At the tender age of seven, Cara put Alina in ballet classes. At first, Alina was a little behind, her hand-eye coordination was not always the best and she wanted to give up, but with a little push from her mommy, Alina began to perform well in classes. Alina went on to attend an arts high school where her long legs and slim figure were exactly what the admissions department was looking for in modern dance, ballet and even pointe. At every one of Alina's ballet recitals, Cara always had to bring a ridiculous amount of tissue, because, well, when it came to her daughter, Cara was a crier, and she could not hide it. Instead of judging her mom, after Alina left the stage, she simply hugged her and they cried together, it became their ritual. A smile came to Cara, watching this movie in her mind's eye. Without a doubt she was going to die here, in this bed, in these chains, and having hope, only to have it crushed moments later, was another torture of its own.

"Hey..." a soft voice said. The owner of the voice shocked the hell out of Cara. It was her, the girl with the freckles, she was awake. "Where are we?"

"I was hoping you could tell me. How long have you been down here?"

"I don't know, but the last time I was awake they said they had to push my procedure back a few hours, and that the next time I wake up, might be my last."

If someone had said that to Cara, she would have killed herself before they'd had the chance to, but in doing so, in this hellhole, it only sped up the process. Even in death, there was no escaping this.

"What is the procedure they are talking about?"

"They haven't told you?" The girl's voice became faint, so gentle Cara could barely hear. "They keep us drugged up so even if we get free, we won't get far. That's what happened to Tanisha."

"Tanisha?" Cara whispered. The girl pointed.

"She was the girl on the other side of you. She... well, they..."

Without finishing her sentence, Cara already knew. The girl did not need to say anything else. Cara balled her fist, enraged. Who could do this to people? And for what reason? Whoever ran this place deserved to die a slow and miserable death.

"She broke free of her handcuffs somehow, but her legs were so weak she couldn't run. They eventually got her."

"Oh my God."

"After a while the handcuffs aren't even necessary, our bodies are no longer our own. I've accepted that now. It brings a certain peace. They may have this vessel, but they'll *never* take my mind."

Cara peered into the girl's brown eyes. They were an ochre color much like the sweet-brown light that bathed autumn forests. Behind the color, was an empty manic gaze. Cara couldn't tell if this woman was strong-willed for her enlightenment or if the place had simply broken her body and mind.

Footsteps closed in on them. In that same slow rhythm accompanied by a whistle. Cara knew exactly who was coming.

"My name is Eva, by the way, what's yours?"

"Cara."

Cara then closed her eyes, pretending to be unconscious as the steps and the whistling stopped near her.

"Good morning, Ms. Esperanza," Dowey said.

Morning? Good morning meant that at least Cara knew the sun was shining outside. Every little breadcrumb this man dropped knowingly or unknowingly, Cara forced herself to remember.

Dowey sat down beside her, glancing at her through thick square glasses.

"How are you today, my dear?" Dowey asked, thinking he was talking to an unconscious woman. He liked the fact she lay still, stayed quiet, and listened to him speak. "I wished that all women were like you, my dear. Sweet, firm, and quiet. I remembered the days before women could get these fast-food abortions. It's ridiculous how far removed we've become as a collective society. As soon as that heartbeat begins, so does life, and only God has the right to take that away. Sometimes women don't make the best choices. I blame the emotions." Dowey chuckled at himself. Then continued at his work. "I watched one of your films recently."

Cara gasped. Her face became warm with embarrassment. She didn't do that kind of work anymore, yet people like him would never let her forget it.

"I believe it was called *Deep Throat* or something like that. Quite remarkable work I must say."

Her film career wasn't her proudest moment, but it paid for a journalism degree that hadn't yet landed her a big girl job. Any day she was going to get a call... only she ended up here. No telling the offers she probably had missed.

Cara began trembling from the downpour of air conditioning, and yet sweat slid from her forehead like rain against a windowpane. Perhaps this was what the nurses had seen on her chart earlier. This felt like a fever coming. Whatever was in those injections, Cara's body was rejecting it, and not only was she fighting to stay optimistic, but now she was also fighting to stay alive.

Dowey popped open that same silver briefcase.

"Maybe you can help me. I don't understand why society puts such an emphasis on the whole getting married concept. I fell for it. My fiancée gave me an ultimatum thirty years ago; I was only twenty-seven when she made me choose her or the door. Looking back, I should've known, any woman that wants you to choose her or else, you take the option of being single. Am I right?" He had the audacity to laugh.

"Why are you doing this?" Cara whispered, but it was loud enough for him to hear.

He stopped his work.

"Somebody's up, good. I think this is something you should know. Well, let's see. I am helping you. When you signed that form at BRT Health Industries you agreed to this treatment. Donating your life to science. I'll admit the whole 'run you off the road' bit is poor taste. If it were up to me, I wouldn't have let you leave after the interview. Anyhow, that was why the interview asked such specific questions. You have no immediate family. You are an only child. You have no children of your own. You were a perfect candidate. If you are to vanish, no one would even notice you were gone."

"I did not sign up for this—"

"Shh." He placed a forefinger on her lips. "It's alright. It'll all be over soon. In three short phases. Phase One is sedation, we like to keep you all unconscious for most of the work since it can be quite invasive." He unlatched his briefcase. "Phase Two is preparation, where we find a proper match with the same blood type, similar cervix structure, and that you are healthy enough to survive through the procedure." He removed the compartments of the syringe. "Lastly, Phase Three is transferal; a doctor, either me or the one who founded the entire project, will donate your womb to a woman in need."

Donate? Did this man just say they were going to take Cara's God-given womb and *donate* it to a woman in need? Did Cara all of a sudden not need hers? No... *this could not be happening*. Cara was so shocked at his cavalier tone and what these people had planned, she had no words.

"For some individuals we can fast-track the process in under twenty-four hours based on their current state of health and certain characteristics like your little friend the other day, to your right, and boy was she healthy. I believe you two came in at the same time. You, however, are full of surprises, some of which we missed in the interview questionnaire. Being so, over the next few hours we must monitor you closely. You were supposed to go into Phase two and get prepped for surgery, but since you're having a bit of a fever, we can't move forward with you right now."

Cara never thought she would say this but *thank God she*

was feeling like crap right now. Goosebumps had formed along her arms bringing with them an unnerving chill through her body. Her face grew hotter by the second. Hopefully, this lasted long enough for them to forget about her altogether, there were at least a dozen other young women around her from what Cara could see, and they brought in new girls almost by the hour.

He took a small syringe full of a clear liquid and inserted the needle tip into Cara's IV bag. As he pushed down on the lever, the transparent substance slid into her veins. Since his work was done, Dowey packed his tools and closed the briefcase.

"Well, until tomorrow, Ms. Esperanza." He stood, but suddenly stopped and looked over his shoulder back at Cara. The glint reflecting off his aviator reading glasses covered his eyes, but she could still feel his chilling gaze. "Even though you made very questionable choices with your life before this, it does not matter. For you will serve a greater purpose. The purpose of all women. God's purpose," he said before walking in the opposite direction.

Chapter 13

Justice: In Between The Lies

G race had been missing for forty-seven hours.
Stuck on paperwork duty, Justice scanned through anything and everything he could find about the sketchy company by the name BRT Health Industries.

On their company website he found:

BRT Health Industries is a pioneering fertility company committed to innovative technologies and providing healthcare alternatives to prestigious clientele...

That was code for, "we only cater to rich people". *Got it.* Moving on, Justice kept reading.

BRT Health Industries has partnered with Mercy Hospital in an attempt to foster a positive influence on the community of Ballantyne. The following internships and programs to help pay for college are available to high school and college students, and even college graduates (student loan repayment programs) have opportunities to grow with us.

This was what Grace had been talking about.

Given our connection to the community, we are committed to diversity and inclusion in our programs. Currently, the student financial aid programs are specifically for female applicants. The scholarships are as follows:

The Aphrodite Scholarship offers up to $15,000 per year for maintaining over a 3.5 GPA and students must demonstrate leadership capabilities within Science, Technology, Engineering, or Math. The Hevinnette scholarship program agrees to pay off any remaining balance of tuition for women of color ranging from ages 17-21. Easy apply and no degree-specific requirement.

This all sounded too good to be true, but if Justice were a desperate female looking for money for school, he probably would have done exactly the same thing Grace had done. He'd told her not to go several times and that there were other ways to pay for school. Justice had filled out a loan application, and even though he only got approved for 11K, he could have picked up an extra job as a nightclub bouncer; he had the look and was no doubt intimidating enough. Or Grace could have worked part time. Justice had heard some college kids worked while in school, that was a thing, right? Why hadn't Grace just listened to him for once? She did not have to go at this alone, there were ways around the tuition. Why couldn't she give him a chance to help her? *Why the fuck didn't she just listen!*

"Dammit!" Justice yelled and slammed on the desk. A stack of folders dropped to the ground, along with paper clippings, photos, pens, sticky notes, a stapler, a binder filled with paper protectors, and tons of crumbled-up old documents from the eighties. Now, all of that, Justice had to pick right back up.

"Hey, Reeves?" Goodchild said.

"What's up?" Justice said, collecting old investigation documents and reports from the gray epoxy flooring, which was now a mountain of white papers and manila folders. Dust and dirt gathered in Justice's fingers, the precinct had seen better, cleaner days. Without asking, Goodchild got down on the ground with his partner and started picking. Perhaps Goodchild was trying to make up for nearly killing someone on his first day or maybe that was Goodchild's style. Justice was still profiling Goodchild, anticipating what kind of partner he would be. He'd never be Mason. Though the two had only been partners for about two weeks now, Goodchild had worked overtime to gain Justice's trust. Right now, Justice needed all the help he could get.

"Do you remember the other day when that lady threw herself out in the middle of the street? I had a guy come in yesterday and he had a strikingly similar story to that woman. The woman who said her daughter went to an interview and never came back home."

Justice stopped and looked at Goodchild. "What did you find?"

Goodchild pulled a bright orange envelope from his desk and handed it to his partner.

"What is all this?" Justice took everything from inside and spread it out atop the desk. One was a picture of a car that had been abandoned. All of the contents included photos, files, documents, and bank statements all belonging to one woman who had just been reported missing.

"A man named Matthew came in with this. Claims she's his ex-wife and he's been trying to reach her but couldn't get a hold of her, so he hired a private investigator. Basically this is what remains of a Ms. Cara Esperanza's vehicle. It was found in a ditch, nearly all but sunk under a shallow creek. I was able to match her license plate, description, and address. The vehicle was found thirty minutes outside the city. We know for certain she's not walking alongside the road desperate for a lift and Mercy Hospital has not documented her entering for emergency services and we definitely know she's not been home or at work in the past forty-eight hours. The important thing here though is that she fits the profile, she's between eighteen and twenty-five, African American, female, with massive debt and in need of financial assistance. Reeves, I think you are on to something."

Another Black woman—gone.

Briana Wilson, Grace Reeves, and now Cara Esperanza all in the same week. Briana was missing for three days now, Grace almost two, and now Cara around eighteen hours. The time between victims was too close for someone to be working alone —which meant that on any given day, at any given hour, another woman could disappear. Someone was deliberately choosing their victims and Grace was at the wrong place at the wrong time.

Justice glanced at the television screen and found the news channel was playing. Front and center, a male reporter was delivering the news headline: **Are Your Shoes Keeping You Overweight?**

Not that America's obesity crisis was not a serious subject, but there were far more pressing issues. Combined with this week's stats, Justice had counted ten Black women who'd vanished in the last ten days, one of which was his sister. However, what did the news choose to discuss? Nonsense. From that lack of coverage, it was clear to him that those women did not matter to society.

Stepping over the still scattered papers on the floor, Justice went back into researching BRT Health Industries, but more importantly, Dr. Jacqui Stevenson.

"What's your working theory of this whole kidnapping situation?"

Typing viciously on the computer, Justice then turned the screen toward Goodchild.

"So, we know between a fifty-mile radius of Claventine Avenue and Thirty-Fifth Street, women have been disappearing. All or most of the victims, that we know of, have gone on some interview with BRT Health Industries and were never seen again after that. Two of the victims' cars have been found outside the city. Either burnt up, or in a body of water, presumably to bury evidence."

"Wait there's Cara Esperanza, who's the other?"

"Grace. Her name is Grace Reeves."

A silence grabbed hold of them both. Justice kept his focus on the screen, but he could sense Goodchild's gaze lingering on him, not quite knowing what to say, but knowing something needed to be said.

"I'm so sorry, Reeves."

"Don't be sorry, help me find the bastards." Justice managed to slide in a joke. In return, Goodchild smiled slightly and then sat on the edge of the desk.

"Here's where it gets weird. The other day I met a Dr. Jacqui Stevenson. Since her daughter is best friends with my sister, I figured who else knew Grace's schedule the best. But when I got there, something strange happened with Dr. Stevenson. This woman exhibited a lot of stressors at the mention of Grace and at first, I thought I was being paranoid by suspecting her, but look here. This woman is the head of BRT Health Industries, the program was founded on her research."

"So, we arrest her, and bring her in for questioning." Goodchild leaned into the screen which now had the face of Jacqui Stevenson on it.

"The woman pays her taxes, does the speed limit, not even parking violations. On paper she's a perfectly law-abiding citizen. Our best bet is to watch her. She'll slip up eventually. If she created BRT Health Industries, then she would know what's happening to those missing women. I just know it."

With his sister gone and the testimony of Briana Wilson's mother, this company, BRT Health Industries, kept emerging.

Silently hiding behind promises of financial freedom, this company was not as it seemed.

"For even Satan disguises himself as an angel of light."

His father's voice came to him. His father was a wall of a man that when he spoke you felt him in the marrow of your bones. Sundays with his father in the pulpit always felt to him more of a performance than teaching. Justice had remembered that day, the "angel of light" sermon. His father had said Satan appeared through our desires, not some red-fleshed horned beast. Desire drove men to madness, desire brought his father to the local gas station, and desire drove that gunman to shoot him. All Justice did was watch as the bullet left the chamber, ripped through his father, and shattered the glass door. His lifeless body had dropped to the ground.

Shaking his head, Justice pushed away the memory.

Justice could feel something was amiss, but only his intuition served as proof. Slowly, the puzzle was coming together. BRT Health Industries. Dr. Jacqui Stevenson. Grace's disappearance. No matter what, Justice was going to figure it out. His sister's life depended on it.

Chapter 14

Jacqui: Overpaid, Overworked

"*I could never repay you.*"

Hearing Angela's voice in her head, Jacqui stood in front of the bathroom mirror repulsed by her reflection. Jacqui was changing. Each passing day, she was burying herself into a hole. On the outside, she was busy convincing herself that every movement driving her deeper into the madness was a necessary evil and that even in the midst of all this mess with Arnold, she was somehow still in control. Inside, she was crumbling. Every time she laid eyes on a new face chained to a hospital bed, or a new Premier Care client seeking a transplant, it pulled Jacqui further into mania. Slowly, she was unraveling, cracking under the pressure from it all.

Who am I? Jacqui studied her hands.

As a child, people had told her she had piano fingers; long, slender and suited for the elegance of producing music, even though she never learned to play. Instead she transformed her hands into an instrument of good. These hands had delivered hundreds of children, some of which were now in high school and college. These were the same hands that had resuscitated countless lives from the edge of death. The same hands that held her daughter as a newborn. And these same hands had murdered Ivery. She had spent her whole life abiding by the rules. Whoever she was now, completely disgusted her.

Enough of being the victim, today Jacqui had to do something, sneak out a sample, take a picture, or recording. Anything that could exonerate her if this went to trial.

Jacqui had gone back to the research and development department. With the new discovery of three previous patients with this Premier Vaccine, she knew there was a connection. Now it was time to find evidence. The best place to start was the trials.

Literature Review of Premier Vaccine 2012

"Since the outbreak of the Lemmia pandemic, the Premier Vaccine has been offered as prevention of infection in an attempt to eradicate the disease through herd immunity. The association between fertility and vaccinations: it can be assumed that the vaccine effects on pregnancy would be minimal, but more data would be needed for confirmation."

To Jacqui, the lack of research in this area meant no one even considered it to be an issue. What she stumbled across in the next article proved her theory correct.

Literature Review of Premier Vaccine 2012

"The fertility loss within those with a completed pregnancy included a spontaneous abortion (<20 weeks) rate of 85.6% (702 out of 827) and stillbirth (≥20 weeks) incidence of 92.1% (591 out of 643)."

Whoa.

With numbers like these, thought Jacqui, someone should have gone to jail. But she only found a few lawsuits that nearly bankrupted Lanzran Inc. Maybe that was why Arnold started BRT Health Industries, to dig himself out of a hole. At the bottom of the article was the biography of the author. This same author had been fired from Lanzran Inc. the year this study was published. Definitely not a coincidence. Jacqui found contact details for the author. Most importantly a phone number. Right away she dialed.

Voicemail.

"Hi, Dr. Seymore, this is Dr. Jacqui Stevenson, I have a few questions about your research with Lanzran Inc. that you published back in 2012, please call me back." Jacqui ended the phone call. Dr. Seymore was Jacqui's last hope. If anybody knew what the hell was going on with Lanzran Inc. it would be him.

While on the elevator, Jacqui opened her phone and for the first time in a while, looked at her bank statement. Her bi-weekly deposits had an additional three zeros in them. This should have brought happiness, but instead, she quickly closed out of the app. She finally understood that saying of more money, more problems.

<hr>

THE ELEVATOR STOPPED AT level UG of the Colony. The lobby level of BRT Health Industries. As she performed her daily walk-through of the chained women in the Transition Room, she watched each passing monitor looking for declining numbers, discoloration of the IV bag, changes in blood pressure, and resting heart rate. Anything out of the norm. She stopped her slow stride when the number 7048 came into her vision. That was Grace Reeves. Jacqui pulled out the business card from the detective, Grace's brother. She thought again about him showing up at her house and how she'd blatantly lied to the man. She'd lied to Grace's brother about where she was. Only an evil person was capable of doing that to someone else, but Jacqui was not evil. She was a good person—somewhat. She liked to think of herself as a person who helped others in need. But good people tell the truth, no matter what. That was something Jacqui did not have the heart to do, not with her daughter's life on the line. She just couldn't risk it. She had a plan. *Keep Grace out of Phase Two.*

A nurse in teal scrubs, a white cap, and a surgical mask was sitting next to Grace in a backless chair. In her hand was a luminous silver briefcase.

No. This was too soon, especially for Grace. The contents of that box would begin Grace's downfall. Jacqui may not have created the serum, but given her short time with BRT Health Industries, she had learned of the true evil this company was capable of doing. Phase One: the serum would first attack Grace's ovaries and essentially remove all trace of her DNA in her uterus. The second dose in Phase Two would move her uterus and fallopian tubes into a detachment status and her own organs would no longer recognize her as a host. Some women died in this phase, like Ivery, or turned hot with a fever. Phase Three was the removal and would ultimately be the end for Grace. Once Phase One started, Jacqui would have less than twenty-four hours to get Grace out of the hospital, or she would be dead.

Jacqui stopped in place, watching the nurse unpack the silver briefcase. Each medical tool she placed on the teal cloth shimmered like untouched diamonds when the light hit it. Grace was supposed to be unpacking her countless amounts of shoes in her college dorm room or bonding with a foreign exchange student who was her new roommate. Grace was supposed to be getting lost on campus while looking for her classes and stressing about papers, assignments, and midterms. Instead, she was here, thrust into a living hell all because of what? Being born a woman! Or was her true crime the amount of melanin in her skin? Either way, if Jacqui did not intervene now, Grace would die from her cowardice.

"Excuse me, nurse. What are you doing?" Jacqui asked, but it was not a question.

"Um... she cleared Phase One, over the night shift, and I am initiating Phase Two preparation," the nurse said as she held the syringe dangerously close to Grace's shoulder. A few centimeters more and the countdown on Grace's life would begin.

Jacqui marched over to Grace's chart.

The nurse watched Jacqui's every move. She knew exactly who Dr. Jacqui Stevenson was, everyone in the hospital knew.

Inspecting Grace's chart, Jacqui could see that every box had the word *"no"* checked off. No additional medications. No antibiotics. Not overweight or underweight. No prior STIs. Grace was a virgin. She was the ideal candidate and Jacqui knew they would try to fast-track her.

"She's not ready," Jacqui said.

"But all her results came back normal—"

"I *said* she is not ready. We must run another test on her pancreas."

"I already double-checked and—"

"Look, I have been in your shoes before. Wanting to prove you can be assertive and you figure if you act like one of the boys you get the same respect. Do you want to be responsible for *killing* this woman because she wasn't properly vetted?"

The nurse sighed, glanced over at Grace then looked back at

Jacqui. Hesitantly, she put the syringe away, and moved the serum back into its casing. Though she said nothing, she merely responded with a slight nod of the head.

"You're right, Dr. Stevenson, I apologize. I will rerun the test once more and check the stats." The nurse snatched the clipboard from in front of the monitor, clearly annoyed.

The nurse closed the silver case and left Grace's proximity. Finally, Jacqui could breathe again. Grace needed to be protected at all costs. She could do this; she could keep the vultures at bay. Jacqui had the authority and the clearance. As long as she could save someone from this nightmare, it would be worth it.

"She's gorgeous," a deep voice surprised Jacqui from behind.

It was Arnold's voice.

Arnold stepped from around her and strolled over to Grace's bedside.

"Lovely cheekbones, almond eyes, nearly symmetrical face. I don't really care for the wild lavender hair color, and you know, usually, I don't find African American women all that attractive, but this one..." Arnold said, running the back of his hand against her cheek. "I would pay good money for her."

Realizing what had brought Arnold to this girl's side, Jacqui had to stay calm. If she showed favoritism, he would push Grace to the front of the line just for his amusement.

"She's not ready to enter Phase One. Her medical history indicates high-risk exposure for high blood pressure, diabetes, high cholesterol, and not to mention her paternal genome sequence. She runs an even higher possibility for developing early-onset pancreatic cancer. We only want the best for clients, yes? And we definitely don't want another loss, do we?"

Arnold tugged at his collar. "No, of course not."

Satisfied with his answer, Jacqui turned to walk away. "She'll be ready soon enough, don't worry."

"Oh, I am not worried." His sarcasm stopped Jacqui in place. "Not with you on my side. You are on *my* side, right?"

"Yes." Jacqui bit down on her bottom lip.

"I heard the police paid you a visit the other night. What was that about?"

Shocked, Jacqui turned to face Arnold. Then again, she should not be that surprised, surveying her house sounded just like Arnold. But what could she tell him? The patient he was standing beside had a brother who worked in law enforcement and was desperately looking for her. Or maybe she should leave that out. Why did she not think about Arnold finding this out? Now, no matter her answer, she looked guilty of something.

"He is a friend of the family. He's a sweet guy, likes to check on us from time to time."

Arnold narrowed eyes at Jacqui.

Did he buy it?

He stood there, silent. The man had a strong poker face. She could never decipher his expression.

"Of course, being a single woman gets lonely I imagine," Arnold then smiled, "I just would hate for anything bad to happen. To you or to anyone you love." His words dipped in false promises.

Jacqui, having had enough of Arnold's threats, imagined taking the scalpel out of her coat pocket and jamming it into his neck, slicing his jugular vein wide open. She imagined his blood splattering across her face, warm against her flesh like it was her reward for acting on impulse. She thought about how she would feel watching him fall to his knees then back onto his spine, grasping at his neck before he collapsed in a pool of his own blood. Finally, her daughter would be safe, and she would be free of this mess, well, after cleaning up the body and producing an alibi of course. But the important thing to her was that it would be over, not to mention how satisfying it would be to watch him die slowly and painfully. But that was the only place where she could watch this man bleed out. In her dreams.

"Jacqui?" Arnold said. "Can I call you Jacqui?"

Arnold took a few steps closer to her and glanced back at Grace.

"She's a friend of your daughter?"

Jacqui kept her best straight face, but she had worked for Arnold long enough for him to know her. He had found Jacqui's exposed nerve and even in her silence, she knew he'd found another way to manipulate her.

"I will take that as a yes. Well, Jacqui, let me make this clear and I will only say this once. Everything I do is for a reason. Have her in Phase One by the end of day, or your daughter will be in her place by tomorrow. Do I make myself clear?"

Jacqui glanced at Grace and understood now that she had not been placed here by chance. No, she was a warning. Well, this time Jacqui had a message for him.

"Why did you stop producing the Premier Vaccine in 2020?"

"What makes you ask about that? That was so long ago," Arnold replied. "Look, I would love to stay and chat, but I have meetings to attend."

Jacqui had never seen that look from him. He thinned his lips and cut his eyes at her as though she took him by surprise. She watched him as he marched off through the double doors. A smile came to her savoring the small victory, but more than that, Jacqui was beginning to play Arnold at his own game, and he had shown her his hand. By his response alone, she knew there was much more to this vaccine and that she was merely scraping the surface. In doing so, she would now have to be careful, Arnold would be watching her even more closely.

In the pocket of her lab coat, Jacqui's phone vibrated one

time then nothing. Glancing at the screen she had a missed call. Upon looking at the number, her eyes widened. This person was a key to this whole Lanzran Inc. and BRT Health puzzle. It was from Dr. Anthony Seymore.

Chapter 15

Justice: Seventy-one Hours Missing

Where is Grace? the social media post read. Justice created and shared every hour on the hour in search of his sister hoping that someone, anyone would see and say something, only for him to be put on restriction all within twenty-four hours. *These fucking social sites and their stupid ass rules about how often someone can post.* If Justice found his sister's body in a ditch all because Twitter wanted to play stupid games, Justice was gonna find the person responsible and shoot them at point-blank range. No, that was not Justice. It was his anxiety, stress, and grief trying to overtake his actions, but as a big brother not knowing where his sister was, tore at him. What if he never saw his sister's smile again? Or if he never heard her laugh, saw her crazy hair color, or her tiny wrists and threw subtle jabs at her obnoxious cackle ever again? All he was asking for was one more chance. The world was so cruel.

Within the four walls of his apartment, he sifted through documents, photos, newspaper clippings, bank statements, and other clues spread out along the wooden floor. His living room was now a mosaic of pictures, numbers, aligned dates, missing posters, and various images of young missing Black women. There was a trend. He knew it. He could feel it in his gut. It was like food he could not digest, yet there remained not enough evidence to prove anything that would hold up in court. Regardless, this was a puzzle and Justice was not going to be able to sleep until he'd solved it.

Hunched over the scattered papers on the carpet floor, the keyhole to his door rustled until it unlocked, cracking open.

Justice leapt to his feet and took cover beside the kitchen wall. Whoever thought they were about to walk up in here and steal from him had Justice confused for a fool.

Moments later, a face poked through an opening of the door.

"Hello?" a soft voice said.

Justice sighed with relief. Consumed with finding his sister, he'd forgotten that he'd given Cindy a key. Okay, maybe they were rushing things, a little, but the first night he found out his sister was missing, Cindy had stood by him. She'd given him his first lead, brought him lunch while he was stuck on desk duty at work, and above all, embraced him during his weakest moments and anger venting that often turned into crying spells at night over his sister's disappearance.

"Hey, Cindy," Justice said, and she snapped her head towards him.

"Um, what are you doing hiding behind the door?" Cindy said, before closing the door behind herself. Her high heels clicked against the oak floorboards. She thrust her purse on the couch, and stepped in front of him, careful of the documents on the floor. "I brought Chinese since I'm sure you haven't eaten all day."

Cindy looked at Justice but was quickly distracted by the massive wall of gathered evidence behind him. It was full of pictures, reports, and documents and a blood-red tape stretched across the entire wall. It was a spider web of his own making. A tapestry of truth to uncover a conspiracy hiding amidst the quiet society of Ballantyne. Though Cindy did not speak, her silence said it all.

"It's how I think," Justice replied.

"Fascinating. Wait a minute." A picture on the wall had snatched Cindy's attention. She walked over to it, running her fingers over the smooth shiny surface. Her eyes expanded as she approached the person's face.

"Why do you have a picture of Jacqui?" Cindy asked, genuinely confused. "Is she a suspect or something?" Cindy gasped. "She is! Isn't she... Okay, whatever you think is going on, you need to tell me right now."

"Don't touch that." Justice ran over to her and seized the picture from her fingers. "Cindy, listen, I went to visit your friend, Dr. Jacqui Stevenson, right? I saw Ashley. She got home right as I was leaving but listen to me." Justice gently placed his hands on Cindy's shoulders.

"Your friend is not who you think. And I have reason to believe she knows where Grace is."

From the wide-eyed expression, Justice knew he had dropped Cindy in an ocean of truth. The two of them had been friends for five years. Cindy was not ready to see this side of Jacqui.

"No, no that's impossible. She would tell someone, especially me. Jacqui is like my mentor, my closest friend, the godmother of my children when they are born, of course. Whenever I need advice on anything, I trust Jacqui's word over my own mother's. I know everything there is to know about Jacqui. Yes, she's a highly intelligent doctor who is wildly successful in her field, divorced, a single mother raising her only girl; loves wine and any show that starts with the words *The*

Real Housewives. Allergic to pollen and apples, loves romantic comedies, absolutely despises social media, and does not even have a Facebook. What are you talking about? What am I missing?"

"It seems like you know about her, but do you know *her*. I am not saying you're wrong but be honest with yourself. You haven't noticed anything different? Not the new program she's working for?"

"Program? BRT Health Industries, yeah, what about it? Wait, how do you know about that? It's been real hush-hush at the job."

Justice could see the wheels turning. Cindy *had* noticed a difference.

"Well, now that you mention it, Jacqui has been spending a lot more time in the research department and the times I do see her, Jacqui rarely speaks or makes eye contact. I guess things have become a little weird, but Jacqui wouldn't kidnap Grace? That would be unthinkable. Grace is like family to her."

Justice crossed his arms. Between Jacqui's body language from their interaction and now her strange behavior at work, his profile now had another component: isolation from friends and family. Something was definitely off. Perhaps Cindy needed to see what he had learned.

"You may want to have a seat." Justice took Cindy by the hand and led her to the couch.

"What did you find? I am so confused, Justice. I don't know if I *want* to know."

Slowly, Justice pulled a document from the wall and handed it to Cindy. Justice knew by showing this to her it would shatter her entire perception of her best friend, but Cindy deserved to know.

"What am I looking at?" Cindy scanned the piece of paper.

At the top was Jacqui's name, phone number, address, and bank account. "This does not mean anything. She started working with this private company and so she spends a good amount of time down there, so of course, they are paying her."

"That's not the problem, look at the company endorsement on the check. Lanzran Inc. and BRT Health Industries are financially backed by the Aphaia Corporation, a for-profit organization. Does that sound familiar?"

Cindy shook her head from side to side.

"The Aphaia Corporation is the largest multinational conglomerate with subsidiaries active in a variety of industries from the 1950s to the 2000s. Aphaia influences the production and sale of chemicals, industrial machines, private prison management, pharmaceuticals, and other industries."

The more Justice learned about Jacqui Stevenson's finances, the more he discovered about the Aphaia Corporation. Jacqui had been receiving six-figure weekly deposits from an offshore account. The payments had begun just weeks before Grace had gone missing. According to Cindy, it had been the very same week she'd started working with BRT Health Industries. Also around the same time Jacqui's behavior started changing.

"This company at which your friend works, I'm thinking most of these businesses are purposely built to cover up illegal activities," Justice said.

"Jacqui is many things, but she's not a criminal." Cindy jumped to her feet, panicked, trying to make sense of it all. "How do you know BRT Health is illegitimate?"

"From the testimonies of the families of these missing women. All have mentioned that after the interview with BRT Health Industries, the women disappeared. One time is a coincidence. Three out of three? I don't think so."

Justice stood in front of the wall, analyzing his findings once more. During his investigation, a pattern of names had materialized. Mr. Khizar was one in particular. His name had intertwined itself between the Aphaia Corporation and BRT like a seam of fabric.

"The man, Mr. Khizar, twenty years ago, was tried for crimes against humanity by the International Criminal Court. His brigade raided villages, traded ammunition, and was charged with..." Justice paused in place. Wait, something just clicked.

"What else?" Cindy asked.

"Human trafficking."

The room fell deathly quiet. Grace could be halfway across the world by now, thought Justice. She could have been shipped off to some foreign country. Those two men could be degrading her right now. Or worst of it all... Grace could already be... dead.

"Alright, so, wait let me get this straight. This Khizar guy, who is a known human trafficker, his name is tied to a for-profit organization, the Aphaia Corporation, that pretty much controls everything and funds BRT Health Industries and Lanzran Inc. Somehow this money ended up in Jacqui's bank account?" Cindy said. "Well first of all, how is this man not in prison?"

Yes, the pieces were coming together. The major players had been established. Mr. Khizar the trafficker, Aphaia Corporation financially supporting him, BRT kidnapping women, then there still was Dr. Jacqui Stevenson's involvement, but to what end? Their motives remained unclear. Justice had a theory, all he needed now was solid proof.

A knock at the door forced them both silent.

Justice rushed to the door and checked out the peephole. He opened the door and walked back over to his wall of evidence. Goodchild closed the door behind him.

"Hey, Cindy—Is that shrimp fried rice I smell?" He waved then walked toward the dining table. "Reeves, man."

"Did you get anything?" Justice asked, straight to business.

"I tailed her. Watched her, and she has a regular routine. In the morning, her daughter leaves for school at like 5:00am. Thirty minutes later she's out the door behind her and goes straight to work. She doesn't seem to get off work until at least ten at night."

Justice took Goodchild's intel then studied his wall of evidence once more. *How is this possible?* Justice thought. *How are they doing this?* He stared at the picture of Jacqui Stevenson. It was mid-afternoon and she was exiting a revolving door of Mercy Hospital.

"That's it!" Justice said.

Goodchild and Cindy regarded one another then looked back at Justice at the same time, both confused.

"What's... what?" Cindy asked.

"I know how they're doing it now. It's inside the hospital. Mercy Hospital falls right within the fifty-mile radius of where women have gone missing."

Goodchild stood next to Justice as they both stared at the web of red lines of tape sprawled out against the wall.

"Walk me through it," Goodchild said, stepping closer to the picture of Jacqui on the wall.

"Arnold owns Lanzran Inc. which already has a relationship with the hospital. Khizar approaches Arnold with some idea of how to make money. The two have gone into other businesses together, look here." Justice pointed to a series of massage parlors. "Arnold was a silent partner in these businesses, but over here, Arnold then recruits Dr. Stevenson for her work in medicine and hires her to work for his second company, BRT Health Industries, which for some reason lures primarily Black women in with the promise of free education or removal of student loan debt." Justice concluded by pointing at Mercy Hospital, which ironically, landed in the epicenter of his wall tapestry of proof.

"I tell you what, these people are pretty fucking bold to do it in a hospital," Goodchild said. "Granted, say you're right, how do we prove any of this? Chief wouldn't even hear you out about the one piece of evidence regarding the missing women radius."

A picture placed against the wall caught Cindy's eye, it was of a woman. Cindy pulled the picture from the connected lines of red tape. Covering her mouth, Cindy began shaking and dropped the photo.

"Justice, I know this woman."

Justice picked up the same photo. It was a headshot of a woman with honey complexion, brown hair past her shoulders and eyes black as midnight.

"You know Cara Esperanza?"

"Not exactly, I...I." Cindy pulled away from the wall, sat on the sofa, and put her chin into her chest. Her brown curls became a fortress, shielding her face from everyone in the room. "They tell us to mention the name, that's it."

"What are you talking about?" Justice said, inching closer to her. He could hear tears falling from her, there was a certain crack in her voice.

"They tell us to mention patients who fit a certain criteria. Women with certain insurance companies or who are at high-risk for infertility. I did my job. I did what they told me to do."

"Who told you to do what?"

"I don't remember, I just know during our Monday meetings they tell us to say certain things. They tell us if they 'fit the profile' to recommend to the program. I referred her to BRT Health. I thought they helped women with fertility treatments, I didn't know. I swear I didn't know," Cindy said, hysterical. Justice encased her in his arms, trying to soothe her.

"Hey, it's okay. We'll figure this out. First, I need you to tell me what they are doing with those women."

"On the flyers they gave us, it says that BRT Health is some fertility company aimed at providing a solution for women having difficulty conceiving. And Cara was headed down that path and I thought they could help her. I don't know what they do exactly... but I haven't seen Cara since."

Was that the reason BRT was kidnapping women? To experiment on them?

An idea came to Justice. If his theory was true, then Cara was somewhere in the hospital, and if Cara was there then Grace would be also. Their presence would serve as enough proof that this whole operation existed.

"Cindy, I hate to ask this."

"Then don't. I'll save you the trouble." Cindy smiled. "I'll go to where the BRT Health sector is, and I'll find Grace."

Damn. She just knew. Still, sending Cindy behind enemy lines left Justice uneasy. She was his light in all of this darkness, his peace amidst the chaos. If anything happened to her after tonight, he was going to that hospital, warrant or not, and knocking doors for some damn answers. He would not let these people take his sister and his Cindy.

A call came through to Cindy's phone, and she answered in Spanish. "Hello, hey Ivan, what's up? Wait, calm down, slow down, you know I can't understand your Puerto Rican ass." Cindy laughed, but suddenly, her smile crashed into something horrified. "What do you mean? They did what?! Why? Okay, call me back."

Nervous to ask, but he had to know.

"Who was that?" Justice asked.

"Ivan, he's actually a co-worker who was recently hired to work for BRT Health Industries, but apparently, they, including the hospital, let him go. They didn't say why."

This was the perfect opportunity. Maybe Cindy didn't have to put herself in harm's way.

"Ask him if he's free tomorrow morning, I have a few questions for him," Justice said.

"I'm pretty sure he will be," Goodchild interjected. "He's got no job."

Chapter 16

Cara: Dreaming

In her dream, Cara awoke alongside her lover, Matthew. Glancing at the gold wedding band around her ring finger, she gazed at him fondly. He was, no questions asked, her best relationship. He was a country boy from the rural bushlands of North Carolina and Cara was a city girl, but their differences had somehow brought them together. Matthew was patient, such a good listener, and a hard worker, he would have made a great father to the children. Zen and Zach would get his athleticism, charm, and sense of humor, while Alina would be his little princess spoiled rotten, but in a good way, where Matthew at least tried to say no occasionally to her. Lying there entangled in Matthew's arms at the start of a lazy Saturday morning, it felt like true love; a soothing, peaceful, and warm kind of love. Matthew awoke and slid his hand down her arm, relaxing to the touch. He lowered himself down to her waist, leaving imprints of his lips along the way. To her surprise, he pulled a set of handcuffs from his pocket.

"What are you doing?" Cara laughed, knowing the kids were up and in the next room over. It was only a matter of time before they came bursting through the door unannounced. She enjoyed trying new things, but motherhood had turned her into a cautious woman and ever since the kids were big enough to walk and talk on their own, bondage was strictly a no-no when they were around.

The metal dangled between his fingers and the biggest smile rested upon his face.

"What? Oh, c'mon, Cici, let's try it," Matthew begged, his knees on opposite sides of her thighs.

Cara threw her arms straight in the air, ready and willing for whatever Matthew was plotting. One by one he cuffed her hands to each side of the bed. Her skin flushed with heat, watching him secure her wrists, and though Cara would not admit it, this was getting her excited. He slid under her nightgown and pulled down her panties. His kisses between her legs sent waves of pleasure up her spine, and then Matthew did something that shocked her, he replaced his warm tongue with a serrated knife.

BURSTING FROM SLUMBER, CARA screamed at the top of her lungs. The pain from Matthew's knife in her dream was something else in reality; something much worse than a knife but just as jarring. This time when Cara looked down at who was between her legs, it was not Matthew. It was someone in a white lab coat with long dark hair tied off their shoulders.

Cara's vision was groggy and blurred as she looked at her wrists. In place of those sexy handcuffs were chains securing her to the bed in the exact same place Matthew had tied her, but this was no dream. Someone was running tests on her, prodding her inner crevice by what felt like stabbing her insides. These people could do anything they wanted, and Cara knew she was forced to endure it.

Glancing at her side, Cara noticed a slight change. In the bed beside her was a young woman with lilac-colored coils for hair, thin wrists and ankles, and a white hospital gown on her body. But what happened to the other young woman? The girl before, the one with the freckles sprinkled across her nose and cheekbones. *They can't have my mind.* Yes, that strong-willed girl. When Cara first met her, she didn't know if she should be intrigued at the woman's mental fortitude or terrified at her deranged expression. Terror came easier. As Cara remembered the strange woman, the desolation behind her eyes, the more it seemed that girl's silent departure was Cara's likely future. A slow descent into insanity parading itself as optimism. If this place didn't kill Cara, her mind would leave her first.

Eva, Cara remembered. That was her name. She was... gone.

Cara's stomach churned at the thought of Eva's current whereabouts. Thinking of Eva's parents who were probably wondering where their daughter had gone, spending every minute crying, praying, and hoping their daughter would return to them. But in reality, Eva was already dead.

The pain hit again.

Cara's legs jerked back. Stopping the procedure, the doctor working on her pulled away.

"Sorry about that," the doctor muffled through her mask. Sitting on a rolling chair, the doctor slid into Cara's line of sight. Just below the chest pocket of her lab coat, Cara caught a glimpse of a striking image. A pale woman from the shoulders up, sea green eyes, blossoming peach petals in place of hair. In the middle of the woman's forehead was a slit like the beginnings of a black hole. The logo embroidered into the doctor's lab coat reminded Cara of Medusa, but a more polished, clean, family-friendly version. Despite its pastel color combo and pristine appearance, the image gave Cara the chills along her skin. There was something creepy about the logo.

Above the chest pocket of the doctor's shoulder, Cara caught a name.

"Perhaps we'll pause for now, yeah?" The doctor stood and snatched off her latex gloves. The woman walked over to the wash station and rinsed excess baby powder off her hands.

"Dr. Stevenson."

"It's Jacqui." Slowly, she faced Cara. "Just call me Jacqui."

Under the woman's eyes were two black circles, the doctor looked like hell that was for sure. The subtle hint of wrinkles had formed around her lips. Her copper complexion was without blemish, but the most noticeable thing about this woman was the sadness she carried with her. Just by being in Dr. Stevenson's presence, Cara felt even more hopeless.

"Where am I?"

Dr. Stevenson brushed her hands off the sides of her lab coat. Clearing her throat, she formed a response, "Well, you're in a hospital and you were brought in after a car accident."

The way the woman talked sounded like she was a mom. Each of her words were slow and carefully chosen as though Cara was a first-grade student. The doctor's calm and polite nature, for some odd reason, infuriated Cara. At least with the other creepy doctor guy she got the truth, but Cara got the sense that Jacqui was lying to her.

Cara narrowed her eyes at the Dr. Stevenson. "Then why are my hands and feet bound?"

"Well, that's because we, umm—"

"Don't fucking lie to me!" Cara shouted, her voice echoed against the walls, but no one from the dozens upon dozens of unconscious women in that same room heard her.

Using what little strength she had, Cara launched herself

toward the doctor, but she did not get very far. Her shoulder blades had hardly made it off the bed before her restraints forced her backward. Cara fell back into the stiff mattress and stared at the ceiling lights. Fighting against the metal cuffs was a futile effort. The sedation had taken a toll and when Cara demanded her legs to move, they refused. Command of her own body had been lost. All she had left was her voice just like her mother, but Lenora's voice was not enough to save her.

Cara then thought back about her mother's last moments. Maybe if Lenora had been more persistent, more confrontational, louder, and perhaps... angrier, then the doctors and nurses would have listened to her.

"You know, being down here with nothing but my own thoughts I realized something. My entire life I have fought so hard to be the opposite of what people expected of me. To be the nice, sweet, docile Black girl that no one has to worry about. To not be a stereotype, to not be the 'Angry Black Woman,' but I finally get it."

Cara's voice simmered to a low volume. Dr. Stevenson had stopped her work and gave Cara all her attention, it was the least she could do for her.

"They call us angry because deep down they know. With everything that's happened in our history." Cara's frustration released from her in the form of tears. "They know we have every right to be."

Jacqui nodded, silently agreeing with her. She rolled the backless chair closer to Cara's bedside.

"Alright, you want the truth?" Jacqui whispered.

The two synced eye contact. Neither said a word. "You, whether you realized it or not, signed up for an experimental fertility treatment. But what they didn't tell you as that upon completion of the treatment, your womb will be donated. Your recipient has been notified and will be here tomorrow morning for the surgery."

"Surgery? Wait... what?!"

"I'm so sorry about all this. If I could change anything I swear I would."

If Jacqui were searching for comfort, Cara was the last person she would get it from. Disgusted by Jacqui, a Black woman betraying a fellow sister, Cara turned her sight toward the overhead lights.

A few moments ago, Cara had been just another patient, no, just another womb that Dr. Jacqui Stevenson was about to extract for her old college roommate, Evelyn. It was nothing personal, but it was a choice between Cara and her daughter, Ashley. All of Jacqui's other patients were unconscious most of the time she interacted with them, but Cara had responded differently to the serum. While others had succumbed to sedation rather quickly, Cara's body had fought through a fever and resisted the Phase Two medicine. If what Jacqui suspected was to be true, then Cara might have the strength to escape this madness.

"I am so sorry Ms.—"

"Save it," Cara said. Her nose ran, but she was so helpless she could not even wipe her own face. "But I wonder..."

"And what's that?" Jacqui moved closer, drying Cara's upper lip with soft tissue.

"How can you live with yourself?"

She pushed her rolling chair back and tossed the tissue in the trash. Jacqui said absolutely nothing, but in her silence, Cara spotted a difference between Jacqui and the male doctor. See, he was chipper and enjoyed torturing Cara, but with Jacqui, there lingered something she could only make out as regret.

"I know this is not right, believe me. Do you think I want to do this? I can't even sleep at night."

If Jacqui wanted remorse or sympathy from Cara, she was going to have to do a whole lot better than that.

Cara did not know which she hated worse: falling asleep resulting from the drugs and still feeling they were doing only God knows what to her. Or waking up and living through the nightmare, thinking every time she awoke was her last.

"How can you stand by and watch them do this to me? To all of us down here?"

Cara searched her face for answers. To her shock, Jacqui's eyebrows gathered, both confused and saddened.

"Don't you *dare* think about shedding a tear in front of me."

"The only difference between us is that you can see your chains. You don't get it. This is not a choice for me. They threatened me. They said if I did not get involved in the process, they would do terrible things to my daughter."

The idea that this woman was being forced to do this had never even crossed Cara's mind. It was that nurse who'd referred Cara to this program, and the other doctor seemed to love this line of work, and they both did not seem forced into doing any of that.

"But I have an idea. After looking at your chart, it seems your body is rejecting the serum, that's why you keep waking up every so often. Which leads me to believe that if I don't give you this injection you're due for now, I think you'll have enough strength to make it out of here," Jacqui said. "You have to promise as soon as you get out of here, you will tell people what's going on."

"Are you being serious right now?" Cara uttered, stuck in disbelief.

"Look, I know you're angry and I get that I want to help you, but you have to trust me."

Trust. Cara could not trust anyone involved in a human trafficking ring running underneath a hospital. Yet, this Jacqui

Stevenson was the only one willing to help Cara. The only one who talked to her like a human being. The only other person who treated her like she had a future outside of these four walls. That was the dangerous thing about hope, as quickly as it arrived, it could be taken away.

Chapter 17

Justice: Seventy-Nine Hours Missing

Under the red umbrellas on the café patio, Justice waited patiently for his arrival.

Professionals breezed past with their eyes glued to their phones. The bottom of their shoes clapped against the stone tiles. A fountain rested at the center of the plaza. It was a luxurious but quiet reminder of the sophisticated status of those who worked in this area. A symbol of Ballantyne's bourgeoisie.

Through the trickling waters, Justice spotted a man in khakis and a burgundy button-up, his hair slicked back in a thick coat of gel that shone in the sun's presence. That had to be him, thought Justice. He stood around five foot nine inches, Hispanic male with a nice build. Justice guessed he took good care of himself. Ivan Cuevas.

"You're officer Reeves. Cindy's boyfriend?" Ivan asked, approaching the table with dark shades covering his eyes. His voice was small and curt, like he thought Justice was wearing a wire.

"Yes," Justice said to both, proudly, lifting from his seat as he initiated a handshake. "Please have a seat."

"She's a good girl, man, take care of her," Ivan said as he

seated himself in the chair. "So, I'm guessing she told you the whole situation?"

"Not really, I was hoping I could hear it from you. How was your experience with BRT Health?"

A server emerged from the double doors. Preppy and bursting with energy, she had long black hair tied into a ponytail reaching her waist.

"Hello, gentlemen, what can I get for you today?" she asked, in a high-pitched voice.

"I will take a cappuccino," Ivan said.

"Just coffee, black." Justice took his attention back to Ivan. "Like I was saying—"

"Sir, we sell every type of coffee imaginable. Cafe lattes, frappuccinos, espressos, anything you want, we have it." Justice had seen expressions like this girl's before, hiding her frustration behind a forced smile.

"Listen, I just want regular coffee, nothing special."

The server and Ivan paused in unison. They stared at Justice like he'd offended the both of them. Justice was a fish stuck in the forest on this side of town. Was his order truly that out of the norm? The girl pursed her lips together and furrowed her brows at him. All he wanted was just some damn coffee. Since he could not sleep, he needed something to keep him awake.

Ivan faced the young brunette woman. "He'll take an americano."

The girl nodded and disappeared within the thick double doors of the establishment.

"Okay, so where were we? Hmm... BRT Health. Let me tell you, these people are so good at getting you to do something with you not realizing what you are doing, I swear. I can't believe I didn't see it sooner." Ivan leaned back into the chair. He stopped talking. Something about this meeting drew his concern. "Wait a second. Are the police investigating the hospital, or like, what's going on?"

Ivan had a noticeable lisp when he spoke. Combined with the accent, how fast his words flew from him, and feminine flair natural to his persona, the man was quite difficult for Justice to understand. He knew a little bit of Spanish from what Cindy had taught him, but not nearly enough to hold a conversation with Ivan.

"Not exactly, now when you say, 'without realizing what you are doing,' what did you mean by that?"

"None of this is going on the record, right? Because, when they fired me yesterday, technically, they made me sign this NDA thing, so I guess there are some things I can't tell you, and I honestly shouldn't be here, but the way they went about the whole letting me go process was so unprofessional. I can't believe they did this to me, like I have a certain lifestyle to maintain. Someone has to know what's going on in there."

Justice knew it. Ivan was going to be the missing piece connecting everything together.

"But anyways, where was I... Oh yes, the guy who hired me he told us, the nurses, that we were just taking vitals and blood samples from these women, nothing more. My first day, I'm down there with these women in what's called the Transition Room. There are like hundreds of women in there and my job was to keep them sedated, but what's really strange about that room is that all the women were handcuffed or secured to the beds in there. I thought that was weird, and when I asked the manager about it he said, it's for the protection of the nurses, so I left it at that."

Ivan was a talker. In Justice's eyes, he carried himself in a way like he was telling a story on his YouTube channel or something. But if what this man was saying was indeed true, BRT Health Industries had been doing this for a while.

Trafficking girls inside a hospital was genius. No one would look there for a criminal. A hospital was the safest place anyone could go. Arnold and Jacqui among others had perfected a flawless system.

"Another thing," Ivan said. "So, majority of my time in the Transition Room, the women were unconscious, but one day, one of them woke up; it was the only time I managed to have a conversation with one of them. Her name was Eva. The girl woke up, looked me in the eyes, and she said to me," Ivan leaned across the small wooden table, "help me, I don't know how I got here."

If Justice was working and a patient said that to him, he would have reported it. Surely, Ivan had enough sense to do the same.

"I just assumed she had lost her mind or something."

"What?!" Justice shouted. His volume drew unnecessary attention from a nearby table. Ivan pulled back into his chair, startled. In the same moment, their server returned with drinks. She quietly delivered them and disappeared back into the restaurant.

"I'm sorry, I just can't believe what I'm hearing. A patient begged for your help and what did you do?" Justice took a sip from the coffee mug.

Ivan clicked his tongue against his inner cheek, clearly irritated. "My job, is what I did. I mean what else was I supposed to do? Find the key to her handcuffs and break her out of there? We both would not have gotten far. Not with all those surveillance cameras and security everywhere. Besides, I'm no hero and even if I did, they would have replaced her within the day's end." Ivan pursed his lips at Justice, perhaps realizing this was a mistake.

"Replaced?" Justice released a frustrated sigh. "And what did you lose your job for?"

Ivan crossed his arms. "Well, one of the patients had caught a fever, and while her symptoms were in the process of subsiding, the doctor asked me to retrieve the keys to her handcuffs. When I returned from my break, a very buff security guard began asking me questions, lots of questions like, what was I doing there? Whose restraints are those? Mind you, I was just doing what I was asked. Next thing I know, I'm being escorted off the premises."

"They fired you over some keys? And who was this doctor that ordered you to take the keys?"

"Dr. Jacqui Stevenson." Ivan snapped his head both ways as though searching for lingering ears. "Well, yeah, but it gets worse. The last week I was there, I swear I saw them disposing of bodies."

Grace.

"Every Thursday night, a big container comes at around ten o'clock. At first, I thought it was like the shipment for medical tools, so I went down there just to check it out. Even though they said we were not supposed to go down there, I went because why the hell not, it gets boring around there. Anyways, I saw these big, strong, muscular guys just tossing bloody bodies wrapped in white sheets onto the back of a truck. Now it is a huge hospital, it's like bigger than a sports venue, and people die every day, but this... It was like they were throwing slabs of meat around. It was really hard to watch. But honestly, Justice, I think if you want proof that what I'm saying is true, I would watch the loading dock of Mercy Hospital."

If Ivan was right, Justice had a small window of opportunity to find out the truth. Tomorrow was Thursday. He would have the answers he sought. One way or another.

"And like none of this will come back on me, right?" Ivan drew in a long sip from his straw.

"If what you're saying is true, I won't need anything else."

This was unlike Justice. Accusing doctors. Looking into a fertility company for crimes against humanity. Discussing confidential details with someone who was violating their NDA. Justice always followed procedure. But if Justice played by the book, he would lose his sister in the politics of the game. If he had to choose between his career and Grace, the choice was easy. If that was the price of loyalty, then fuck it. He knew his next move.

Chapter 18

Jacqui: The Choice

As the sun broke the horizon, Jacqui awoke with one clear intention on her mind: find the smoking gun on Arnold.

A knock pulled Jacqui's attention back to the present.

"Hey, Mom?" Ashley said, standing in the doorway with her backpack on. "Are you okay?"

Sitting upright in bed and wiping the sleep from the corners of her eyes, Jacqui replied, "Yes, honey, why do you ask?"

Ashley walked over to the bed and sat at the corner. "I don't know, you just seem really, really stressed all the time, I never see you smile or laugh anymore. I don't know what it is, but you're different."

Jacqui pulled Ashley to her as hard as she could. Her daughter was so skinny in her arms. Was Jacqui feeding her enough? The smell of her grapefruit-scented body spray overwhelmed her senses. Every little thing mattered. Moments like this were more precious than life itself.

"Mom, you know if you don't let me go, I'll be late for school, right?"

"I know, I know, honey," Jacqui said, releasing her. She watched Ashley leave.

"Bye, Mom, have a good day," Ashley said before slamming the front door. Once Jacqui heard those words she sighed with immense relief, especially after having asked Arnold that question about the vaccine; that was a risk. An uncalculated risk at that.

Glancing at the time, Jacqui got dressed for the day ahead.

JACQUI HAD BEEN PLAYING a vicious game of phone tag with Dr. Seymore since the previous day. It seemed the only way they could communicate was via voicemail. No matter what, she had to get a meeting with this man. She had left a message for him to meet her at Reisser park a few miles from Mercy Hospital. Thinking of the meeting, her chest swelled with anxiety. *What if he changed his mind?* It was now 6:01 AM. One minute past their agreed meeting time.

Surrounded by glorious chestnut trees and cobblestone pathways, at the center of the park stood a twenty-foot fountain with a pool of clear water enclosing it. The casual cigarette smoke in the breeze, morning joggers, suits on their phones power walking to work, and the bustling sounds of cars passing by the main road filled the park with a professional stiffness. Under the warm touch of the sun, the vibrant flowers, leaves, and even the weeds sprouting from the cracks in the concrete, glimmered a brighter hue of green like they knew the beauty they possessed. Reisser Park was quite peaceful. Jacqui found a bench near the sidewalk that encircled the entire park.

Now she waited.

Jacqui wondered what this Dr. Anthony Seymore would be like. Based on the hoarseness in his voice, the man was definitely a smoker—a pack-a-day kind of smoker. But through the harshness of his tone, the articulateness and specificity of his choice words proved his competence. With twenty years of experience, what could the man have done to lose his job? Lanzran Inc. and BRT Health Industries were an intricately sewn pattern. Seam by seam, Jacqui, with Seymore's intel, was going to rip it apart.

"Dr. Stevenson?" a man said. He stood a few feet apart. Wearing a beige fedora and square sunglasses that even a polygraph could not see through; this man was overly cautious. Or perhaps, Jacqui was not cautious enough. If Arnold had known about Grace's brother visiting her the day after it happened, there was no telling who was following her.

"Yes, Dr. Seymore?" Jacqui said.

The man did not say a thing, he simply nodded in response as he sat beside her. Like two strangers who happened to be sitting on the same bench, neither made eye contact.

"Let's make this quick, you've got work, and I've got a life I still want to live. What do you want to know?"

"What do you know about the Premier Vaccine?"

"In 1975 Arnold's father founded Lanzran Inc. the company was supposed to stick to making medical equipment, syringes, forceps, IV bags, etcetera, but when Arnold came of age in the nineties, his father stepped down and let him take the reins. Big mistake. The boy tried his hand at creating vaccines in his attempt to expand the business. It was a terrible idea doomed from the start. In 1995, I started working with Lanzran Inc. in their R&D department. About a decade later, Arnold started production of what would be called the Premier Vaccine. Now, my position: I was basically quality control for the company's medical products and services. Any serum, steroid cream, new painkiller, anything, I had to sign off on it before it went to the market. In the early 2010s I started noticing something with the select few who could afford this prestigious medication."

"Did Arnold ever explain his reasoning for making the immunization so expensive?"

"No, he never told me why, but with a man like that you know his reasonings boiled down to the dollar bill. He wanted to prove something to his father was my best guess. Back to my point, these same patients paying top prices for premium healthcare were not receiving the best quality product. Many of these same patients began developing fertility issues, but more specifically, the issue was prominent in females. A one-stop shop vaccine was not possible. Period. I presented my research to Arnold. It had been peer-reviewed, and a thorough quantitative analysis had been conducted. I made sure of it. But Arnold did not want to hear any of it, and the same day, I was let go. I either had the choice of signing away my rights through an NDA and taking the severance package or... walking."

Dr. Seymore explained he was a twenty-year US Army veteran who'd started as a medic in the lowest rank possible, but by the time his service was up he had obtained the credentials M.D. next to his name. There was no question of the man's competency or his sense of pride, but Jacqui wondered what had motivated him to speak with her after nearly twenty years of silence. Was it the guilt of having not done more when he'd had the chance? Perhaps this was his redemption.

Seymore retrieved a small green-white carton from his inner coat pocket and pulled out a cigarette. He drew in a long inhale and kept talking.

"I walked. I had my military pension and TSP, and that man was *mad* when he realized not everybody had a price." Seymore let out a sly laugh. "One thing for sure, that man Arnold has connections. Months after I was fired, he had my research discredited. So, when you called me, I was very surprised at the fact you believed the data. Not only that, but people followed me, I received threatening phone calls and death threats through the mail."

"Oh my God." Jacqui could imagine how terrifying this must have been. Seymore reminded her so much of her father. He looked to be over sixty years old. Despite his cigarette habit, he was still in running shape. And there was a certain confidence he had when he spoke that put Jacqui at ease. The meeting felt more like catching up with an old family member rather than discussing how to take down the second-largest pharmaceutical company in the industry.

"Little lady, I spent time in Afghanistan, somebody playing on my phone does not scare me. But like I was saying, these women who received the Premier Vaccine from 2005 to 2020, were not able to have children or even maintain a pregnancy afterward. My research found a direct correlation between the two, no doubt about it. Then I heard Arnold had founded another organization in 2019 called BRT Health Industries and was claiming it was a pioneering fertility treatment company, and like sheep, these people flocked to his health services. It was unbelievable."

All of this was a tidal wave of information and Jacqui was lost at sea without a paddle. It was too much to take in at once. If all of this was true, Jacqui had stumbled across a ghastly realization.

"You're saying Lanzran Inc. created the problem and BRT Health Industries is selling the solution."

"Ding, ding, ding, we have a winner folks." Seymore chuckled. "Ya, damn right."

Jacqui leaned back into the wooden bench. The morning chill burrowed through her lab coat. She crossed her arms, trying to make sense of it all.

"It's not enough. I need proof that Arnold knew there was a connection and did nothing about it."

"You must really not know who I am. That's fine, I can show you better than I can tell you. Give me your card. I'll send you everything I have. Just know, once you do this they'll be coming after you, Jacqui. You've got to be careful. There's only so much they could do to get to me, but these people are evil. They would kill a newborn baby if it meant covering their asses."

Jacqui nodded. Her short time working for Arnold had showed her enough of what the man was capable of doing. Threats were a daily occurrence. But her experience failed in comparison with Dr. Seymore. They had destroyed his career and tried to kill him. She needed to tread carefully if this plan was to work.

"But what about the Aphaia Corporation?"

Dr. Seymore said nothing. Though this was a serious conversation his tone kept the discussion light and comical almost... until Jacqui said the Aphaia Corporation. It was as though she found his sore spot, a sensitive topic like the death of a loved one that was too soon to speak about. His sudden silence brought more questions.

"What about them? Aphaia controls everything. From the material in your clothing to the food you shit. That's all I have to say about that."

There was one thing about BRT Health Industries that confused Jacqui the most. Maybe Dr. Seymore had some inclination. "Have you heard of the Colony? I never understood why it was underground."

Dr. Seymore threw his gaze at Jacqui. The cigarette dangerously close to falling from his mouth. During their entire conversation Dr. Seymore had not once made eye contact until she'd brought up the Aphaia Corporation. Quickly, he snapped his sight back to the fountain in front of them.

"They have one right here in the city?" From the slight

panic in his tone, Jacqui could only assume he knew of the Colony.

"Yes, under Mercy Hospital."

"Dr. Stevenson, you're in much deeper than you know." Seymore finished his cigarette. "Give me your contact info, I'll be in touch."

Jacqui placed her business card on the bench. Dr. Seymore casually stood and snatched it from the wooden seat. Before he walked off, he stopped and kept his gaze on the horizon away from Jacqui. "Know this, Dr. Stevenson, once you blow the lid on this, you won't be safe anywhere."

As Dr. Seymore strolled off through the park, Jacqui watched him walk away. He moved about with a faltering step. Perhaps it was an injury from service. No, it was not, Jacqui knew where she had seen it before. It looked so much like that of her father's. Seymore and Jacqui's dad were roughly the same age, and both were from that era where men walked with a limp to look cool. Jacqui smiled as Dr. Seymore's fedora disappeared into the crowd.

As Jacqui stood up, an eighteen-wheeled truck drove past the park. The hum of the exhaust startled her, but what truly grabbed her nerves was something else. On the side of the commercial vehicle was a symbol of a pale woman with peach petals for hair, moss green eyes, and a black slit in the middle of her forehead. Jacqui had seen that image before. Level three, the lecture hall, the image was the Aphaia Corporation logo. *Seymore was right.* The Aphaia Corporation was everywhere. How had she not noticed this before? It was such a hair-raising design, but in the midst of staring at the emblem Jacqui came to the realization that after her meeting with Dr. Anthony Seymore, she was one step closer to the truth. One step closer to taking down Arnold. One step closer to freedom.

INSIDE MERCY HOSPITAL, JACQUI rushed down to level UG. Every day Arnold came in at exactly 7:00am, and every day, the first thing on his checklist was the new Phase One initiates. The man was painfully disciplined in that way. It was 6:32am. Knowing what Jacqui had learned from Dr. Seymore and the threats Arnold had made regarding her daughter, he was going to make do on his promises if Jacqui failed to deliver—and right now, Jacqui had less than thirty minutes to uphold her end of the bargain about a specific patient. Sifting between moving bodies, and nearly pushing the elevator button into its metal socket, Jacqui raced to her next destination: Grace.

Her heels clapped against the ground as she entered the Transition Room. Three aisles down, nine rows back, Jacqui turned a corner and found that Grace's number had been moved. Spotting a nurse nearby, she stopped her.

"What happened to Grace—I mean—7048?"

Yesterday, Jacqui had put Grace's name down for Phase One, but only in order to satisfy Arnold's demands. Afterward, she had planned to remove her name from the list. *But had she?* She tried hard to recall. *She must have done it?* It wasn't something she would have forgotten?

Crap.

Jacqui ran her fingers through her hair, thinking. Then it came to her. Yesterday she'd spent so much time planning for the patient named Cara, that she couldn't remember if she'd ever taken Grace off the list.

Cara was hard to forget. Even bound to the hospital bed with metal restraints without any hope of freedom, there was a certain strength in Cara's eyes. By Phase Two most of girls in the Transition Room had given up hope. They were already dead. Jacqui knew it and so did they. But not Cara. *They call us* "*angry" because they know we have every right to be.* Cara's words resonated with Jacqui. She had to do something to help her.

"Unit 7048 has been expedited to Phase Two."

Expedited.

Arnold must have been working overtime, thought Jacqui. *How did Grace already complete Phase One overnight unless Jacqui's colleague, if she dared call him that, Dr. Dowey, had taken one of her patients? The sick bastard.* He was a little too eager to do this job. Jacqui had heard stories about Dowey. A husband of thirty years and a devout Christian, Dowey was forced out of the medical community for complaints and unethical experiments on female patients. He was a genius or a madman dependent upon whom was asked. Dowey had spent his days hunting, fishing, and playing chess with his spoiled grandchildren until Arnold had offered him a position at BRT Health Industries. *What had Arnold promised him that made Dowey enjoy this so much?* There was no time for that, Jacqui needed to find Grace and fast.

Hearing that news, Jacqui knew exactly where she would be headed next. Power walking down the long bright blue halls, Jacqui hoped to God that there was still time.

Jacqui entered a room with a triangle and the Roman numeral two on the front. Inside were a dozen women chained to their own individual beds and organized into three columns like they were cattle. At the front of each column was a white tube large enough to fit a human body through with alarming precision. To the untrained eye, the tubes looked like MRI machines. These tubes were medical imaging machines that could see into the DNA structure of the organs inside the body. This was Phase Two, analyzing the genome sequence of the host and pinpointing which client had the most similar characteristics leading to minimal damage to the recipient.

These tube machines were matchmakers, searching for vulnerabilities and comparing patients through a sophisticated database. And now, Grace was inside this room.

By the time Jacqui reached the room it was too late.

Two nurses were working together from behind a one-way mirror. Their workspace took up half the room. On the nurses' side, there were two monitors. One provided a single patient's vital signs and the other kept track of the scans from the machines. Despite there being only two nurses, they worked with speed and efficiency.

By pressing a few buttons on the keyboards, a needle emerged from a wall panel and injected Grace's wrist at a pivotal point of her bloodstream. Even if Grace found the chip, she would bleed out before she could remove it. The tiny object was embedded in between her arteries. It was over for Grace. Her wrist flashed with a red dot three times before the small circle fell silent under her brown flesh.

Jacqui was too late.

Even if Jacqui managed to get her out of here and Grace tried to run, they would always find her. Now, in one simple prick of her skin, hope for Grace's escape was gone.

Jacqui slid behind the nurses, watching them at work. The women were lined up like cattle, there were at least five beds in front of each machine. Jacqui grabbed the chart that rested between the two nurses, and just as she feared, Grace had been put at the front. Grace was trapped down here with her.

Panicked, Jacqui paced back and forth in the small space. She was too busy caught in a web of lies and now, so was Grace. Maybe there was a way to remove the implant, Jacqui had performed much riskier surgeries before. Regardless, Jacqui could not find the heart to give up on her. Even so, Jacqui had to handle this carefully. The slightest slip up and Ashley would be down here next.

"Patient 7048 might be a problem," one of the nurses said.

"What is it?" Jacqui said.

The nurse began typing a note on a separate screen. "Patient 7048 needs to go to level four of the hospital. It seems the serum may have irritated her pancreas."

"I'll do it," Jacqui said.

"Are you sure, Dr. Stevenson? I can have one of the newer nurses do it for you. It's just transporting her, monitoring her, and removing her restraints."

"It's not an issue. It's fine."

The nurse gave her no further protest. Pushing select icons on the monitor, Jacqui brought the machinery to a halt. She then moved Grace's bed out of the Phase Two room.

With her heart pounding ferociously in her chest, Jacqui pushed Grace through the never-ending halls. The last time Jacqui had seen her in the real world, prior to all this mess was when Ashley invited her for a sleepover. That night, Jacqui had made spaghetti and they'd watched Lifetime movies. They'd all pretended they were not crying and had hidden their sniffles under blankets and oversized T-shirts. Later on that same night, Cindy had showed up with a bottle of wine for Jacqui as she'd dished about her latest boy drama. Who knew that Grace would end up here? As Jacqui studied Grace, she saw her chestnut complexion had taken on a slight hue of pale gray and dark circles had formed under her eyes. The serum they'd given her by rushing Grace into Phase Two, was indeed killing her. Jacqui blamed herself. This was all her fault... there was no other way to look at it.

At the end of each corridor, Jacqui watched the cameras staring back at her. By the fifth corner she turned, she knew no one was coming after her; security down there was much faster than that. Soon, Jacqui found the entrance, the sight of those transparent doors bringing instant relief. She waited for the elevator to the main floor, looking back over her shoulder, every five seconds. Grace did not deserve this. To be treated, probed, and strapped down like an animal. She should have been studying all that computer stuff she loved so much, thought Jacqui. The elevator had stopped on their floor. *This was it.* Jacqui was going to get Grace upstairs, perform the necessary immediate surgery, then have her transferred to another hospital to recover. At least somewhere she would be safe. They were so close to freedom, but it could still be ripped from them.

Jacqui kept checking to see if anyone was approaching from behind. Until someone did notice them.

"Dr. Stevenson!"

Not again. The sound of her name, down here, never meant anything good.

"Dr. Stevenson, we need you. Her heart rate spiked. Patient 8052," Farra, a nurse, said.

"Patient 8052?" Jacqui whispered to herself. "Cara."

The last time a young woman's heart rate had spiked, shortly afterward she'd died on the table. That woman's name was Ivery. This time it was Cara. *No, not her.* Cara had hope of getting out of here. Jacqui could not let another patient die. This time she knew what to do. However, in doing so, this meant leaving Grace's side.

"Farra, I need a favor."

"I was about to go on lunch—"

"Farra," Jacqui said, pleading with her. "You are the only one I trust down here. There's something I need you to do for me."

Upon hearing the favor, Farra twisted her face and said, "I can't promise she won't end up right back in the Transition Room."

Chapter 19

Justice: Ninety-One Hours Missing

G one.
A word, both soft and subtle, yet one which had brought Justice so much pain. Every living moment he had to spare he spent searching for Grace. Instead of hours in the gym he did push-ups in his apartment reading articles in between, and while he laid awake at night next to Cindy watching her sleep, all he could think about was Grace.

"Sir, I think you should see something," Justice said, tossing a proposal in front of the Chief. The documents landed atop the thick stack on Glassman's desk, the bold font reflected in his glasses. Justice then took a step back and placed his hands behind himself. Considering the fact Justice was strictly on desk duty, his presence was a risk. But with all of this evidence, there was no way Glassman would not see it from Justice's angle.

Glassman pushed his glasses up the bridge of his nose and reviewed the proposal in front of him.

"You have reason to believe that Mercy Hospital is storing missing Black women," Glassman read and looked over his lenses at Justice.

"That is correct, sir."

Glassman leaned back into his chair. The old seat creaked and groaned under the pressure of his weight.

"And what do you think is going on down there?"

Justice filtered through his notes and found one page in particular. "Sir, according to the floor plans submitted to City Hall there is considerable additional space beneath the building."

"Okay and?"

"If you look here." Justice flipped to a set of pictures. "Back in 2019, when Mercy Hospital began a partnership with BRT Health Industries under the Aphaia Corporation, the company poured millions into reconstructing and utilizing that same space. I believe that is where they are keeping the missing women," Justice said.

The Chief became quiet. In the pupils of Chief Glassman's bright blue eyes, Justice found the reflection of his proposal as he scanned the documents in front of him. Glassman released a sigh. He then took a coffee mug to his lips and placed the papers back on his desk.

"Chief, based on the evidence I've collected, it appears that the hospital is an underground human trafficking ring. For what purpose I am not sure, but I have documentation and two witnesses who can testify to this—"

Glassman choked on his coffee and cleared his throat. "Did you say a human trafficking ring?" he repeated, laughing almost. "Look, Officer Reeves, I think you're seeing conspiracies everywhere. What's next? You're going to tell me that private prisons are sterilizing female inmates? C'mon now, Reeves. I appreciate all you do here, I do."

"Thank you, sir." Justice nodded, ignoring the first half of the Chief's statement.

"And I am terribly sorry about what happened to your sister. We're desperately searching for her."

"I appreciate your support, sir."

Bullshit.

That was a load of crap and Justice knew it. The other day he'd walked in on a conversation that two officers were having and there was one phrase that stood out to Justice in particular:

"She probably went off with some thug, the drug dealer type, you know."

To them, Grace had run away, simple as that. These were his sworn brothers in blue and they could not even be bothered to help him. In that moment, Justice had known there was only one person looking for Grace. Himself.

"But I just feel like you're grasping at straws here. Yeah, there is a flaw in the floor plan, so what? They could've built anything. And as far as these witnesses, what can they prove really?"

"Chief, if you—"

"I don't know, Reeves, this seems like a witch hunt."

"Chief, I have a gut feeling about this. I can prove to you the truth. All I am asking for is just a little faith."

Glassman sat in silence.

The chief stroked his beard, thinking. "Reeves, I like ya, but I cannot afford to have an officer going rogue on me. And as far as I'm concerned, you're still on desk duty. Did you get that report for Rogers?"

Slam.

Justice closed the door behind him upon the end of their conversation.

Glassman had dismissed him—again.

From the first meeting, Justice should have known the second would turn out the same. He should have come better prepared. Instead of hunches and assumptions he should have brought more facts and data. As well as Glassman's indifference, this outcome was also Justice's fault. *Damn it.* Now Grace was going to suffer from this mistake.

It was a hard pill to swallow, knowing his co-workers and boss did not have his back. Despite all he had accomplished. All the respect from the higher-ups he had earned. Hell Justice had a medal from the mayor hanging up in his apartment. Still, he had to prove himself.

In the process of storming out of the precinct, Justice marched past Goodchild's cubicle.

"Hey, Reeves, where are you headed?"

Justice kept walking. He did not have time for Goodchild's chipper mood as he was far too furious to speak. Grabbing his keys and a few file folders, he left the precinct.

JUSTICE PARKED HIS CAR outside of Mercy Hospital. In a spot away from streetlights and parallel to the side of the road, he watched the loading dock. It was 9:56PM. Any minute now *it* was about to happen. He did not know what he was looking for in particular, but he was not leaving this spot until he found something. Anything would count, sudden movements, things out of place or abnormal for a hospital. Someone was going to slip up.

"...Guys just tossing bloody bodies wrapped in white sheets onto the back of a truck."

From the conversation with Ivan, Justice hoped he wasn't wasting time chasing a dead end. Ninety-four percent of missing persons were found within the first three days. Grace was on day four. Including his sister, those other women were being snatched off the street and murdered, all for what purpose?

Justice's phone vibrated. He answered it quickly, upon seeing the caller's name.

"Cindy, are you okay?"

"Hey, I'm fine, but listen, everything you were saying, Justice, you are definitely onto something. The other day, I saw one of the girls from your wall, not Cara, but a different one. I think her name was Briana. I'm not sure."

"What about Grace?"

A beat of silence.

"Well, Justice..."

Cindy was a naturally outspoken woman, so when she was quiet, something was terribly wrong. Why wasn't she saying anything? *Unless... she'd found her. Cindy had found her body. Oh, God.* Justice could not handle this. How was he going to tell their mother that Grace, like their father, was dead? Justice waited for her response.

"No. I haven't seen any sign of Grace."

Justice released a sign of relief. No sign could still be a good sign. There was still time.

"But, babe, you were basically right. The other day I was chopping it up with one of the security guards, because if anyone would see something it's them, right? So, while in the office with all the cameras and stuff, I saw Jacqui get on the elevator, but she pulled out a key and put it in a secret hole under the regular buttons and the elevator took her to some deep underground level. Some place I didn't even know existed."

Justice's theory was right. Whatever was happening to those women was happening underground.

That was enough. Cindy needed to take no further part in this, even her doing this much gave Justice anxiety. But he knew Cindy loved Grace like a little sister. With all that Justice had told her, combined with the strange way Jacqui had been acting lately, she was not going to stop until she found the truth. Despite the danger she did not know she was about to set foot in.

"Thank you, Cindy, but please be careful. Don't do anything silly or reckless."

"Of course, but any ways gotta go."

"Okay, love you," Justice said, without realizing it.

There was a short pause after he spoke, but within that brief delay of mere seconds an entire lifetime had passed. Though Justice had no intention of saying he loved someone after only dating for a full week, he now valued the precious time he had with his loved ones. People were here today and being snatched off the street tomorrow. He could not stand by and not say what he was thinking or feeling any longer.

"Love you too."

She said it back...

It was one thing for him to recklessly blurt out the "L-word," but it was something else for her to return it. Did she truly mean it, or did she say it back out of some pity or obligation? Either way, there was too much to unpack and the only concern that mattered was finding his sister.

The call ended.

A knock at the passenger side window grabbed his attention. He could only make out a figure standing with the streetlight behind them. With the dingy yellow light at their back, their face was completely blacked out. By his broad shoulders it had to be a man. His collar was ironed to perfection. Maybe they were a fellow officer. Maybe just someone looking for directions, or maybe a lookout. No matter who it was, his presence confirmed Justice's suspicion. Something incriminating was taking place at this hospital, but more than that, someone had discovered his hiding spot.

"Hey, Reeves," a voice said. "It's me. Open up."

Standing before him was a man with blonde coils so tightly wound, that his hair looked like steel wool. He lowered his head to the window, bursting with a smile. Justice sighed. The last thing he needed was a talker.

"Goodchild?" Justice said, unlocking the door. Goodchild then jumped in but not empty-handed, two disposable cups and a foil-wrapped sandwich in his hands.

"I brought coffee," he said, handing Justice a cup.

One glance at the clock, it was eleven-thirty. Not only had Justice been here all day, but if Ivan's intel was accurate, something should have happened by now. Justice was losing his patience.

"Thanks," Justice said. "I haven't eaten since lunch. Hold up. I didn't tell you where I was going. How'd you know where I would be?"

Goodchild took a sip from his coffee. He winced at the hot beverage and placed it in the cupholder.

"First off, I am a cop like you." His attempt to be humorous, fell flat. "And also, we still share locations or did you forget."

Ever since that night when he'd searched for his sister's whereabout using that app Justice looked at that tech differently. When the words *no location found* had appeared, to Justice, that shit was no longer reliable. The time when he needed it to work it failed him. He'd meant to uninstall the app a while ago, but it had slipped his mind.

"Reeves, you think you're this untouchable dude, but you're pretty easy to read. You put your all into everything and that's part of the reason why I admire you. But at the same time, you have tunnel vision. Which makes you *very* predictable. Plus, I overheard your talk with Chief. You think something crazy is going on at this hospital. I figured you'd need backup."

Before now, if someone had asked Justice to describe Goodchild, he would have said he was a goofy, scrawny cop who should not have made it through the academy. However, he was the only one who believed Justice. Goodchild was the only one who had helped him put clues together and right now he was the only one who had his back. Like his old partner, Mason.

Goodchild unwrapped his sandwich. The putrid stench of day-old tomatoes and hot onion swarmed Justice's Camaro. Goodchild then took a massive bite out of his sub.

"Oh, hell no! You can't eat that shit in here."

Creamy lettuce and mayo dripped from Goodchild's chin. The two of them had been spending a lot of time together, as with most partners, but regardless, Goodchild was supposed to ask before eating in someone else's car. Call Justice old-fashioned, but it was common courtesy.

"Damn, my bad," Goodchild said. "Do you mind?"

Shaking his head in disbelief, Justice gave him the okay. *What the hell.* Justice turned his attention back to the loading dock. There were five overhead doors each with a black dock seal. A canopy light—positioned atop each individual loading bay door—projected an eerie light. The light itself wasn't creepy but thinking of the operation hiding inside the hospital was chilling. As Justice watched bugs fight for a single canopy light's warmth, he recalled his theory. BRT Health Industries' false promises lured a certain demographic of women: Briana, Cara, and his sister. After an interview, Mr. Khizar trafficked the women, bringing them to an underground operation. Then there was Dr. Jacqui Stevenson's research and some type of experimentation which had yet to be determined. Lastly, their bodies, according to Ivan, were disposed here at the loading dock.

"What are we looking for exactly?" Goodchild said with his mouth full.

"That part I am not sure. I just know Ivan said they have a

truck come through around this time, and if we wanted proof tonight was the night to get it."

"Hmm." Goodchild didn't seem fully convinced.

"What's the 'hmm' for? Speak up."

"You know what is so strange about this whole case to me. Why hasn't the news picked it up yet? We've received a wild number of missing persons reports. More than enough to draw someone's attention at least. From just the past week we've been going hard on this case, the count is at what? Thirty women now? Just disappearing? It's crazy when you think about it."

Goodchild, the youngest of three siblings, had been born with privilege and opportunities, but Justice thought he was so ignorant to the world around him. The two of them had grown up on opposite sides of town, had nothing in common, and had been thrown together thanks to Justice's old partner getting shot in the back. However, the one thing about Goodchild that separated him from the rest of their so-called brothers in blue, was empathy. Goodchild had a willingness to see someone else's side and that alone was what Justice needed in a partner.

"Do you have any siblings, Goodchild?"

"Two older sisters. Nani and Erica."

"And have either of them ever tried to run away?"

Goodchild smiled and chuckled. "Yea, when Nani turned seventeen she claimed she was going to New York City to pursue her dreams of modeling and she ran away. No one heard from her for days. My parents assumed the worst."

"And what happened to her?"

"Umm, well my mom called the cops and they found her at a friend's place like two days later. She was on punishment for like a whole year after that." Goodchild paused, picked up a piece of tomato from his shirt and said, "Why do you ask?"

"You see, that's the difference. When your light-eyed, light-skinned sister disappeared, the cops moved heaven and earth to find her. Thank God she was at a friend's place. But when my little sister goes missing, *actually missing*, what do they do?" Justice clenched his teeth and bit down on the inside of his cheek. "They assume she's run away; they don't even look."

"That's... heavy."

A deep silence swelled between them. Minutes passed and still nothing. Normally, Justice hated Goodchild's constant need to speak. He talked—a lot. However, right now Justice wished he would say something... anything to push this blood-curling silence away.

The clock read midnight, officially two hours had passed since the alleged drop-off. Justice did not want to believe it, but Ivan, his new lead, had forced him down the wrong path.

Slipping into a daydream, Justice faded from the moment. A light came from Justice's phone. It was from Chief Glassman.

Justice got a call. The call that only came in the early hours of the morning. The call that was never the good kind of news. Justice started the car and raced to the location. Him and Goodchild ended up at a field of winter-brown grass and long-legged trees off the main road. His colleagues had already issued out yellow do-not-cross tape while there were K-9s sniffing along the patchy ground.

Chief Glassman came up to Justice, and with a solemn expression on his face he said, "Follow me, Reeves."

As Justice stepped over twigs, ant piles, dirt mounds, and broken branches, his heart began beating faster. Nothing good ever came from a crime scene that had police cars and no ambulance.

Chief Glassman stopped.

He turned around to Justice, and said, "Take all the time you need." As Glassman moved his beer belly out of the way, there she was. Her Carden University sweatshirt had been riddled with dirt and debris from a shallow grave. Her skin tone, once a rich and smooth chestnut, had turned pale with dark circles under her eyes. But worst of all she had no pants. Her underwear had been ripped and hung from a single leg. The girl laying before him was the one girl he swore to protect. She was Grace. And Grace was dead—

"Justice?" Goodchild said. "You still with me?"

With that single question, Goodchild broke through the nightmare playing in Justice's mind.

"Yeah, I'm good." Justice blinked several times before slumping down into the driver's seat, fully sinking back into reality. His mind tended to drift off in the worst way, scaring him into movement for if Justice sat too still for too long doing nothing, the guilt consumed him. Though Justice would never say it aloud, it was a good thing that his partner was here. Justice needed someone to keep him grounded.

Goodchild took a careful sip from his coffee. He sucked in his upper lip before responding, "I think we got something, look, six o'clock."

An eighteen-wheeler pulled into the hospital loading dock. Its headlights blinded Justice as it made a wide right turn into a secured spot. With a cherry-red exterior and a chrome-tinted radiator grill, even the transport spared no expense. Seeing this truck reminded Justice of a piece of evidence. *The Aphaia Corporation.* They were financially supporting Mr. Khizar, that part he could prove, but something about this mysterious investor bothered Justice. *What else was this corporation funding?*

The truck stopped right in between two broccoli-green steel overhead doors. Soon, men dressed in all black jumped from loading bay and directed the operator to park in place. With a single light pole illuminating the entire area, the pictures Justice snapped from afar were no good. The pictures came out too blurry and without fine details. None of these would hold up in court. Justice undid his seat belt. This was exactly what Justice had been waiting on—action.

"Whoa, hold on, Reeves, I thought we were just gathering intel."

They were... initially, but when was the next time Justice would have an opening like this? The circumstances had changed and the plan along with it.

"I need a better look," Justice said quietly, as he propped open the door. "Listen, I know my sister is in there and if you think I'm about to let them do this to her, you don't know me at all. I'll keep my phone on so you can reach me but, Goodchild, I need you to find Cindy and get her out of here. When this all goes down, I want her safe and as far away from this place as possible. Can you do that?"

Justice was always a loner, in fact, he did his best work on his own. Right now, he needed backup whether he realized it or not, and the only person in his corner was Goodchild. This was the first time Justice was relying on him for something, and this something was huge to Justice. He could only pray the man would not let him down.

"I got you."

Justice nodded, hoping Goodchild meant what he said. With that one subtle exchange, they had made a pact.

Then Justice looked both ways and bolted across the street. He took cover behind a concrete wall just around the corner from the loading area. Peeking his head around the thick wall and through the wire fence, what Justice laid eyes on was worse than what he could ever have imagined. He counted eight men. All had a medium build, nothing to be intimidated by, but it was what they were doing that horrified him. In an assembly line, the men tossed brown bodies wrapped in white cloth from inside the hospital down into the truck. Each thud and bump of flesh that slammed into the back of the eighteen-wheeler, made

Justice even more determined to find his sister. While it was too late for these women, Justice still had hope for Grace.

The truck's lights started again, the drum of the engine roared as it pulled out onto the road and the loaders had retreated inside the loading dock. This was his chance. The doors were closing. His heart began hammering in his chest. Justice turned the corner and sprinted to the overhead doors that were closing second by second. He pushed himself as fast as he could run, stretching his legs, and breathing so hard his lungs felt like they were about to explode. None of that mattered, not even in the slightest, for he was within arm's reach of his sister.

The steel doors closed.

Justice was now on the inside of Mercy Hospital.

Chapter 20

Cara: The Red Dot

W aking up, her head was pounding.

Cara had never felt such pain slamming into her forehead over and over again. With each breath, the pain continued in waves, crashing against the shore of her body. She was helpless against the suffering.

The hard part was waking up. The frigid metal clung to her wrists and ankles, a clear-cut reminder of reality. She was trapped, but this time she wasn't alone. Cara didn't know if that was better or worse considering that female doctor said she was going to have surgery soon. *Oh no... was this the room?* Muffled voices and bodies in burgundy scrubs surrounded her. Her eyesight was fuzzy, everything just out of focus, but one thing she made out was a tall wooden rectangle in the corner. *A door!* Cara was too tired to be excited. Instead her attention was set on one thing: What phase had these terrible people moved her to now.

"She's stable, for now," a nurse said.

"How are you feeling?" A doctor flashed a light in Cara's face. Her eyes then focused on the piercing gaze of the flashlight, forcing her awake.

"Where am I?"

"You're in a hospital. Now, look at me."

Out of all the questions to ask, Cara could have thought of a better one. But be it the drowsiness scattering to her mind, or the fatigue setting in from the serum, everything Cara was fighting against was beginning to get the best of her. Turning her chin up, she found a familiar face looking back down at her.

"Good, your vitals are looking normal," Jacqui said.

"What happened to me?" Cara whispered. Her lips had become dry and cracked and peeled at the edges. Even talking brought bouts of despair.

"A few hours ago, your heart stopped twice."

This was bad. And things were only going to get worse. She needed to leave this place. Slowly, in the most painful way imaginable, these serums, injections, and experiments were starting to kill her. Panic was settling on her chest. Her breathing ran quick and short. How much longer before she would be dead? How was Jacqui planning on getting her out of here? Nothing made sense.

"It took several hours of monitoring you, but it worked. You will feel some slight discomfort, but it will pass," Jacqui said.

Jacqui popped the flashlight into a socket against the wall. She then took the stethoscope and placed the end on Cara's chest, listening to her ragged breath.

The person who'd promised Cara an escape and the doctor standing before Cara at this moment were two totally different people. The regretful and remorseful woman that Cara had shared a true and honest moment with was gone. A calculated, serious, and emotionally distant person had taken Jacqui's place. As Cara watched Dr. Stevenson type in numbers and other data into a clear clipboard, only one word came to her mind: *Sociopath*. The woman had to be crazy. She was able to switch between emotions like changing clothes. Cara should have known better than to trust her, and yet she did. She was always so forgiving of others, while she herself had no room for imperfection.

Still, Cara could not help but feel that being here was nothing short of God punishing her. She felt she'd been reckless with her body in her late teens into her early twenties, but she was done with that behavior and for good. Adult films had paid for her textbooks, tuition, and campus parking passes. No, she did not know her true body count, but did that mean she was a second-class citizen? Apparently, to a few frat boys, that was all it took.

Being trapped down here unlocked a memory. Years before, at a house party right off campus, Cara had gone with two of her friends... well, Cara learned the hard way what the word friend meant. Friends would not have allowed what happened to Cara that night, to happen at all. Inside there were thousands of red cups strewn everywhere, two huge speakers playing EDM, and kegs at every corner of the house. Students were packed in every inch; it was like moving through a club just to reach the bathroom. Eventually, Cara and her friends had found their way to the kitchen, and it was not long before guys offered them drinks. However, her secret admirer had a special recipe in Cara's drink.

Cara went from clinking cups one minute to a dark room with her legs spread apart and her jeans slid down to her ankles. Then Cara realized that she was not alone. Some guy was on top of her. He was panting as his third arm had gotten stuck between her thighs. He did not exactly reach her sacred crevice, in fact, he was barely above her knees, but he was too drunk to care. She still remembered his breath and the disgusting mix of tequila and puke that made up his cologne that night. Seconds later he'd finished and was out the door. Cara found a bathroom and written across her stomach were the words *Deep Throat*. A film she had just finished only a year prior. Strangely of that night, seeing the insult written across her skin in black permanent marker was not the worst of it. She could handle the insults back then, she was strong enough, but what stuck with Cara after all these years was one question: why didn't she fight back? She just laid there. She did not scream. She did not move. She did not hit him. She only mumbled the word "stop" a few times. He probably did not hear her over the sound of his own moaning. She never understood why she just froze and accepted it.

Like she was doing right now. Cara had made mistakes, but did that mean she deserved to be assaulted? Or that anyone could have her? Still, Cara got the sense that this place, in the evil that it was doing, she had brought this on herself. This was some sort of divine version of karma. With her hands and ankles bound, she was mentally back at that party all over again. Only this time it was a doctor taking advantage of her.

"Dr. Stevenson," a nurse said. "Since her fever broke, I've updated her records. Once she leaves this room, she is cleared to go right into surgery."

Jacqui simply nodded and went back to examining Cara.

Cara's eyes widened at the mention of surgery. Jacqui held no change in her expression. What the hell was going on? Wait. Maybe Jacqui was playing a role in front of the nurses. *Yes, of course, that was it!* Jacqui did not seem like the type to lie. She'd promised she would help. Agony spread throughout Cara's chest like an oil spill. She hoped her suspicion was true. But as time went on and these nurses kept pushing buttons, staring at screens, and whispering numbers and alphanumeric codes to one another, time was running out. This was what Cara deserved for believing someone. When was she going to learn to trust no one? Absolutely no one, no matter how comfortable she felt with them. *Stupid, stupid girl.* Her naiveté was going to kill her. Once again, that hope Cara held, had slipped from her grasp. Cara knew that when she left this room, from that point on it would be out of Jacqui's hands.

Dr. Stevenson leaned down and whispered to Cara, "Listen, there is not much time..."

Jacqui's words were faint and delicate, hardly making it the long trek to Cara's comprehension. Slowly, Jacqui grabbed a scalpel from nearby and hid the sharp object within Cara's hands.

"What are you doing?" Cara asked.

"Trust me," Jacqui paused, looked at the nurses, then back at Cara, "you're going to need something if you plan to make it out of here."

Despite her reluctance, Cara nodded. Jacqui uncuffed her wrists one at a time, in a calm fashion so as not to alert the others in the room. When the metal pulled away from her body, Cara could have cried right there and then. Instant relief from the icy sting, the hope she had waited so long for was beginning to unfold before her. Cara laid quietly on the bed and followed Jacqui's every instruction.

"Open the door," Jacqui said to the nurse by the exit and without further protest one of the nurses opened the door, allowing Cara and Jacqui to leave.

They made it to the elevator. Once inside, the door closed, encasing them in a small haven. Jacqui then pushed level one, escaping from the Colony into the lobby of Mercy Hospital.

"Where am I really?" Cara asked. Her voice was snuffy and hoarse. "Tell me the truth."

Cara stared into the brown of Jacqui's eyes.

"You are in what's called the Colony, an underground facility fifty floors deep. This place was built for the sole purpose of preserving life through womb transplantation. Through any means necessary. Even if you did manage to break free from your restraints, escape the Transition Room, and find your way out of the maze of the Colony, there was no way you were getting out of here unnoticed."

Cara watched the floor numbers turn, but instead of the elevator taking Cara straight to the first floor of Mercy Hospital it continued on until reaching level two.

"Dammit," Jacqui said.

Cara turned to the side, looking at her. Something was not right. Heat poured from Jacqui like a furnace. The thought of going back to that Transition Room pumped angst through her veins. From the worry in Jacqui's face, Cara knew this was not a part of her plan.

The doors parted.

The elevator became flooded with lab coats, suits, and briefcases. Though the metal box could hold up to twenty or so height-weight proportionate individuals, Jacqui could not risk being seen. Level two was now their off-boarding point.

Moving rather quickly through the porcelain white halls, Jacqui tucked her chin into her chest, hiding her face, and rolled Cara into an empty room. Off-white tile flooring, a two-panel window in the corner with a single pale blue exam table filled the tiny room. Jacqui stood next to Cara and wrapped an arm around her shoulder, lifting Cara from the bed. Together, the two staggered over to the exam table. As Cara's back touched the stiff surface behind her, she fell back onto the seat and Jacqui dropped to the floor, labored breathing consumed them both. Jacqui had made good on her promise.

Jacqui leaned against the wall with her hands on her knees, taking in deep breaths. She looked at Cara with a slight smile, like the two had accomplished something impossible. At least for the time being, Cara felt safe. No one knew where they were.

"Here's the thing," Jacqui said. Then her expression took a

nosedive. "While you were unconscious, they moved you into Phase Two. They'll realize you are missing, and they'll come for you. That shouldn't happen for another hour or so, and by then, hopefully, you'll be long gone."

Cara had no words. She knew she was not out of the woods yet. But more importantly, she could barely move her appendages. Like the signal from her brain to her arms and legs had been disconnected from the Wi-Fi. She hoped the feeling to her legs would return soon.

"You were about to kill me... weren't you?"

The room fell quiet. Reluctantly, Jacqui made eye contact for a second then turned away. She was too ashamed to speak, but in her silence Cara found the answer.

"Why didn't you? Why are you helping me?"

Leaning against the door, Jacqui crossed her arms and tucked her chin to her chest. She said nothing for a long time.

"I've performed that surgery one too many times." Jacqui's voice began cracking, but even with that weakness in her voice there was an anger, a power hidden within her words. "Enough is enough."

With the back end of her wrist, Jacqui wiped her nose and cleared her throat. A tiny smile came across her face. "I'll be right back, I promise," Jacqui said opening the door.

"Hey, Jacqui." Cara stopped her. The time Cara had spent down there, reflecting on her life, she realized that the career she wanted so bad meant nothing in comparison to the family she desired. It had been three months since her and Matthew had gone their separate ways. And though Cara always waited for the guy to make the first move, if he was still single Cara would reach out first. Having been thrust into an experiment by a sick old man in a wrinkled lab coat, it was clear to Cara what she wanted. Jacqui had given her the opportunity to live again, Cara would not waste it.

"Thank you."

Jacqui didn't say a word, she nodded, closed the door behind her and locked it.

Upon hearing that twist and click of the knob, Cara was relieved. That sound meant she had time, which had become a precious commodity in a place like this. The only thing standing between safety and certain death was now her sheer will to live.

Roughly ten minutes had passed. Then something happened. A miracle had begun to unfold. A tingling sensation ran through her legs which she could also feel in her forearms. Though it was very slow, like watching a caterpillar move kind of slow, there was no mistaking it, her strength was returning.

Cara scanned her surroundings. This room felt familiar. Yes, she had been in this room before. The white walls, razor-thin monitors, medical equipment and posters, and the ice-cold linoleum floors stared at her now just as they did back then. This was where she first got the news about her diagnosis and how much the treatment would cost in dollars. Cara still remembered that total. It was as fresh as yesterday. Anger bubbled in her chest by just thinking about it again. Here she was, back where she'd started.

None of that mattered now, not even in the slightest, she had to get moving before—

Knock. Knock. Knock.

Like a knee-jerk reaction, Cara gasped.

Someone was at the door.

What could she do? She could not move more than rolling her ankles and snapping her fingers. Then again, no telling who was behind the door.

The person knocked again, only this time, they began banging on the door. Only one person knew she was here. And that person did not need to knock.

Cara covered her mouth trying to be as quiet as possible.

She then saw something out of her peripheral vision. At the base of her wrist and entangled amidst the green vines that were her veins, a red dot the size of a dime was flashing underneath her skin. It was so quiet, so subtle, no wonder she did not see it sooner. *Oh, God...* What had these people done to her? She knew that it did not matter how silent she remained, they knew where she was. They would always find her.

Chapter 21

Justice: Ninety-Three Hours Missing

J ustice slid through the overhead doors right before they closed.

The interior was the spitting image of a warehouse. Inside were forklifts, pallets, electric-powered pallet trucks, and metal shelves that reached as high as the ceiling. Industrial strip lights reflected off the metallic gray concrete flooring. Men dressed in all black, reflector vests and hard hats walked briskly throughout the industrial space. Clearly, these men were kept busy at all hours.

Walking briskly between two shelves, Justice moved with silence and stealth. His first time, in a new place, and the slightest slip-up could mean the death of his sister. He crouched down and watched two workers as they stood idly beside a coffee maker.

"You know, for this to be a hospital I don't think these doctors know what they be doing," one worker said. This one was taller, stockier, and Justice imagined that he could definitely bench press at least 250lbs.

"What makes you say that?" a co-worker responded. This one was shorter, but his biceps were as defined as an ancient statue of some Greek god. If he had to fight them both at the same time, Justice could take them head on. It wouldn't be easy, but it wasn't impossible either.

"Every week, we dispose of hella lot of bodies. Come on, I know I'm not the only one seeing this. If we keep doing as many as we did today, I might throw my back out."

"It's a big hospital. I wouldn't think too much about it," the shorter worker said. He then looked at his watch. Then they both rushed through the exit behind them. Wherever they were headed off to in such a hurry, Justice knew it meant something terrible.

"Hey, hey you!" a man wearing a highlighter orange vest said.

Every muscle in Justice's body stiffened at once. To Justice's left, there was a man seated behind a thick desktop computer made two decades ago. Judging by his beer belly, low haircut, and the mountain of paperwork stashed across his desk, the guy had to be some sort of manager. Justice realized the man was talking to him.

"What the hell are you doing?" the manager shouted.

Justice stood up and rubbed the back of his head. Running would make it obvious that Justice did not belong. Hiding was out of the question since the man had already seen his face. There was only one thing left for Justice to do.

"I was—"

"You're supposed to be upstairs in the meeting, it's for all security personnel, remember?"

"I guess I got lost." Justice cracked a smile.

"And you look like it too," the man grumbled. "It's downstairs you have to take the fancy elevator with all the floors. Go to the main floor. Then go past the bathroom and it's two doors down from the right. You can't miss it."

Justice hated when people said "you can't miss it" because,

well, if you left it up to him, he would miss it. Though he was diligent, strong-minded, and hardworking, anything related to directions and using a map was not Justice's forte.

"Where's your ID badge?"

"I don't have one yet." Sometimes Justice surprised himself with how quick he was on his feet. The words came out faster than his mind processed it. Good. He needed that type of cunning. No telling what traps awaited him inside this place.

"Here's a visitor's badge. But bring it back." The manager handed Justice a white badge with red letters on it.

Justice marched towards the entryway of the warehouse and on his way out snatched an orange vest in the process. Racing down the metal stringer staircase, he found what he assumed was the "fancy" elevator. He scanned the manager's ID badge and the doors split open. Decorated with lustrous stone flooring, and the stainless-steel interior shone to perfection. This was without question the right one.

A fifty-button panel sat at the entrance. None of them read "main floor" each had a number—except number one. Justice hadn't a clue which floor to go to and if Grace was down here, how was he going to find her in a facility fifty floors deep? She was probably already dead.

Justice shook his head, clearing his mind of any thoughts of Grace's death. There was enough time. Even though the first forty-eight hours had passed, there had been cases where women were found years after disappearing.

A case he worked a few years back stuck out in particular. A twenty-year-old woman had disappeared from college campus. No one had seen her, not classmates, professors, friends, not a single soul. The case went cold. Until five years later a neighbor made a noise complaint about the man next door. Upon checking out the situation, Justice found the man's demeanor too anxious, he claimed he lived alone, but at the kitchen table there were three cups sitting out. Justice left the man's home but stayed parked outside to satisfy this itch of curiosity. Something told him the man was lying. Within the hour, Justice spotted the silhouette of a woman from the window. She was being choked and tossed around. Justice then stormed the house, only later to discover that the woman being abused by this man was the same woman who had gone missing from class five years earlier. If it was possible for her, Justice had to believe it was possible for his sister.

Confused, Justice did the only thing he could do; he pushed a random elevator button.

The screen above the doors read:

Level UG

When the doors opened, he was overcome with wide-eyed horror of the maze that existed down here.

Tons of nurses in burgundy, black, and teal scrubs and surgical masks swarmed the hallway. It was so crowded that Justice could not see five paces ahead of him without having to say, "excuse me," or "sorry" for stepping on someone's shoes. Tall ceilings, ashen gray walls, and mute-colored floors, not a lot of artistic influence went into creating this place. No wonder everyone looked depressed, thought Justice, the dull shades simply sucked the life out of them. One thing for sure, he needed to blend in, and this bright orange vest had lost its charm.

He spotted a dark blue door that looked home to nothing but cleaning materials. Perfect for his plan. Now he was only missing one thing.

Justice scanned the countless faces strolling through the narrow hallway. Mostly slender female nurses in scrubs filled the space. He was approaching the dark blue door. Time was running out before it became clear that he was not supposed to be there. Then he found it, or *him*, rather.

"Hey, can I ask you a question?" Justice approached a male nurse in scrubs. The two were roughly the same height and stood eye to eye as they held a conversation. "Do you know where I'm supposed to be? I think he said the conference room, or something, there's a meeting I'm supposed to be in..."

"No worries." The young man eyed Justice up and down, assessing his attire. "I know where you have to be. It's about three doors down and on the right." The male nurse pointed.

"I know you're busy, but do you mind showing me?"

The man paused, and his shoulder dropped slightly in response as though irritated. Nonetheless, he agreed and began walking in that direction.

Justice had to time this perfectly. Now that they were away from the flow of traffic, Justice had one chance to get it right. *Three... two... and... Now!*

"So where are you from—" As the young man turned, Justice shoved him into the door frame with his shoulder. Forcing the door open and knocking him unconscious. Quickly, Justice swung it shut behind them.

"I am sorry about this, man," Justice said.

Justice snatched the man's shirt from around his neck and changed into his bottoms. The man laid unconscious with nothing but boxers on and a necklace with a cross on it. The holy symbol fell down to his chest. Seeing the crucifix showered Justice with shame. He looked at his hands, then back at the nurse who was out cold. This was unlike him, to lie, manipulate, and steal from someone. Who was he becoming? His mother wore a very similar chain. He could not begin to imagine what she would say.

Grace.

No. Now was not the time. Justice had worse problems than his conscience.

With all that noise, he was certain he'd drawn some

attention. He propped the edge open, looking through the slit in the door for security or anyone who might have seen him. Closing the door behind himself, Justice brushed himself clean of debris and maneuvered his way within the sea of moving faces. No one looked perplexed by his presence, or by his new name which was now... Andre. Whatever these people did, it consumed all of their attention and perhaps their lives.

Justice emerged from the room and back into the halls wearing thin turquoise scrubs, a surgeon hat, and a white surgical mask over his mouth. He walked briskly between passersby and kept at his search. The long halls and high ceilings continued for days. It was a labyrinth down here, full of secured doors, bright lights, secret dead ends, and keycode entryways. It would be a while before he learned any information anywhere.

While walking, Justice found a group of what looked like students taking notes. The group stood in front of a floor-length glass window. Justice pulled away from the main strip of traffic and drew closer to the students and in doing so, found a surgery taking place inside of a transparent room. An old man with an age spot in the middle of his neck, thick aviator reading glasses, a head full of ghost-white hair, and a microphone attached to his ear, moved about in the secluded room with two nurses following every command. On one side of the doctor was a petite woman with blond hair. She was unconscious with baby blue fabric covering her chest and thighs while her navel area down to between her legs was exposed. Justice could see everything. Literally everything. Pink pieces of flesh, bloody scalpels, obstetrical forceps, clamps, suction devices sprinkled with dried blood, and thin needles with black thread. The light overhead spared no detail.

What Justice found on the other side of the room consumed him with utter, primal rage. A girl of copper complexion. She had to be no older than eighteen. While the majority of the group kept their focus with the doctor and the blond-haired woman, Justice stepped over to the other side. His attention was fixed solely on the brown girl. Her skin held no blemish, scratch, or scarring, but there was something in her face that frustrated him. Did he know her? She looked familiar, but from where kept evading him.

"My baby, someone took my sweet girl!"

And just like that, it came back to him.

Justice reached for his shoulder, remembering that woman's touch. The same woman who'd rushed out in the middle of the road with no regard for her own life. The woman who was screaming and crying and pleading with Justice to find her baby. The woman with those bright pink acrylic claws. The woman who started him down this path. The mother of Briana Wilson. As promised, Justice had found her daughter. Only it was too late.

"That is a complete womb transplant. Any questions?" Dowey said. His tone was so full of life and excitement. And while all the other students jostled for Dr. Dowey's scrutiny, dread coiled in the pit of Justice's stomach. He wondered what he was going to say to her mother. How was he going to explain this? Never would he ever have believed he was going to find Briana here of all places.

The monitor behind Briana's bed began showing red symbols and numbers. While the doctor sat and answered questions, the nurses did nothing. A straight line had formed on Briana's screen, and she took her last breath. This was unreal; like Justice was in another universe down here. Staring at her swollen face, matted hair, her closed sunken eyes, and the respirator tube protruding from her mouth, all boiled his blood to the point he could see the logic behind mass shootings. He imagined carrying an AR-15 into this place and killing every single person on sight. If they were down here, then they were responsible. The doctors, the students, the nurses, the technicians, the loaders, even the managers who sat on their fat asses, all of these people were all guilty in Justice's eyes.

Now it all made sense about BRT Health Industries and what they were doing down here. Justice knew that if he didn't act fast, his sister was about to share the same fate as Briana. If she hadn't already.

Chapter 22

Jacqui: A New Notification

Using her face ID, Jacqui logged in to her desktop and went straight to her email. The meeting with Dr. Seymore had given Jacqui a sense of hope, and also validation. Having three of her patients rendered barren from the same vaccine was one thing, but Dr. Seymore's research was a testament reassuring Jacqui that she was not going crazy. Even so, Jacqui needed absolute proof and that was not going to reveal itself easily.

An email message appeared.

```
From: Seymore, Anthony Dr.
   Subject: What Do You Think of this?
   I have sat on this for too long. See
Attached.
   Get that sucker.
```

Clicking on the attached message, Jacqui read the first piece of documentation inside a zip file.

```
From: Seymore, Anthony
```

Subject: Quality Control Review - Premier Vaccine

To: Reisser Jr., Arnold

Mr. Reisser,

As senior Quality Assurance Engineer, I have found the following concerns regarding the Premier Vaccine production (est. 2005).

The effectiveness in the vaccine does not outweigh the long-term risks posed to the recipient of the vaccine.

From a thoroughly reviewed quantitative analysis, it was evident that the Premier Vaccine has an over 80% probability of causing infertility complications in recipients of the vaccine.

It is my recommendation to stop production and immediately cease further administration of the Premier Vaccine to patients.

RE: Quality Control Review - Premier Vaccine

From: Reisser Jr., Arnold

To: Seymore, Anthony

Dr. Seymore,

According to your research, which I don't doubt, I am aware some rare instances can cause temporary fertility issues, but I have not seen any reason to prohibit further continuation of

```
Lanzran Inc's best healthcare service
currently available on the market. While
I appreciate your research and
meticulousness in this matter, we will
continue production as planned.
    Best
```

Holy crap. This man knew. Arnold absolutely knew and did nothing, Jacqui thought.

Attached to the email were countless more conversations between Dr. Seymore and Arnold and their escalating disagreement.

Glancing at the time, Jacqui had twenty-five minutes until she needed to get back to Cara on the second floor, but first, she retrieved the card the police officer gave her, entered the Thirty-Fifth precinct's email, and began typing.

With each stroke of the keyboard, Jacqui drafted her version of events. The email compiled of all her evidence against Arnold. Every detail from his original company Lanzran Inc., the Premier Vaccine, the research proving its inefficacy, and Arnold's refusal to remove the dangerous product from the market.

She made sure to include the additional details Dr. Seymore had provided, but something had caught Jacqui by surprise.

```
From: Reisser Jr., Arnold (Lanzran
Inc. USA)
    To: Vargos, Ted (Federal Bureau of
Drug and Food Administration)
    Cc: Dowey, Jonathan (MD, Obstetrics)
    Ted,
    On behalf of Lanzran Inc., we welcome
you to the team. I cannot thank you
```

```
enough   for   your   assistance   with   the
Premier   Vaccine.   See   your   benefits
package   along   with   other   onboarding
information attached…
```

Jacqui continued reading the exchanges between Arnold and Ted, she fell further into disbelief. Arnold had no bounds. This among other emails proved that Arnold had paid off Ted, the director of the Federal Administrative Bureau of Drug Administration, and then had given him a job the same year the vaccine was approved. This network of lies ran deep. Deep as nerves connected to a single brain that was the Aphaia Corporation.

Jacqui eventually reached the most difficult portion. Her involvement. This was the moment of truth. She laid out everything, detailing how BRT Health Industries lured in candidates through scholarships and debt relief programs to a false interview. Then, there was a separate team that abducted the young women, ensuring they never made it home after the interview. After that, the women would be placed under 24/7 surveillance in the Transition Room, supervised by Dr. Dowey and herself. Jacqui outlined the three phases of the womb transferal process, from the sedation tactics, trackers embedded in the girl's wrists, and what happened to them once the procedure was completed...

Jacqui stopped typing.

She hated this part. How the loading team tossed the girls' bodies around like trash into a garbage truck. Each thud and clap of their flesh made Jacqui retch. And yet, for the sake of keeping her daughter alive, she'd been willing to send others to the slaughter. No more. Today it stopped. Jacqui resumed typing, finishing the email stating where anyone could find the bodies of these missing women, the ones that had not been cremated. Girls like Ivery, however, were now merely ash and embers.

Lastly, she mentioned how Arnold had manipulated her into working for him and threatened her daughter's life if she'd refused. To anyone reading this, after seeing Jacqui's involvement it would seem like Arnold threatening her daughter was a false claim, a way to weasel out of any guilt. A part of Jacqui knew this day would come. On her second or third day on the job, Arnold was already too arrogant. In his cockiness, he made a mistake. A simple mistake that Jacqui had recorded.

"She's a friend of your daughter?"

Silence...

"I will take that as a yes. Well, Jacqui, let me make this clear and I will only say this once. Everything I do is for a reason. Have her in Phase One by the end of day, or your daughter will be in her place by tomorrow. Do I make myself clear?"

There was no debate. That was Arnold's voice. And that was a threat against her daughter. Anything of value she spared no detail too small.

As she uploaded the voice recording, Jacqui wondered if all of this would be enough to hold up in court. She was no lawyer by any means, but she had watched enough *Law & Order* to learn a few official words. Probable cause was one of them. Perhaps all of this evidence was not sufficient to charge Arnold, but maybe it could start an investigation at least. That was all Jacqui could hope for at this point.

Jacqui stopped typing for good. She glanced over the email for typos and poorly structured sentences. It was one thing to be a criminal, she could not afford to have bad grammar too.

It was done. The email had everything. All the attachments, evidence, and information Jacqui had gathered to destroy Arnold. Even so, her finger hovered over the enter key. She could not do it. Why was she hesitating? Sitting in front of her was what she had dreamed of finding from day one—the truth, but this was more like a heaping pile of shit with Arnold's signature all over it. She'd finally found it. Yet, with all of that success came a frightening realization. If she pushed enter, Jacqui would certainly be rotting in some federal prison with Arnold if he was serious about his threat. However, if she did like Dr. Seymore, Jacqui would have to go on the run with Ashley, forever looking over her shoulder. In the end, Jacqui could either dismantle Lanzran Inc. and BRT Health Industries or remain an active parent in her daughter's life, but she could not do both.

She had made up her mind. A part of her did not know if this was selfish or selfless.

Sent.

Chapter 23

Justice: Ninety-Five Hours Missing

Proof. A simple word but required a mountain of effort.

This place was ridiculously huge, thought Justice. High ceilings with cameras at every turn. Painfully bright lights sparing no corners or crevices of darkness. Hallways that seemed to stretch for miles at a time with countless doors. There were so many doors and there was no meaningful numbering system in Justice's eyes. Some had standard numbers of one, two, three written in plain English, while others used Roman numerals, and some had nothing at all. One thing Justice noticed was that next to each door was a smooth black surface the size of an index card. One nurse stepped in front of the door and swiped her badge against the black device and a green light appeared above the door as the woman walked through it. Justice glanced at the badge hanging from his shirt pocket. Hopefully, with Andre's card, he had similar access.

Without a clue of where to even begin looking for his sister, Justice stopped in front of a door with the Roman numeral sign "two" written front and center. He wiped his card against the black surface, then waited, looking at the colored light bulbs above the door: one green, one red.

"Come on," Justice muttered under his breath.

As nurses walked by him, Justice saw a tour group headed his way. At the front was a man with salt-and-pepper hair, a black suit that was no doubt made by some foreign designer, and a watch that looked like it had cost half a million on his wrist. Behind the man was a herd of suits and high heels taking in their surroundings with awed expressions and quiet conversations amongst themselves. The man leading them... his face... he looked familiar, but from where? In the same breath, an image from Justice's wall of evidence surfaced. It was an image of a gentleman with crow's feet at the corners of his hooded eyes, black-gray hair low cut, and a black suit—he always wore a black suit.

The man's name was Arnold.

Justice made the mistake of maintaining eye contact with Arnold for a second too long. He then pulled his attention back to the lights above the door; however, it was too late.

Buzz.

The answer Justice had waited for. The light had turned green. Justice pushed down on the handle and the entrance began to unfold—

"Young man, may I borrow you for a second?" Arnold said.

Justice stopped dead and looked to his right. There were dozens, no more like hundreds of people walking through these hallways. Surely, Justice thought, there was no way in hell this man was talking to him, that would be absurd. Still, to be sure, Justice pointed at his chest, maybe the man would not even notice.

"You, yes you by the door."

Fuck.

"Come here I want to introduce you to a few people."

As Justice walked away from the door, the green light faded back into its black silence. He was so close to answers yet so far.

"Everyone I'd like you all to meet, umm..."

"Justice... I mean..." Justice looked down at his name tag. "Andre. My name is Andre."

Arnold lifted an eyebrow at Justice.

"Andre, nice, alright these are some investors who have some questions about BRT Health Industries. Now I may have founded the organization, but it is nothing without the hard work that people like yourself do down here every day that make this place possible. So, for anything I can't answer, I'll rely on your expertise. Sound like a fair deal?"

To the untrained eye, Justice could see how people would fall for this man's charisma. Arnold had a way about him that made someone feel comfortable in his presence, like a father figure of sorts, but Justice knew better. He knew too much about Arnold and this place to believe a word coming out of his mouth.

"If you all will follow me," Arnold said, continuing the tour.

For any other nurse this was the opportunity of a lifetime. To meet Arnold, have him remember your first name and show you off to his peers would ignite anyone's career. But Justice was only in this place for one reason alone, and it damn sure was not for a raise.

Together Arnold and Justice led the group, serving as the tour guides.

They walked through the hallways, long, bright lights and spilling with nurses and doctors in scrubs; IV bags, carts full of medical supplies and protective gear. Despite his disgust for what this place was doing, it amazed Justice how everything seemed legitimate.

"This is the sampling room," Arnold announced, and the stampede of footsteps came to a staggering stop.

To the right was a floor-length window. Inside were slim-figured bodies covered in white plastic, with surgical masks over their mouths, and clear goggles covering their faces. Dealing with blood, saliva, other bodily fluids, and sharp objects required such protection.

"Here is step one. The beginning of the process. Andre, if you could?"

Justice gazed inside the room in astonishment. One scientist placed two vials inside of a digital rotator. The object looked like a tiny Ferris wheel with each small vial filled with a clear substance orbiting around the center. What were these people doing? Step one seemed to have something to do with this serum, but this demonstration left Justice with more questions. Mainly, how was this related to what happened to Briana Wilson? Seeing her body lay without life while that doctor had operated on her, tore at Justice's heart. He'd been too late to save her. How much longer before his sister ended up like her? Staring at these people had consumed Justice with so much anger that he'd forgotten his cover name—again.

"Andre?"

"Oh right, Andre, that's me." Justice chuckled.

From the menacing gaze upon Arnold's face, Justice could tell that this man saw through his disguise. Reluctantly, Justice turned around to face the group. Justice had never liked science. He'd barely passed the class his entire time in high school. He'd never needed to know the organic compound structure of salt or water and hydrogen or whatever. At the time, he'd wondered how any of that could play a part in his daily life. Well, life had a funny way of working itself out. Right now, he wished he'd paid more attention. These people were the brightest of Ballantyne, with doctorate degrees in finance, science, and technology, while Justice stood in front of them with only a high school diploma. It would take a miracle for Justice to fool them.

"Um, well, as you can see here... and as Mr. Arnold pointed out this is... this is... what we call the sampling room... the ugh...

the start of the entire process for the company... I've worked with Dr. Jacqui Stevenson and she... she is the one who is the reason we are all here today, um... you know with her work in fertility and with women."

Silence. A long eerie silence followed his last word. Justice could only hope it was enough.

Arnold nodded along. He then leaned into Justice's ear, "Meet me in my office, I need a word with you separately." Taking the group's attention, Arnold turned around. "Great, now moving on." The group followed behind Arnold, and though Arnold said nothing, Justice imagined that mentally, this incompetence was strike two, and there would not be another.

The group passed by an opening, another hallway, but down a few doors to the right, Justice spotted a door with male signage on it. Perfect. This was his chance. Justice made a break for it.

Rushing into the male restroom, the door quietly closed behind him. Justice then made a phone call.

"Goodchild, did you find Cindy?"

"Reeves, man, you won't believe this."

"What's going on?"

"Cindy is fine, but listen to me, the precinct just got an email from some doctor. I think this is the missing link for your case. Some higher-ups just went into the Chief's office just now, they've been in there for a while..."

The higher-ups could jump into a ditch, break every bone, and bleed out in a slow and agonizing death for all Justice cared. He had given a decade of his life to his community and when Justice had tried bringing a case to them what did they do? They turned a blind eye, so fuck them. The only person who mattered was Grace.

"Goodchild, find Cindy."

Click.

Justice had given Goodchild one job, and the man could not even do that. This was the exact reason why Justice never put too much faith in others. They always let him down.

Peeking out of the restroom, Justice slid back into the crowded hallway. A young man stood at an intersection of pathways with a clear clipboard in his hand, surely, he had answers. The young man's badge indicated that his name was Mark.

Justice tapped Mark on the shoulder. Irritated, Mark turned to meet him face to face.

"Can you show me back to the umm... lobby... I am so lost and everywhere looks exactly the same."

Mark crossed his arms, looked down at Justice's feet, his plain black tennis shoes, back up to his face then down at his name tag. He rolled his eyes at Justice. With such sassiness in Mark's personality, Justice imagined that Mark often made enemies and friends quite easily this way.

"Andre, huh?" Mark uncrossed his arms and began scrolling on the clear clipboard as though searching for something specific. "Yeah, it's pretty easy to get lost down here, let me show you back to the front."

Mark marched off and Justice kept pace beside him.

"So what group are you with?"

"Um, well I'm not sure." Justice kept looking over his shoulder, hoping that Arnold would not find him.

"How long have you been working here?" Mark asked, while walking and looking down at the clipboard. Mark had no concern for whoever was unfortunate enough to be in front of him.

"It's... my first day."

"It's your first day and you led a tour group with Arnold? Must be nice." Mark seemed like the type to know everything about everybody. Justice figured if anyone would know where Grace was, it would be Mark.

"They told me I was supposed to go to the room where they had all the women stored, but I forgot what it was called."

"You're talking about the Transition Room. We are terribly understaffed down there. Ooh, have you heard? The Aphaia Corporation is going to expand the donor process."

Aphaia Corporation, Justice thought. *The corporation financing all of this... plans on expanding.*

"Expand the donor process?"

"Well, ya know, offer more services, and become a separate organ donation supply chain of sorts. Like imagine this operation here, but one in each state. It is way too fancy for me to understand. Anyways, the Transition Room is at the end of this hall, then you make two rights. Follow the corridor until you reach a dead-end, then swipe your badge. You will see the Aphaia logo, and you should be good to go from there, bye," Mark said, before power walking in the opposite direction from which they'd come.

As Justice walked through the hallways, he took in the sights around him and every word from conversations he could catch off lips. Two words, in particular, kept bouncing off the walls:

Transition Room.

By that fact alone, Justice needed to see what was in this room.

He turned left down a hall and to his luck, Justice ran into a dead-end. Only an ashy gray wall rested in front of him, no signs, not a symbol, no Roman numerals, nothing.

Dammit, Justice thought.

Wait a minute. This was supposed to happen if Justice remembered correctly.

Slowly, Justice inched closer to this mysterious wall. He ran his fingers across the surface and wherever his hand went, a ribbon of iridescent light followed. This wall was not made from concrete. No, it reacted to him like a touchscreen computer. If there was a computer, then there had to be a monitor or some kind of output device. Justice walked to the corner and then, as predicted, a black surface the size of a playing card, appeared from a wall panel.

But something unexpected happened when he touched the digital screen. An image appeared. The image was of a pale woman from the shoulders up, with piercing green eyes and blossoming peach petals in place of hair. In the middle of the woman's forehead was a slit like the beginnings of a new universe. At the bottom read: The Aphaia Corporation.

From that one small symbol, Justice knew he was without doubt headed the right direction.

Justice grabbed onto the badge and swiped it against the black device. The device grew quiet while processing his information. Seconds afterward, the dead-end split in two, parting like elevator doors.

This place was full of secrets. The kind of hidden pathways that could bury the truth. Once he stepped through, he found signs upon his entrance.

LEFT -> RESTROOMS

RIGHT -> TRANSITION ROOM

Justice did not know it yet, but he got the sense everything he was searching for was within reach. The further he went into this place, it became clear, it was anything but a hospital.

Chapter 24

Cara: Alone And Afraid

K *nock. Knock.*
    The door handle jingled but did not give way.
Oh. My. God, Cara thought.

A wave of adrenaline rushed through her body. Her chest flooded with a thousand heartbeats per second as she regained control over her breath. The walls began to close in from all sides. To her right was a window big enough for her to see the entire skyline of the city. At the center of the opening was a thick line of intricate clasps securing the window shut. This was it. If she wanted to escape this nightmare, that window had now become her only hope.

A voice approached from behind the door on the opposite side of the room. Cara refused to stay and find out who it was. She'd had enough of strangers and enough of hospitals.

Pushing past fatigue, she got up from the bed, throwing her legs over the sides and dropping bare toes atop the chilling linoleum ground. She limped towards the window. Desperately, Cara searched for clues of how to unlock the only barrier standing between herself and freedom.

The door handle twisted. Someone wanted to open the door, but to her fortune they did not have the key.

The clasp broke loose, and Cara slid the window open, bringing the chilly breeze crashing onto her skin. Cara had not a clue of the little things about life that she had missed. That sweet tangy taste of air polluted by a nearby gas station and mostly scented with trees shaking off the sheath of winter, coated her sense of smell. It was such a simple thing to notice, but in this moment, it meant she was close to having her life back again.

Clenching the scalpel in her hand, anger bubbled in her chest. The time she had lost at the hands of this place, the powerlessness she had felt for days at a time, for a second, this place had broken her, but there was no time for that. The doorknob lowered. Someone else had entered.

Without thinking, Cara stepped out onto the ledge, securing her backside against the gritty flesh-toned wall. Her long hair billowed, twisting, and turning around her head by the wind's desire. Those thoughts of anger diminished as fear grabbed hold of her. Watching the traffic below move in a melancholy fashion, the tip of her toes tucked at the end of the surface. One wrong move and Cara would not need to worry about the person chasing her, she would already be dead.

Cara hooked her fingernails into the corner of the ledge and dug them into a chipped concrete crevice, holding on for the sake of what time she had left on earth. Jacqui said this would be on the first floor, the sight below did not look like it. Cara was at least another story up. Close enough to see the highlights of a woman entering the hospital, but too far to jump without certain injury. Taking a deep breath, Cara had to make her next move. The wind recklessly flung her hair around her face. Shaking. Her heart pounding. Ravaged with anxiety knowing that one wrong move was a trip to the cemetery, Cara could not go through with this. The cold air paralyzed her in place, there was no way she could scale this building and make it to the bottom in one piece. Carefully, she eased her gaze over the ledge.

Beneath her was a cerulean glass visor attached to the level below. If she could reach that, then maybe, just maybe she could do this. At least, she hoped so. It was the only escape possible at this point. If she could somehow turn around and face the wall then climb down, then there was a chance. But, dear God, this was terrifying. Cara did not have a fear of heights—at least, for the most part, she thought she did not. She enjoyed that frightening drop of a rollercoaster like the rest of the world. However, here, right at this moment, her heart was thumping so hard she could have sworn it would throw her off balance. New plan: she was going to wait it out, and go back inside, like in the movies. *Yes, she could do that, no problem.* It was far more possible than this plan on the ledge.

As she moved closer to the window, suddenly, a man's head poked out of the opening. It was a thick-necked, burly fellow with his hair styled in a topknot. Then, seeing his face triggered a memory... It was him! He was the last face she'd seen before passing out in her car. He was the one who'd driven her into the ditch. He was the one who had pulled her from the wreckage. This man was going to be the end of her.

Clutching the ledge, she lowered her bottom onto the end of the small protruding surface. Her feet dangled from over the edge. Taking a deep breath, she threw a glance back at the burly man, seeing how long she had before he found her. A part of her was surprised he had not looked her way.

While watching the back of the fine hairs of his neck, one wrong move and he would spot her. One of her feet hovered above the transparent visor. She was close enough to see the remnants of pollen and debris scattered across the blue-tinted surface, but her feet could not touch it. Right then, Cara made up her mind that she had to jump for it. She had to go for it, with both wind and gravity against her, unsure of how she would land atop the surface below. The only thing she knew for certain, if she stayed, he would kill her.

With a quick push, she hopped off the edge without regard for landing. Wind flew through her hair as she dropped through the air. She was weightless falling through the breeze. Finally, she was free.

A hand grabbed her wrist, stopping the rest of her body in mid-air. She looked up and saw this man, holding her, pulling her back into the window. A sudden numbness began taking over her fingers. He was too strong to stop.

No, no, no, this could not be happening. She had to think quick. If he pulled her back into that window, she was as good as dead.

"You're going to need this..." Jacqui's words reminded Cara of a gift.

Cara pulled the scalpel Jacqui gave her from the front pocket of her hospital gown. She sliced and cut and sliced into his wrist. She then sunk the thin, razor-sharp weapon into his tattooed flesh until she drew blood, hoping she would hit a vein somewhere important.

His grip turned loose.

Cara fell through the whipping winds and landed back first onto the visor. The crushing impact shot a mind-numbing pain up her spine. She looked up. *Oh, how lovely*, Cara thought. The sun was setting. Fruity reds and plush pink clouds painted the sky. The sun had cast a soft shadow around his head, but Cara could still see his face. The man's eyebrows had curled into two lines of worry. He pulled out a black item and spoke words into it. Cara smiled. The man could do nothing to harm her now, however, she had another growing concern. The blue-tinted glass beneath her had cracked into a million slivers of tiny lines, like lightning. Every tiny move sent a hundred more further away from her.

Through the spider web of silver lines underneath, she had no idea how far up she was. This could not be how she was going to die. Cara refused to believe it.

The visor shattered.

Cara closed her eyes bracing for the worst.

Moments passed in the air as she began her fall once more, slipping between flying shards of ice-blue glass and the steel beams once supporting her.

Clap.

Darkness.

Her body slammed hard into the earth, but not where she expected. She was anticipating much more pain having just slammed into fresh concrete. The impact alone should have broken every bone in her body or maybe it had, and she was now paralyzed from the neck down, maybe that was why she did not feel any pain. All she could see was a blanket of blackness. No life in her limbs and barely clinging to breath, two hands pulled her from the gravel.

As this person retrieved Cara, sharp leaves, rose petals, and thorns scraped against her skin. At the same time, she heard a voice. Soft. Feminine. The woman helping her looked familiar. Light-skinned, bright-colored eyes, and a gentle voice anyone could confide in.

"Ma'am... you... Hurt?" she asked, but the words were muffled.

A man stepped into her sight. With one hand around her waist, and the other around the back of her knees, he scooped Cara off the hard ground. The light-eyed nurse beside him.

Still disoriented by the fall, Cara had no words to speak.

"Hey, stay with me." The nurse placed a hand on her forehead. "She's burning up."

The nurse leaned toward Cara and upon a closer look, her eyes expanded.

"Goodchild, this is one of the girls Justice has been looking for. One of the girls on that wall. It's... Cara," Cindy said. "Hurry, bring her here." Cindy directed Goodchild, who was carrying Cara, to Cindy's car. For Cindy knew, inside of the hospital Cara would not be safe.

"Go. I'll meet back up with you in a little bit. I think Reeves might need me," Goodchild said before running into the hospital. Cindy turned her attention back to the woman in her passenger seat. Her hospital gown had torn at the seams from her fall. Her bones rattled. Her lower back screamed. Cara slipped in and out of consciousness, but she managed to say a few words to Cindy.

"I need you to call someone for me," Cara whispered.

"Who?"

Cara looked out of the window, staring at Mercy Hospital. The evening sun shone against the windows of the building as broken shards of ice-blue glass laid across the front entrance. Cara had her freedom back. She was free to do anything. Free to live, to make mistakes, but the one thing on her mind—other than some sleep—was him. Tears formed in Cara's eyes just thinking of him. He used to send flowers to her job when she worked as a server and her co-workers used to hate it, but she did not care. A sweet man. She loved his deep southern accent, country-fried chicken, his good manners, and even better sex. No, sex was not everything to Cara, but one thing she wanted was a life free of regret. He was the one she married and the one that got away, and if she let this man walk out of her life, again, she would carry that heartache to the grave.

"His name is Matthew. I need to see him."

Chapter 25

Justice: Ninety-Six Hours Missing

What the hell? Justice thought.

Lone square lights sat at the intersection of the low ceilings and the walls. The halls were gray with dingy concrete, stretching around a seemingly never-ending curve. His footsteps echoed against the quiet emptiness before him. This place sounded like the perfect place to take someone, so quiet, and so isolated.

Watching a string of water slide down from a crack in the ceiling, this part of the infrastructure was not as neatly maintained as the other side. Dust had accumulated in the corners and the place had dozens of shallow water puddles mixed with a brown substance that Justice hoped was not sewage. This part was not going to be on Arnold's tour, that was certain.

At the end of the hall, a door appeared. The front of the double doors read:

TRANSITION ROOM
CAUTION: INHABITANTS MAY EXHIBIT

RADICAL/IRRATIONAL BEHAVIOR, PROCEED
CAREFULLY.

This did not seem right. Perhaps this Transition Room was more that of a psych ward. On the other side could be poop caked along the walls, screaming voices too loud for the common ear, and wild-haired individuals undergoing drug withdrawal. He must have made a wrong turn.

"Leave no stone unturned." A saying from his old partner, Mason, whispered in Justice's ear. If he had to go through hell to get to his sister, then that was what he had to do.

The doors to the Transition Room parted, splitting the two words directly in half in the process. The first thing that appeared in his sight was the armed guard standing in the right corner. He stood well over six feet, a black short-sleeved shirt showed off the thick veins in his biceps and forearms, and a beard that swallowed his lips whole. A loaded black handgun sat in his holder. The bald wide-shouldered man stood close enough for Justice to make out the details of his face, but too far for him to lunge at him or disarm him. Justice would deal with this threat later.

The most notable attribute of the space was that the people in this Transition Room were chained to their hospital beds. All of them were unconscious. Beside each bed were monitors, sanitary stations, medical equipment, and IV bags.

Justice stopped mid-stride.

He noticed something. A characteristic each of these women had in common. Melanin skin. All shades. High yellow, bronze, russet, and everything else in between. And then it hit him.

Justice had found them.

All of those missing women were here. Hundreds of beds,

each with numbers instead of names which led him to just one conclusion.

Grace must be down here!

She was stuck in this hell. Justice glanced back over at the lone sentry. Immediately, the two locked eyes. Without a sliver of doubt, that guard kept his attention on Justice's every move.

"You're the nurse for the next shift?" the armed guard said. His features were masked by a dense growth of a dark beard.

Justice nodded.

"That one over there—the bed has been making noises."

Justice looked over at the bed in the distance then back at the armed guard. "A semi-automatic handgun seems a little excessive for a bunch of unconscious females, don't you think?"

The man took a few steps closer with an eyebrow lifted. "I have my job, you have yours." Ceiling lights danced on the bald man's head in a shiny obnoxious reflection. The guard placed his finger just outside of the trigger, a wordless threat Justice understood too well.

Justice further analyzed the weapon. All black, clean design, lightweight, and looked like a Glock 19, which meant the guy was either law enforcement or ex-military.

Around Justice were several other entrances scattered on the four walls. An industrial staircase led to the second floor and another door sat at the top. Each door withheld a secret.

Justice began walking over towards the woman the guard mentioned, in between, he studied the charts of each bed he passed in the process. Scanning between women, he stopped at one. A young woman. Her cherrywood complexion glistened like it had been doused in gasoline. The harsh lighting from above exaggerated every pimple, scar, and ounce of sweat. She looked young, no older than eighteen. The girl's chest heaved up and down, taking in a hundred breaths per minute. She was clearly in need of medical attention, and with only a near expired CPR certificate, Justice was the last person who could provide any help. *God this was terrible.* This was inhumane to keep someone like this.

In the distance, something stole his attention.

Three rows down.

Five beds from the front.

Could it be? Was that... her?

Justice rushed over to the woman's bedside. With his heart pounding ferociously as he drew near, he hoped his eyes were not playing tricks on him. He prayed this was not some mirage he was seeing after being in the desert for weeks without water. He slowed his pace as he got closer to her bed. His eyebrows shot to the ceiling. It couldn't be...

Shallow breaths. Skin flushed a shade brighter than her usual deep shade of brown. Her eyelashes closed to the brutal world around her. Most importantly, those lilac coils sprouting from her hair. It was her. Justice had found her. He'd found Grace.

A sudden rush of water shrouded his vision. Justice had encountered so many bodies along the way here, but somehow Grace was alive. The short lilac curls of her hair were tiny tulips growing out of her scalp. Gorgeous. He scooped her limp body into his arms. Unfazed by the metal cuffs on her thin wrists, he cradled her back and forth, vowing that as long as he drew breath, he would protect her with his life, always.

Justice had his sister, but she was not safe just yet. There still remained the issue, how was Justice going to get her out of here—discretely. First, the armed guard had to go.

"I need some help!" Justice shouted to the guard.

The broad-shouldered man stared at him but did not move.

Gently, Justice placed Grace back down on the bed. He slid between the other rows of monitors and bed rails to get back to the entrance. By the time he reached the guard, instead of a stoic expression greeting him, it was a loaded barrel.

"Whoa, don't shoot!" Justice lifted his arms above his head. "I just need an extra set of hands."

Gradually, Justice moved closer to the man. Closing the gap of empty space between them and using a friendly smile, he was hopeful it would remove the man's finger from the trigger. If only he was so lucky.

"What do you need help with?"

Justice did not notice the thick accent before, it was maybe Eastern European. It was harsh, even his kindness sounded threatening.

As Justice moved closer, he kept watch on the loaded weapon. The barrel was aimed straight at his chest with plenty of arteries and organs to take a bullet. He had this feeling before of a gun pointed at him. Even with that experience, the fear felt the same. Last time it was at a gas station past midnight. Justice remembered it like it was yesterday. The panic surging through his blood, the sweat pouring from his palms and face, and the despair—true horror of someone else holding his life between their fingers—all from not knowing if the man would kill him after he handed over the money. Justice tossed him his wallet, the man scurried off with all three hundred dollars of his life savings, and Justice lived to see another day. This moment had driven Justice straight into the arms of the police force. There, he would never be a victim again.

"I need you to hold her for me, we need to transfer her to another location."

"Why? I have worked this shift before, they never needed my help." The guard's grip on the gun drew tighter. The guard took a small step toward him and in doing so he exposed himself. His left leg had a limp, a subtle limp, but it was noticeable.

"There's a first time for everything," Justice said.

Sweat slid down his armpits and forehead. His heart thumped with adrenaline running rampant in his chest. Studying this man with the gun aimed straight at his skull, Justice's arms grew heavy with anxiety, but he kept his focus on the armed guard, waiting for the right moment. And since the man had not yet shot him dead, there was still hope.

"I really need your help, man, it's just me. My partner had to step out for a little bit and hey, look at you? I wouldn't try it."

In this fight, Justice's only weapon was humor.

Slowly, the end of the gun lowered, inch by inch. Good. Justice was within arm's reach. Now the only concern left was making it out alive. If he grabbed the wrong end of the gun, he would not live to see his sister again. Justice did not come all this way only to die right in front of her.

Without hesitating, Justice launched a flying tackle.

Justice pushed him against the wall. He grabbed the man by his wrist, spun the gun upward, and yanked it from the guard. Quickly, he shoved him with an elbow to his nose, shattering the thin bone upon impact. The man fell back into the wall behind him with blood pouring from the center of his face. He slid down to his knees, unconscious.

Justice grabbed the keys dangling from his waist. Not knowing exactly what they were for, he figured any keys located down here unlocked something. He secured the handgun in the back of his scrub trousers and raced back over to Grace. He began trying every key on the ring. First try, failed. Second attempt, failed. Third, it fit but did not turn to unlock anything. Justice would be down here a while, there were at least fifty keys on this one ring.

Dammit.

A single slow clap broke out.

Justice threw his gaze upward and found Arnold walking

down a black steel staircase. Casually, he took his time down the steps.

"I knew you looked familiar." Arnold squinted. "My God, you'd make a terrible nurse. I really should have known. How did you do it?" Arnold said, reaching the bottom of the steps.

Justice stuffed the keys inside his pant pockets. He looked at Grace, her innocent sleeping face, then turned his sight back to Arnold.

"Why are you doing this? What have these women done to you?" Justice yelled, approaching Arnold, moving between beds and monitors.

Arnold stood still, waiting leisurely. Justice could tell that through Arnold's dark suit, he had a sinewy build. Clearly he was in his fifties, judging by the gray-black low cut and he stood an inch or two shorter than Justice. Perhaps the man knew some form of martial arts. Few people would see an angry Justice walking towards them and remain this unafraid. The man must have something up his sleeves. Regardless, Justice had thrown all of his police procedures out the window. He couldn't give a damn about the consequences of his actions. It was just him and Arnold now.

"Well, that's kind of the point, is it not? I have the right to do *whatever* I want, when I can afford to do *anything* I want. This is my colony."

"Colony..." Justice uttered under his breath.

"Humans are like ants. Ants have their own colonies, and do you know what happens when two colonies collide? War. Just like us. Only one will survive."

Is that what this project was to him? That's what he thinks he's doing down here... surviving. Justice thought.

"In any war, there will be casualties." Arnold smirked. "No one is looking for these women. At least down here their lives will serve a greater purpose."

236

Justice was so insulted he stopped walking toward the man. It was a harsh truth that even he as an officer had recognized. Justice would have moved heaven and earth for these women, but to society, they were just another face, another poster, another post on a long list of other things that occupied their time on social media.

"I have worked for people like you my entire life. Without your privilege, without your position. You're nothing."

Arnold chuckled to himself. The sound of that subtle breathy laugh boiled Justice's blood.

"You may not realize it because it does not, in particular, affect you. But we're in a birth crisis. Children are dying before they even live and if you don't care about the wealth of this great city then whose side are you on?"

"Their side." Justice pointed to an unconscious woman chained to a hospital bed.

Arnold smiled slyly. "Of course you are. You fight for the working-class man. All while the ones who own the banks and the ones who sign your checks are incapable of having children. Why should they have to pay for the services of the ones who can? Why should they pour hundreds of thousands of their hard-earned dollars into a system they'll never use, or into clinics and public institutions they'll never step foot into? Or fund lower end hospitals birthing thousands of poor children while they cannot have one of their own. Does that sound fair to you?"

"I don't give a fuck."

His phone vibrated in his pocket, but Justice was far too busy to answer. Any calls would have to wait.

"I'm sure these women matter... to someone. But not to enough people to make a difference."

And that was Justice's breaking point. He retrieved the gun from his backside and aimed it at Arnold. His finger, a thought away from pulling the trigger. A moment from the life of a cop to a life in prison. Arnold deserved to die. Justice could, and he should, end this man's life. Only one pull of his forefinger and it could be done.

But he hesitated. *"Take care of your mother and sister. They need you."*

The dying words of Justice's father held his hand steady. Often Justice wondered what his father would think of the man he had become. He thought of himself as a good person. He helped old ladies across the street, he volunteered on his off days at homeless shelters, and had never stolen anything in his entire life, not even candy from a liquor store. But right now, Justice had every right to shoot this man. He was the one who orchestrated the kidnapping and experimentation on his sister and countless other women like her. The only regret Justice had was that he could not kill Arnold more than once. Would his father think less of him if he killed this man or let the law handle him?

Narrowing his eyes at Justice, Arnold worked up the nerve to part his lips to speak.

"Don't think I won't shoot you," Justice threatened through clenched teeth. Biting down on his bottom lip, tension locked his jaw in place. He was no murderer, but someone had to answer for what happened to Grace. Justice's finger began shaking. There were simply some things in life worth living for and worth dying for, which category did his sister fall under? He was willing to die to protect her, but who would be there at her graduation and to give her away at her wedding? It was clear to him what he must do in that moment. His family was worth killing for.

Arnold held out his arms defensively, then he made a bold decision. One that would cost someone their life. He lunged forward, grabbing the gun from Justice. They fumbled the deadly metal object between their hands, struggling for the handle.

Justice heard the bullet enter the chamber. It was only a matter of time before...

A round fired.

The scream of gunfire reminded Justice of the gas station, to the day that changed his life in a split second. From the passenger seat, he had watched it unfold. His father had left the gas station, a tiny white bag with a single packet of pink candy in hand. The joy of his favorite treat had worn off as his father left the store and found a barrel pointed at him, but what Justice remembered most was the look in his father's eyes. There was a terror-stricken gaze that rattled Justice with guilt. Justice yelled and banged on the window. By the time he had reached for the handle, it was already too late. His father grabbed the pistol and, shortly after, a round echoed within the gas station pavilion. A bullet had burst through his chest. Police sirens rang in the distance. The gunman scurried off. Blood poured onto the concrete like running water. Justice ran to his father, holding his hand drenched in warm blood. His father smiled, grabbed onto Justice's forearm, and whispered to him to take care of the family. And with that, life disappeared from his eyes.

As Justice struggled with Arnold for the gun, he refused to die like his father.

The two shoved each other back and forth into monitors, machinery, and beds. They struggled, jostled, and fought for the weapon and then... it went off.

The round missed Arnold.

A slight sting grazed Justice's shoulder.

The bullet buried into the concrete wall. Justice knocked the gun from Arnold's grip. The weapon slid under a bed—just out of reach. Justice and Arnold glanced at one another then scrambled after the gun. Within a few moments, every door in the lower level flung open. A team dressed in all black tactical attire, bulletproof vests, helmets, goggles, shoulder and knee pads, stormed the Transition Room. Thick combat boots stomped across the solid concrete floor. Quickly, the armed group surrounded Arnold and Justice.

A smirk came to Arnold's face.

What was he smiling about? Justice thought and took his gaze around the circle. *No...* It dawned on him. It should have come as no surprise. Arnold seemed like the kind of man who had police on payroll and this moment was proof. This was no average SWAT team. They were hired mercenaries. Now the truth would die with Justice.

"Make it quick," Arnold said, adjusting his blazer. He walked beside a SWAT personnel. They were sleek, tall, intimidating men in jet-black attire. "It pays to have friends."

The men looked at Justice with blank stares, like they could kill him and forget about it tomorrow. Arnold grabbed one of their guns, ensuring that it was loaded. He stepped in front of Justice and placed the gun against his scalp. Its cold metal sunk into his skin.

"I'll take *good* care of these girls."

As Justice looked at the mercenaries surrounding him, he realized his mistake. Alone and outnumbered. It was clear he was going to die. Within his head he apologized to his mother and Grace, hoping they could forgive him for leaving them behind. He had let them both down. Then there was Cindy. Poor Cindy. She would never forgive him for this, especially since she had told him to do the very opposite thing he was currently wrapped up in. It was his end. Justice had let rash decision-making pull him into darkness, and now he would never see Cindy walking down the aisle towards him at a chapel.

A separate door opened. More bodies flooded the room, but

Justice was too focused on the loaded gun against his skull to notice.

"Go to hell!" Justice's words meant nothing to Arnold. It was over.

A young man broke through the crowd.

Unlike the soldiers of Arnold's team, he was a slender, green-eyed individual in an all-black police uniform a size too big for his shoulders. Defiantly, he parted the SWAT team that had crowded around Arnold and Justice. The man put a gun behind Arnold's head.

"Put the gun down," Goodchild said. One click and Goodchild's firearm was itching to release.

"You pull that trigger and I'll—"

"I doubt you're faster than me."

Seconds passed, but they felt to Justice like hours. Two guns. Arnold and Goodchild. Each waited for the other to make a move.

A single bead of sweat left a snail's trail down Arnold's face. A glassy sheen of indecision in his eyes. Even the air within the room watched with anticipation. Someone was going to die. Justice could only pray it wasn't himself.

Arnold sighed through his nostrils and then gave up his weapon.

"Arnold Reisser," Goodchild snatched the gun from his hand and placed it in his belt, "you are under arrest." Goodchild cuffed Arnold's wrist behind his back and handed Arnold off to a colleague.

Justice stood up, adjusted his scrubs, and found the entire thirty-fifth precinct had swarmed the room. Officers were uncuffing young women and studying medical charts. The Forensics team had begun taking photos and gathering evidence. Chief Glassman stopped in front of him.

"Tomorrow, I need to see you in my office." The firmness in his voice faded. "Good job."

Goodchild walked over to Justice. "I told you I got you."

"How did you know where to find me?"

"Like I was telling you about that email, before you hung up. Within the hour the judge gave us a warrant to search the entire hospital and from our surveillance last night, I knew where to look." Goodchild then handed Justice his phone.

As Justice read the words on the screen, disbelief struck him. An article about Mercy Hospital went viral.

Human Trafficking Fronts As A Hospital

A whistleblower claimed medical abuse inside Mercy Hospital, alleging that at least two doctors performed "medically unnecessary" surgery without consent, on dozens of women, including procedures affecting victims' reproductive health. The report shares radiology reports, surgical impressions, a textbook-thick consent packet and prescriptions. Together, this information highlighted an alarming pattern of an alleged organ harvesting operation by a company called BRT Health Industries whose sister company, Lanzran Inc., is the primary supplier of medical equipment to Mercy Hospital.

"You were right, about the missing women," Goodchild said.

Two officers escorted Arnold up the switchback staircase. His once condescending demeanor had evolved into a red-faced tantrum. He was a silver-haired man-child in a twenty-thousand-dollar suit, kicking, spitting, shoving the officers, and yelling obscenities.

"You think by stopping me you've made anything change?

Do you honestly believe arresting me will stop anything here? You have no idea what's going on."

"Yeah, yeah, heard it all before, pal," Goodchild said. The officers pushed Arnold upstairs.

"You have no idea what's going on." Repeated in his mind.

There was truth in that. Justice would have never guessed that this place existed. Despite the part of himself wanting to label this day as a "win," he got a sickening feeling there was more to Arnold's last-ditch diatribe. The idea that Arnold was merely a cog in a well-oiled machine took root in his mind and angst swelled in him like heartburn. All of these conflicting feelings had led Justice to believe that this operation was merely the surface. He knew it. But for now, he was content with this small victory. He was happy to see his little sister again.

He uncuffed her and shook her by the shoulders. Grace finally awoke from her slumber.

"Justice?" Grace's eyes fluttered open in a creepy, ventriloquist doll-like fashion. "Where am I?"

Tears flooded his eyes at finally seeing his sister once more. Justice hugged Grace the hardest he had ever done in his life. "You're safe, Grace, you're safe."

Chapter 26

Jacqui: No News Is Bad News

Jacqui leaned back in her desk chair and took a long exhale. Knowing her freedom was numbered, she had a sudden urge for something bad for her health. *Maybe a drink would do it,* Jacqui thought. Who knew when the next time would be that she could have a neat bourbon or a stiff martini?

She signed out of her account for the last time and studied her reflection in the transparent computer screen. Only an outline of her straight hair and white lab coat stared back at her like it was her alter ego, the alternate version of herself that had committed these crimes instead of her. Looking down at her name that was sewn in with a cursive calligraphy, Jacqui truly realized everything she was about to lose. Countless hours of cramming information before exams, sleepless nights of working, days she would go without seeing her daughter due to long shifts—all that hard work and all those years of her life now meant nothing. She would be barred from practicing medicine. And that was the least of her problems.

Disbelief was setting in. That email was enough to destroy Lanzran Inc. and BRT Health Industries engulfing all of Arnold's decades of research and so-called progress within the medical community, in an inferno of blistering guilt. And Jacqui would burn right alongside him.

She sat there in the chair, still and silent, enjoying the quietness. Around her were rows of white desks, their cleanliness held on to a glint of the ceiling light. The quiet hum of computer hard drives was the only sound that kept her company. She was alone.

Around her was so calm and peaceful that she allowed her mind to wonder what would happen next. Would she be killed in a not-so-random car crash while on her way to work? Would it be a bullet from an experienced sniper sitting in some hotel across the hospital? Or would he plant a bomb under her car or in her house? All options seemed possible, and Arnold had the means to get it done.

Then the doors to the entrance slid open. Three men dressed in black suits—like Arnold's colleagues the first day she met him—appeared. Two of them marched through the empty rows until they found Jacqui, while one blocked the doorway. One man stood in front of her, and one took the space behind her. This was it. She knew there would be one of two outcomes if she betrayed Arnold. Prison or the morgue. Still, she did not think they had the audacity to murder her right here. Then again, if these people worked for Arnold, they were capable of anything.

The one standing in front of her pulled out a syringe.

Jacqui's eyes widened. They would not dare do this.

The one behind her grabbed her, forcing her arms against her body. He had trapped her like an anaconda did its prey. She squirmed, kicked, and fought, but his biceps covered her entire abdomen. She would never get free, not without his permission. The other man then stuck her neck with the syringe and pushed the empty vial of pure oxygen into her bloodstream. With the cool air mindlessly running through her veins, the man behind her released her back into the chair. His work was done. Jacqui only had ten minutes of life left maybe less. Arnold must have ordered the hit. An embolism. Arnold was right. He might not have been a doctor, but he knew enough to kill her like one.

A sharp pain stabbed her in the chest. They might as well have taken a machete and sliced her open. Between that and the feeling Jacqui endured right now, the machete would have been the better way to die. Jacqui grabbed onto her chest. Losing air. Unable to take in a single breath. Numbness taking over her arms. Her eyes closed. This time she would never awake.

Beep. Beep.

Back to reality.

Jacqui's pager went off. The noise yanked her back into the present. She was back in the same chair staring at her reflection. Thank God such a terrible death was a hallucination. A sick fragment of thought that had slipped out of her imagination. Even so, thinking like that was not the norm for Jacqui. To willingly give in to her demise was unlike her. She had done the unspeakable to some of those women like Ivery Johnson. Yes, that was true, and she could never undo that, but at the same time, she had done the impossible. She had taken down Arnold. Instead of sitting here, wondering how long it would take for the police to arrive, she had more that needed to be done.

Ashley, Jacqui thought. A flash of her daughter's smile came to mind. Her teeth were so perfectly aligned. Every time Jacqui took Ashley to see a dentist, they'd always ask if she used to wear braces. Nope. It was just Ashley. Her precious little girl. *Oh no. Ashley!* What would Arnold do once he found out Jacqui betrayed him? He already had someone tailing her daughter while she was at school and cheerleading practice. All he would need to do is make a phone call and Ashley was... dead.

The proof had been sent to the authorities. The damage was done. Now, with what little time Jacqui had left, she needed to get her daughter far away from Ballantyne as soon as possible. And there was only one person Jacqui trusted to do that.

She dialed a number from her phone.

"I can't talk right now, Jacqui, I—"

"Damon, I need you to pick Ashley up from school this afternoon. I dropped off a bunch of her things this morning at your place. Do not come by my house for anything. I'm serious, Damon, for nothing, at all," Jacqui said, waiting for his response on the other end.

"No, we agreed that—"

"Please."

Damon sighed. Then there was silence. Now was not the time for silence.

"Damon?"

"All right, fine, but, Jacqui, what's going on? Why can't she go to your house? And how long do you need me to keep her?"

"For goodness' sake, Damon, she's your daughter not some freakin' pet, she should be able to stay there for as long as she needs."

"You know what, Jacqui, I don't have time for this."

Click.

Neither did Jacqui.

Frustrated, Jacqui slammed a fist on the desk. *Why didn't Damon just listen for once?* Jacqui thought. She then rushed through the entrance.

Jacqui took the elevator back to Cara, but when she entered, she found an empty room and an open window stifling the room with chilly air. Jacqui poked her head out the window and refused to believe what she found.

A shattered glass visor. Scraps of hospital gown hanging from the broken beams. At the base of the hospital entrance, a crowd gathered.

Jacqui covered her mouth.

Upon the sight, Jacqui knew Cara was dead. She had to be. No one could have survived the fall without serious trauma. Why did Cara do this? All she had to do was wait a little bit longer. She was so close. Or... maybe Cara was tired of it all.

Jacqui placed her back against the wall. Cara's bloody and broken body from the fall flooded her mind. Cara must have felt so alone in her last moments. All that Jacqui had promised her. And out of all the girls she'd tried to protect, Cara was the one who had hope. A slight sting formed in her eyes. Jacqui had failed her.

Slowly, Jacqui slid down the wall and collapsed onto the floor. What was all of this for? How could Jacqui have been so stupid? So self-righteous to think she could do everything on her own? Classic superwoman syndrome, just like her mother. Jacqui raked a hand through her hair, pulling and tearing at the scalp. Dammit! Had Jacqui gone to the police the first day, Cara would still be alive, and Grace would never have been subjected to any of this. Jacqui had reached her limit. She then broke into a quiet lament; tears ran down her face. Now Jacqui had another woman's death on her hands.

JACQUI WENT TO THE main entrance. Level one of Mercy Hospital. Sooner or later, it was better to simply face her mistakes. She needed to see Cara's face. To see how all of the studies and work she had done, had led Cara to her death. Moving past the still bodies, what awaited Jacqui at the front door was her penance.

Yellow do-not-cross tape barred entry along the outside, but inside Mercy Hospital was chaos. Red and blue emergency lights flashed against the porcelain white walls like fireworks. Officers dressed in all black swarmed the hospital in militant order. Radio chatter from uniformed police coated the halls with their code names and numbers. Patients had become spectators to a front-page conspiracy. Mercy Hospital always held a certain ambiance of calmness and sophistication similar to that of a seven-star hotel only for the one percent of society, but with the authorities running rampant, the place felt more like a motel infested with roaches.

Then she saw him. The scum of them all. Arnold.

Only Arnold was not alone. With his hands secured behind his back, two officers were escorting him toward the exit. His face had turned a terrifying bright red. It was such a stark contrast against his salt-and-pepper hair. Veins popped from his forehead and around the crow's feet of his eyes. He was screaming and yelling and spitting profanities at anyone who dared to lay eyes on him.

Finally, the truth was out. Arnold was receiving a long-overdue sentence. Then again, how long would Arnold actually sit in a jail cell? With his connections, he might never set foot in a prison. No telling what kind of tricks he had in case of this kind of emergency. Still, seeing Arnold get dragged and pushed by the police formed a smile on Jacqui's face. A small and savory victory.

Arnold found her. The two locked eyes.

"You!" Arnold hissed.

His voice brought attention, too much attention from onlookers and idle officers. Time had frozen. All of these strange eyes had fallen upon her. Though the people staring at Jacqui were of different ethnicities, ages, and professions, they shared the same confusion on their faces. A bewilderment that turned poisonous after hearing what Arnold said next.

"You're dead," Arnold said with a glare that could cut glass. Her blood ran cold. The evil in his eyes was unlike anything she had *ever* seen from him. Arnold was going to make good on his threat. She could feel it in the venom of his delivery. Then the officers pushed him out of the main entrance.

"Excuse me, miss," an officer approached her, "is your name Jacqui Stevenson?"

Jacqui's stomach spun into a free fall.

She tilted her head upright to meet his eyes. They were a light brown shade like the color of leaves turning over to autumn. His facial hair was light and well-trimmed, the young man definitely took care of himself. Though Jacqui could tell he weighed no more than a buck fifty, the load-bearing vest made him look thirty pounds heavier. Insignias on each of his short sleeves. Precinct logo patches rested on each of his shoulders. The yellow pommel of his taser stuck out of its holster. If she grabbed it, she might be able to tase him and make a break for it. Who was she kidding? If this was her time, she had to go willingly. It made her look even more guilty if she fought it.

Hesitant, Jacqui nodded in agreement.

The officer reached for his waist. Everything moved in slow motion as he spoke, "You have the right to remain silent. Everything you say can and will..."

The rest of his words drifted off into an abyss of silence. Jacqui became numb. It was like she had slipped out of her body and was watching this happen to someone else. Nurses, receptionists, technicians, patients, parents, children, police officers, and her colleagues stared at Jacqui with both surprise and disappointment.

The officer twisted her arms behind her back and slapped cuffs on her wrists. As he tightened the cuffs, the metal was frigid and unforgiving at its job against her skin and bones. This hurt much more than she anticipated. But in the eyes of the law, she deserved it. Criminals were not afforded the luxury of comfort; these cuffs were the beginning of that lesson Jacqui would learn.

The officer stood behind her and pushed her toward the entrance. As Jacqui walked, she could no longer look anyone in the eye. The crowd became a blur. She could not bear to look at anyone, especially her co-workers who once held her in such high regard.

Dr. Isaiah slowed to a halt as he spotted Jacqui. Oh, God. Though she loathed him in secrecy for getting that promotion over herself, he adored her. Isaiah would never believe that Jacqui was able to hide this from him. But how could she tell him? How could she explain everything so that it would make sense? She never thought everyone would find out like this. His eyes widened, but soon his expression changed and the bewildered look on his face turned into an entirely different emotion.

"This has got to be some mistake," Isaiah shouted at the officer.

"Isaiah, please," Jacqui whispered to him, "I'll explain later—"

"Don't say anything. I'll get you a lawyer."

If only she could tell him. No lawyer would do any good. Jacqui was guilty.

Together, she and the officer continued Jacqui's walk of shame. The glass doors of the entrance were within sight. Sirens, police chatter, mumbles from the crowd outside drew near. Jacqui would now have to face an even worse enemy than her self-loathing. There was the press.

Right before she stepped outside, a voice called to her. It was so soft it was angelic, belonging to only one person. A person she could not face. Not now or ever.

"Jacqui!" Grace said.

Dressed in only a thin hospital gown, Grace was screaming at the officer behind Jacqui.

"Let her go!"

It warmed her heart seeing how people openly defied the police on Jacqui's behalf. If only she deserved such love. Though Grace yelled with all the strength she could muster, after days of sedation, she was no louder than a raspy shriek. Grace's current condition was Jacqui's fault. At this point, Grace needed not to waste her breath.

"No! They made a mistake," Grace said turning to her side.

And that was when Jacqui felt shame wash over her. When she saw him, the one person who knew the truth and how deep Jacqui's involvement went.

Justice.

With his arm around her shoulders, Grace's brother was standing beside her in teal scrubs. He held a disappointed yet not surprised look on his face as he watched Jacqui get carried off by his colleagues. The fact that Grace was still an advocate for Jacqui proved one thing: she did not yet know the truth. Yes, it was better that way, at least for now. Grace had just gotten her freedom back; it was best she did not know Jacqui was the reason she was put there. Jacqui would tell Grace in her own way, perhaps through a letter. Maybe after years in prison, when Jacqui was ready for redemption, she would have the strength, but not now. That sting in the back of Jacqui's eyes crept up once more. No... she dared not cry. No one would have empathy for her. No amount of tears could save her.

Jacqui said nothing to Grace. There was nothing she could use to defend her actions. And now she would stand before a jury and plead her case, but in the eyes of the public, Jacqui was already guilty.

Outside, patrol vehicles crowded the parking lot like a tailgate, and reporters had jostled their way to the front of the yellow tape barrier. News vans had parked on sidewalks with their cameras pointed right at Jacqui while she made her debut.

She knew this day would come but knowing and preparing for it were two different things.

"Out of the way!" the officer behind Jacqui shouted.

Jacqui walked into the crowd. The reporters were a horde of animals hungry for a story and the tale of a doctor turned human trafficker was fresh meat. They had formed a wall of microphones, tape recorders, cameras, and blinding lights, refusing to let her pass. At a slow pace, Jacqui and the officer moved towards the black-and-white patrol car. Though she could see the blue and red lights atop the vehicle, the press was relentless, pushing against her like a mob. They harassed her with questions, hateful questions at that, provoking her. These people had no conscience. They only wanted to use her at the worst moment of her life. Jacqui knew that, but it did not stop her from responding once they found her weakness.

"Didn't you think of your daughter?"

Jacqui snapped her head to her left. There were several faces, but the lights behind them had turned the reporters into moving shadows.

"Everything I did was *for* my daughter!" Jacqui shouted.

The voices stopped. No one said a word for a moment. Maybe they understood. Maybe Jacqui's story would be heard. Maybe they wanted to know the truth of what happened underneath Mercy Hospital. Or maybe, they were waiting for something more.

"Jacqui, over here!"

"Why did you kill those missing girls?"

And Jacqui's one statement created a surge of more questions.

The officer opened the door and shoved Jacqui inside by the top of her head. She leaned back and breathed a sigh of relief. Strangely, sitting against the crinkled black leather interior, Jacqui felt safe. One glance out the window and she did not miss the feeling she'd just experienced. Having the world judge her at the worst moment of her life, was a sentence of its own.

She sat in the patrol car, looking through the barred window in the back seat. Shame bubbled inside her like acid reflux. She looked over at the place that was once her employer. The shiny windows of Mercy Hospital reflected the city skyline of Ballantyne. Nearing dusk, intense corals and peachy oranges draped the sky like falling sheets of fabric. Jacqui had spent so much of her life working, thinking she was healing others, how often did she take the time to enjoy a view like this? To truly appreciate the little things. Now, moments like these were worth more than any currency.

The only thing that brought Jacqui relief was knowing that she'd taken Arnold down with her. He could no longer threaten her little girl anymore. Ashley was safe. She was going to college next semester, majoring in social work or something that involved helping people like her mom. Jacqui could sleep at night knowing that she was far away from this wretched city. Jacqui finally realized the person she had become from this ordeal. This place didn't change her. It didn't break her. Nor did it consume her. This place only made her more of who she already was. Jacqui was a doctor, a great one for many years, but she was much more than that. She was a woman who would do anything for her child. She had suffered in silence, had lived with a terrible truth, and was willing to die protecting her little girl. She wasn't a murderer. No. She was a mother. Ashley's mother. Simple as that.

Epilogue

Staring at the cracked ceiling, she laid on a twin mattress that felt no different from a sheet of brick against her back. Steel bars with chipped white paint from the hands of countless people who had lived before her. Eating yellow-colored mystery substances with bread that could break teeth were her daily meals. A cement room had been her home for about a year now. This was her new life. Jacqui's life. Federal prison.

Between her fingers, she gingerly held a letter, a long-awaited letter she'd received that day. The handwriting was in a neat cursive so well-written it could have been a professional font.

Dear Jacqui,

I hope this letter finds you well. It still feels unreal. Just yesterday was the anniversary of that day. The day you saved my life. Even as I am writing this right now, I can't stop the tears from flowing as I think back on the whole thing. When I was down there all I kept thinking was that I was going to die. Every time I woke up, I didn't want to go back to sleep because

I didn't think I would wake up again. You gave me a second chance. Another opportunity at life, like I seriously can't thank you enough. I don't know how I will ever repay you. I'm hoping these letters are a start.

So, some exciting news, Matthew and I are pregnant! I was so surprised because last time I had a check-up Dr. Isaiah said I was infertile because of what happened to me. For the longest, I thought I couldn't have kids. I'm twelve weeks and we can't wait to find out the gender. It's all so exciting. I'll keep you posted.

With love,

Mrs. Esperanza.

Jacqui held the letter to her chest. She had saved one life and now that same woman was about to add a little person to the world. Cara was Jacqui's one redemption.

A guard came to the door in a stark blue uniform, with a radio, cuffs, and a baton at his waist. His belly hung over his belt.

"You got a visitor."

The guard escorted Jacqui to the visiting room. There, an unlikely guest awaited her.

Jacqui knew exactly who he was at first glance. She sucked in a breath. The white T-shirt he wore clashed with his mahogany complexion like a perfect opposite pair. He was the last person she thought would visit her.

He sat at a lone round table next to a man with a little boy visiting his mother. A sadness clung to this room. Either the cruel muted colors of the walls and doors, the stiff warmth in the room barely kept cool with open windows and broken fans, or the harsh concrete floors were what drew depression out of even the happiest of people here. Jacqui certainly was not one of those cheerful individuals and neither was her visitor.

She sat across from him, both eager and fearful of what had brought him an hour's drive away from Ballantyne to meet her.

"What are you doing here?" Jacqui asked. The metal dangling from her cuffs clinked and bounced into one another like pieces of a chandelier.

"I guess... I came here wanting to figure that out," Justice said.

His expression was solemn and blank like life had left his eyes. He must have discovered something new about Jacqui, but how? A year from the incident, what more was there to uncover? Or maybe he was here to get something off his chest. Either way, Jacqui deserved whatever diatribe Justice had practiced. In the meantime, she needed to delay it, she was not ready to face this. Coming to terms with how she betrayed Grace was the worst punishment of her crime.

"How's Grace?"

His brows furrowed at the sound of Grace's name. He needed not to say anything more as his face told it all. How dare Jacqui even ask such a question? Still, Grace had become a daughter to her and despite the things she had done, above all, she fought as hard as she could to keep her alive.

Jacqui dropped her head into her chest. She could not bring herself to look at him. She was no longer entitled to that privilege.

"Fine." Justice's expression suddenly softened. "I suppose... I have you to thank for that."

Jacqui lifted her head to meet his gaze.

"I keep replaying that night I went to your home, Dr. Stevenson..."

"I've relived those moments several times over. I wished I would have done things differently."

"That's the thing," Justice chuckled humorlessly, "I kept going back to that moment, wondering why you didn't. God, you remind me so much of my mom. After my dad died, she picked up several jobs, lost sleep, did everything she could to keep us afloat. She tried so hard until her body eventually gave out."

Silence. Jacqui peered into the deep mahogany of his eyes and found something strange looking back at her. This man did not come to scold her. In his gaze, she found empathy.

"You went up against an entire organization. Admirable, I'll give you that." He smiled, but then his joy turned somber. "You didn't have to go at it alone."

Jacqui sighed through her nostrils and leaned her elbows against the table. She could not stop herself from wondering how much different things would have been, had she done just that. Instead of lying to him, collaborating with him. Why did the thought not cross her mind sooner?

"You mentioned Ivery Johnson in your email to the precinct." Justice bit his upper lip, trying to hold back sorrow. "Did she suffer?"

Jacqui shook her head "no" but could not find the strength to say her name aloud. She had promised Ivery she would help her, instead, she had killed her. Ivery was the reason she stayed and fought, but the moment she stuck that syringe into Ivery's veins was the moment Jacqui had sealed her fate. She was always going to end up in prison. She was fooling only herself thinking there was any hope otherwise.

Justice leaned forward and motioned for Jacqui to do the same.

"You were never going to win, not against the Aphaia Corporation," he whispered.

"How do you know about that—"

"You haven't gone to trial yet, right?"

"No. They've been dragging their feet with my case."

Justice smiled slyly then pushed away from the table.

"I think we can get your charges dropped." Justice stood up. "I'll be in touch."

THE END

A note from the publisher

Thank you for reading this book. If you enjoyed it please do consider leaving a review on Amazon to help others find it too.

We hate typos. All of our books have been rigorously edited and proofread, but sometimes mistakes do slip through. If you have spotted a typo, please do let us know and we can get it amended within hours.

info@bloodhoundbooks.com

Printed in Great Britain
by Amazon

17264825R00153